ANNE ALETHA

Camille N. Wright

Visit Camille Wright's Author Page
at
www.ArdentWriterPress.com

The Ardent Writer Press
Brownsboro, Alabama

For general information about publishing with The
Ardent Writer Press contact *steve@ardentwriterpress.com*
or forward mail to:
The Ardent Writer Press, Box 25, Brownsboro, Alabama
35741.

This is a first edition of a novel, *Anne Aletha-The Story of a Suffragist's Fight against Racism and the Klan during WWI*, by Camille N. Wright, Smyrna, Georgia. *Anne Aletha* is a novel based on historical events and family history of the author. The story portrays the life of a young schoolteacher, based on a real character from the author's family, in the small Southern town of Ray's Mill, Georgia, at the end of World War I. The role of race relations at that time in history is a prominent point of the book, highlighting the influence of the KKK and the impact of the 1918 flu epidemic. All rights reserved by Camille N. Wright. Excerpts of text may be posted online only for a noncommercial use, provided quotations do not exceed a total of over three hundred (300) words.

Cover art and composition the work of The Ardent Writer Press and Village Green Press using Photoshop techniques. Composition and cover are covered by the same grant for noncommercial use noted above.

Photo of Camille N. Wright is by beth seitz photography.

Library of Congress Cataloging-in-Publication Data

Anne Aletha-The Story of a Suffragist's Fight against Racism and the Klan during WWI by Camille N. Wright

p. cm. - (Ardent Writer Press-2020) ISBN 978-1-64066-081-6 (pbk.); 978-1-64066-082-3 (hdk); 978-1-64066-083-0 (eBook mobi)

Library of Congress Control Number 2019952994

Library of Congress Subject Headings
- Fiction/General
- Fiction and reality
- FICTION / Historical / General.

BISAC Subject Headings

- FIC000000 FICTION / General
- FIC066000 FICTION / Small Town & Rural
- FIC074000 FICTION / Southern
- FIC014040 FICTION / Historical / World War I

First Edition (Copyright Camille N. Wright © 2018)

Acknowledgments

MY DEEPEST THANKS *to my wonderful teacher, mentor, editor, and friend Linda E. Clopton for encouraging me so many years ago when I enrolled in her writing class and for expertly guiding Anne Aletha through every draft of this long journey.*

ALSO, A SPECIAL THANK YOU *to my longtime friend and poet Dianna Eden, who loved Anne Aletha from the beginning and critiqued each chapter telling me that she wanted to grow old with her, which we, in fact, have done.*

AND HEARTFELT THANKS *to Jennifer Yankopolus, my book doctor, for holding my hand and guiding me through the last leg of this journey, not only editing, proofreading, and navigating the publishing/marketing world, but also assisting me with the challenges of the computer. You made it happen.*

TO MY DEAREST FRIENDS *Pat and Jim Wilson, who read every draft and cheered me on. Bella still resides in their barn and Peety is buried with his scavenged booty.*

MANY THANKS TO MY READERS *and dear friends Rose Sims, Rebecca Clements, Beverly McElhinney, and Elise Chase. You gave me courage.*

BOUNDLESS GRATITUDE *to Steve Gierhart, publisher of* The Ardent Writer Press, *for the opportunity to launch Anne Aletha into the world. And special thanks to Doyle Duke, editor at The Ardent Writer, for his gentle and insightful guidance. Both of you are my good fortune.*

And others to whom I am indebted:

MY GREAT AUNT GUSSIE, *one of sixteen O'Quinn children, who shared the stories of the old home place in Odum, Georgia: the sunrise weddings, the timber rafting, and life on their 1,200-acre farm in the early 1900s. Also to my cousin, Ralph O'Quinn Jr., who showed me the remaining property of the old homeplace including our great, great grandfather's grave.*

TO LION MASON, *my amazing neighbor, for sharing his World War I memories for use in Anne Aletha. I embellished his war experiences with cooties, rats, and shrapnel wounds.*

TO SUSAN TUNGATE, *who saw my first notebook and told me I was a writer.*

TO CHRISTINE DRAKE, *novelist and teacher, who was the first person to see my musings and tell me to keep going.*

A SPECIAL APPRECIATION *to Beth Seitz for her generosity of spirit and laughter and for putting me at ease during our afternoon photo shoot on such a lovely spring day. You will be missed.*

Author's Note

PEOPLE SAY WE WRITE stories to better understand ourselves and the world in which we live. I think this is true. My story begins in 1918 in Ray's Mill, Georgia, the birthplace of my beloved mother and the year in which she was born. It was a compelling year for fiction. World War I was raging, the Ku Klux Klan flourishing, women's suffrage struggling, and the deadly Spanish Influenza spreading.

Anne Aletha explores racial injustice and courage, themes still relevant today. In researching Ray's Mill, where I spent my childhood summers, I discovered the horrific May 1918 lynching of Mary Turner and four other African Americans that took place a few miles from Ray's Mill. Mary Turner is now memorialized in the National Memorial for Peace and Justice, aka the Lynching Museum in Montgomery, Alabama, which opened in spring 2018. Because I grew up in the 1950s and '60s in the segregated South, already shamed by Jim Crow, I am grateful for the opportunity to document these despicable acts.

The inspiration for *Anne Aletha* originated with a trunk of Victorian love letters my mother and I acquired for our small antique business. Alex and Nellie, the African American sharecroppers in my novel, are the fictionalized couple whose letters I read so many years ago. Also at this time, my elderly next-door neighbor shared his fascinating stories about fighting in France during the Great War. I embellished his experiences for my book.

Historical events and family history form the backdrop of my story. I stayed true to the facts, except where noted. My maternal grandparents provided the setting for the novel. I grew up enthralled by the family stories of my grandmother's old homeplace on the banks of the Altamaha

River in Odum, Georgia. She was one of sixteen children, and over the years, she and my great aunts delighted me with anecdotes about life on their 1,200-acre farm during the early 1900s: sunrise weddings, timber rafting down the Altamaha, and foot washings in the Primitive Baptist Church. Although the old house burned years ago and the land was divided and sold, I was able to visit the field where my great great grandfather is buried. This is where Anne Aletha escapes to read her books beneath the chinaberry tree next to her grandfather's grave. The ancient oak that divides the road in front of Anne Aletha's farmhouse and symbolizes her divided heart for the twin brothers still stands today on the O'Quinn Loop in Odum. I transposed the tree to Ray's Mill.

Anne Aletha is based on a real person. Her name was an amusing mixup. For years I thought my mother and aunt were calling their aunt "Anne Aletha," but they were in fact saying Aunt Elitha. Aunt Elitha had a Normal School diploma, played the piano, and lived to be a hundred. Though I fictionalized all the characters, my grandfather, Joe Clements and his twin brother and their siblings ran the Clements Lumber Mill in Ray's Mill until the early 1920s. John Henry originates from my imagination, but Uncle Doctor was my grandfather's brother who practiced medicine in nearby Adel. Neville, Patten, Frank, Roena and Jincy are all family names that I borrowed for my characters. The Klan marching down the aisle of New Ramah Primitive Baptist Church is my own invention. Sadly, the church no longer stands.

All newspaper accounts of World War I, the Ku Klux Klan, and the Spanish Influenza are true and taken from the *Atlanta Constitution*. In order to accommodate the time line, I used creative license in the following places:

Mary Turner was lynched on Sunday, May 19, 1918, not Saturday, May 18, 1918. Her husband, Hayes Turner, was hung the day before. There were five lynchings associated with Hampton Smith's murder, not four. The newspaper accounting of the lynchings in Valdosta were taken from the *Atlanta Constitution*, but I attributed them to the fictionalized *Valdosta Tribune*.

Maidee brought newspapers with news of the Suffrage Amendment's defeat to Anne Aletha on Saturday when she picked up the orphans. However, the bill was not defeated until the following Monday, May 6, 1918.

Willa Mae's assault is based on a true incident that took place in Alabama fifty years later.

Ray's Mill became Ray City in 1909, nine years before Anne Aletha arrived.

Two other historical notes: Later accounts of Mary Turner's horrific burning, butchery, and murder of her unborn child were not read in the newspapers by Anne Aletha at that time and therefore not included. Although the heyday of the Klan wasn't until 1920–1922, it is likely Klansmen were involved in the Valdosta mob lynchings.

Lastly, the joy of writing historical fiction for me is the attempt to capture the time and place of a bygone era. I hope my readers will enjoy the journey as much as I have.

Dedication

TO THE TWO GREATEST LOVES *of my life, my mother, Camille Clements, born in Ray's Mill in 1918, whose birthplace and heritage inspired Anne Aletha, and to my husband of fifty years, George, who wept at my scenes and supported my dream.*

Because the story is set in 1918, the novel uses period language, including obsolete terms for race.

1

"ALAPAHA, RAY'S MILL, VALDOSTA ... next stop Alapaha," called the conductor as Anne Aletha leaned forward in the lumpy horsehair seat trying to dislodge the blouse stuck to her back. Perspiration trickled down her midriff and the sultry air from the open window blew hot across her face. She took a deep breath, inhaling the scent of freshly plowed earth of the passing fields. For hours she'd gazed at only tall straight pines and cypress swamps, but now, further south, the red Georgia clay turned loamy and Spanish moss clung to the trees making even the tenant shanties look pretty.

At last, the passenger sitting across from her had fallen asleep. An old woman with a beaked nose, few teeth and a mole with whiskers. Along with endless rude questions: Why was she going to Ray's Mill? Why had her uncle left his farmhouse to Anne Aletha and not one of her seven brothers? Surely her parents wouldn't allow her to live there alone. And why wasn't she yet married? She prayed the nosy lady would get off at the next stop and watched the plumes of the woman's old-fashioned hat rise and fall as she slept. Along with the dead songbirds wired to its rim. A millinery style that had almost brought the small birds to extinction only a few years back. The sight sickened Anne Aletha as she thought of a world without the sweetness of birdsong.

Suddenly, the train lurched and the old lady awoke with a loud snort. Anne Aletha quickly opened the book on her lap, hoping to avoid further conversation. She felt the woman's stare as she paged through her uncle's treasured volume of Plato, searching for his favorite dialogue, *The Republic.*

"I see you got on a yellow rose, Miss. 'Yellow for suffrage and red if opposed.' Ain't that right? Bet you're one of them suffragettes, wanting women to get the vote and all." She leaned over to pull up the stockings rolled down around her ankles and rummaged noisily through an array of hat boxes at her feet. Unwrapping a package folded in wax paper, she offered a peeled boiled egg.

Anne Aletha shook her head, thanking her politely, wondering if the woman could eat it without teeth. She gave no answer to the question about women getting the vote, reluctant to defend her views to this stranger. Gratefully, moments later, the train's whistle and screeching brakes saved her from reply.

"Shame I ain't goin' further with you," said the woman, rewrapping the hard-boiled eggs. "Keep you company and all. Bet them soldiers over yonder on the platform are coming on board. Poor boys, going to Camp Hancock and then off to fight the Kaiser."

Steam hissed and the compartment doors clattered open as Anne Aletha sighed with relief. She looked out the window at the approaching depot and read the war posters lining the platform of the train station:

Buy Liberty Bonds
Do Your Duty!
Make Victory Certain
Save Our Boys in France.

Monday & Wednesday, Eat Wheatless
Tuesday, Eat Meatless
Thursday, Eat Porkless

Could it be only three months since she'd kissed her favorite brother, Frank, goodbye? He was in France by now, the first of the troops to arrive on the one-year anniversary of America's declaration of war. The great German offensive would soon begin.

The old woman stood to gather her tattered carpetbag and hat boxes as the train conductor entered their compartment. "Ten minute stop in Alapaha, ladies. Train departs for Ray's Mill at 4:17."

She turned back to Anne Aletha. "You mind yourself now, young lady, traveling alone and all. A white girl can't be too careful nowadays. The niggers is getting way too uppity. If you ask me, somebody needs to be putting them in their place."

Anne Aletha turned away in disgust, staring out the window as the woman left, angry at the widespread bigotry and appalled by the recent rise of violence and lynchings. Last week's newspaper accounts of the torture of a Negro man in Tennessee still haunted her thoughts. Chained to a tree and branded with hot irons, the man was slowly burned alive. While America and the world denounced Germany's heinous war crimes, people at home continued to condone the shameful treatment of the Negro.

Her Uncle Carter said that most people lived in a world of opinion, like the prisoners in Plato's *Allegory of the Cave*, chained to their ignorance and able to see only the shadows of the cave, never the light of knowledge. But if no one saw the light of Plato's cave, how would prejudice and intolerance ever be overcome?

She waited for the old woman to step down on the platform, then stood to stretch her legs, airing her damp clothes. Minutes later, the whistle blew and she returned to her seat, closing her tired eyes while the train jerked and clanked out of the station.

At home this morning long before the rooster crowed, she had lain awake in the big front bedroom she shared with her sisters, saddened by the thought of goodbye. Toog, the youngest, had snuggled next to her all night, her warm bottom pressed against Anne Aletha's while her other sisters slept nearby in barely discernible mounds in the darkness. But tonight, for the first time, she would sleep alone, in her own bed, and in her own house. And though sad to leave her family, the thought of this newfound freedom and independence thrilled her beyond dreams.

Opening her eyes, she watched two mongrel dogs chase the train's wheels as it gathered momentum, then slow their pursuit when the outskirts of town gave way to field and pastureland. The words of her Uncle Carter's will echoed in her head: *"I, Carter Irving, hereby bequeath my worldly possessions to my niece, Anne Aletha O'Quinn, in the hope that she will accept my legacy and make Ray's Mill her home, bringing her love of knowledge and fine Normal School teaching diploma to the children and townspeople of Ray's Mill."*

Astonishing words to everyone, but especially to her parents and eldest brother. Tears stung her eyes at the loss of her beloved uncle, both mentor and friend. Since childhood, he and his wife, Lily, had been a special part of her life, spending every Christmas with her family in Odum, Georgia. And every month since she could remember, a small parcel of books would arrive from her uncle's library, on loan to her family for their reading and enjoyment. Books that Anne Aletha cherished. Each day she could hardly wait for the hour after their midday meal, when her mother and sisters retired upstairs to rest and her father and brothers went to the porch to smoke before returning to the fields. She would hurry to the back pasture and the tall stand of pines, where her grandfather O'Quinn was buried, and prop herself against his headstone with one of her uncle's favorite books. In summer, she retreated to the shade of the riverbank on the Altamaha, leaning against the swollen bellies of the cypress trees to escape into a world far beyond her own. This hour of solitude was her most treasured of the day.

She blotted her eyes as the memories of her Uncle Carter flooded back, remembering her sixteenth birthday and the letter he'd written saying that now he would include special assignments just for her. "We're going to begin a long journey together, Aletha," he said. "You and I are going to study the world's greatest dead men. The greatest thinkers and philosophers of our time." She looked down at the volume of Plato. Books had changed her life.

"Miss?" interrupted the conductor.

She glanced up, embarrassed by her tears.

"Will you need help with your luggage? We'll be arriving in Ray's Mill at 5:12."

"Oh, no thank you. Someone is meeting me." She felt the pocket of her serge skirt and the telegram from her uncle's executor. Neville Clements had assured her parents he would meet her train.

As the locomotive neared the outskirts of town, purple clover blanketed the sides of the track and wild orange honeysuckle scented the May air, reminding her of home. She thought of Toog, and their recent nightly escapes to the far pasture. Just she and her baby sister knew that the mama raccoon had another litter of babies this year in the old chinaberry tree. Every evening, just after dusk, they would sit quietly together until the nocturnal raccoon left her kittens to forage. Descending the tree with caution, the raccoon would oftentimes have to scamper back up the tree to chastise one of her offspring when a baby head poked out as if to follow. She would miss the tiny raccoons venturing down from their hollow, but Toog would write of their antics. She smiled. Nature made her happy.

STEAM HISSED and the bell clanged as Ray's Mill came up suddenly. The moment the train chugged to a stop by the big wooden water tanks that filled its boilers, Anne Aletha jumped up, smoothed her rumpled skirt and tried with little success to repin the mass of unruly dark hair that went in every direction but the one intended. Next week she planned to bob it like all the young army nurses overseas—regardless of her mother's objections.

Lifting her heavy, cloth-covered suitcase, she stepped down cautiously onto the little iron steps of the locomotive and to the wooden platform. Passengers crowded the station waiting to board the train to Valdosta, the final destination sixteen miles away. Searching the crowd, she walked toward the depot's tiny, red-brick building. A corpulent man with mutton chops and a walrus mustache tipped his hat. She nodded, wondering if he might be Mr. Clements, but the man walked on. Another gentleman with a cane stared at her, but he seemed younger than her uncle's best friend and executor would be. An elderly Negro in overalls and a straw hat stood behind him. He might be Alex, her uncle's longtime servant and sharecropper, but he looked older than he should be.

She approached the Negro man first. "Pardon me, I wonder if you might be Alex Hamilton? I'm Anne Aletha O'Quinn."

"Why Miss Aletha," he said, removing his wide brim hat. "You don't look nothin' like your mama. Course I ain't seen her in years but I told Mr. Neville here we's lookin' for a tall, red-headed young lady."

Anne Aletha smiled, extending her hand. Only her uncle had called her Aletha.

"That would be all four of my sisters, Alex, except me. Even our baby sister is taller."

Alex quickly reached for her suitcase, appearing flustered at shaking the hand of a white woman. "Oh Miss Aletha, let me take that for you and this here is Mr. Neville."

Neville removed his hat. "It's a pleasure, Miss O'Quinn. I'm Neville Clements. Welcome to Ray's Mill."

She took his hand, studying the clean shaven face with the graying temples and clear blue eyes. "Thank you, Mr. Clements. Uncle Carter spoke so fondly of you."

The train's piercing warning whistle blew behind them. "All aboard."

"Miss Aletha, I be gettin' your trunks," said Alex. "How many you got?"

"Just one, Alex. But I'm afraid it's heavy. We might need to help you," she said before remembering Mr. Clements' cane.

"I've brought slates and books for the schoolchildren. I hope to send a book home with every child," she explained.

Neville took her elbow, walking stiff-kneed as they followed Alex to the end of the platform. "I know it's been a long day, Miss O'Quinn, and that you're anxious to get settled in. I asked Alex to bring the wagon for your trunks so he can take you out to the farmhouse. His Nellie's been cooking all day. With your permission, I'll stop by in a few days."

She nodded, thanking him for his consideration. Though filled with questions as she watched him leave, she couldn't wait to see the farmhouse, meet Nellie and have a bath.

AT THE FAR END of the platform, a boney, swaybacked mule watched Anne Aletha and Alex approach. Alex patted the mule's flank with affection and untied the reins from the hitching post. "This here's Sulky, Miss Aletha. He paw and bray a little, especially if the preacher gets long-winded on Sundays, but he a good worker."

She laughed, looking into the big watchful eyes of the scrawny old mule. She stroked him alongside the bristly tufts of hair that ran down the back of his neck, watching the twitch of his enormous ears. Perhaps she could befriend him with leftovers to fatten him, she thought, curious if Alex and the mule were as well along in years as they appeared.

She climbed up on the sagging wagon seat. Alex clucked to the mule and Sulky headed down main street, his tail swishing at flies while Alex pointed out the tiny town of two hundred inhabitants.

"See over yonder, Miss Aletha. We's got us a drugstore, a dry goods and a grocery store," he said with pride as they rode past a two-story red-brick building on their left.

Old timers on a bench outside the corner drugstore stared at her and she smiled back, wondering if every small town had a ubiquitous bench with grizzled old men who gazed and dozed. At the barber shop next door, a freshly shaven gentleman stepped out onto the sidewalk and tipped his hat toward her, while a middle-aged lady came out of the dry goods store vigorously fanning the heated afternoon air with a cardboard advertising fan. She eyed Anne Aletha with curiosity, nodded briefly and strode next door to Willard's Grocery.

Sulky plodded along as Alex continued. "Got a feed and seed store down yonder and a hardware store. The bank and the post office be on the corner. We gonna turn left there. Got us a fancy hat shop too, Miz Mobley's. My Nellie likes to look in the window at all her pretties."

The milliner's shop was fancier than she expected. In the window, iridescent peacock feathers spilled out of a tall vase, and spring hats in every size, shape and color filled the window display, each one festooned with ribbons, flowers, and feathers.

"It's lovely," she said, regretting she'd not brought Nellie something frilly. All four of her sisters could sew, each of them so clever with needle and thread and able to fancy up any old hat or piece of clothing with just the smallest bits of lace or trim. Her own lack of sewing abilities was always a source of great ridicule.

At the corner bank, Alex slowed, the mule turning left off main street. "This here road go all the way out to the Clements Lumber Mill, 'bout a mile down the road. Most folks lives along it."

"Does Mr. Neville read law and run the lumber mill?" she asked, recalling that her uncle said Neville Clements' library surpassed even his own.

"No ma'am. Mr. Neville's brother, Mr. Patten, runs it now, since old Mr. Clements die. They's twins, you know. Ain't nothin' alike though. Mr. Neville, why he's as polite to us colored as he is to any white man. Mr. Patten's fair, but he a hard man. Now, Miz Clements, their mother, she a fine lady and Miss Jincy too, Mr. Patten's daughter. His wife die in child birthin.'"

She wondered how old Neville Clements was, curious about his cane. "Did Mr. Neville have an accident?"

"Yes'um. Mr. Patten lame him when they were youngins. Horsing around a buggy. Mr. Neville climb up on the buggy wheels just as Mr. Patten telling the mare to giddy-up."

A short distance later, Alex tugged on the reins of the old mule to slow him and turned the buggy onto a narrow dirt road. "This here's the old millpond road. Miss Effie live there on the corner."

A small, weathered, gray clapboard house stood behind a privet hedge, and a tiny, stooped lady in an old-fashioned sunbonnet and house slippers hung out washing on a backyard clothes line that was almost as low to the ground as she was. A nanny goat with two white baby goats frolicked around her, and Anne Aletha thought them soon likely to snatch the bloomers and dish towels off the line. The wizened lady turned and waved.

Anne Aletha smiled and waved back.

"Afternoon, Miss Effie," called Alex as they passed.

"Folks call her the goat lady cause she treat 'em like children. Let 'em come in the house, even the billy goat. But she a kind old lady."

Anne Aletha thought about Frank and the pet pig that had followed him everywhere as a child. Once they came through the front door, down the wide hallway and into the big kitchen where the girls squealed and the pig squealed and her mother shooed him out.

"We's a little ways down the road. Only house on it, 'sides the gristmill. Mr. Ray dam up the old cypress pond here years ago and built hisself a gristmill. Used to be a commissary and post office out here too, but now only time folks travel this road is when corn's comin' in."

"Is the millpond large?" she asked.

"Yes'um. These cypress waters go all the way to the Okefenokee swamp. It full of catfish and bream. Mr. Carter and Mr. Neville went fishing every Saturday. Catch a mess of bream and Nellie would fry 'em up. Till Mr. Carter took sick. Then Mr. Neville just come around and read to him."

She heard the catch in his voice and let the silence follow, realizing that he and Nellie had been with her uncle almost a lifetime. Though she'd not told her parents, she intended to deed Alex and Nellie their tenant cottage with a little land. The three of them could farm the land together and she knew her uncle would approve.

"See them fields over yonder? This here used to be all cotton. A real pretty sight when them pink flowers first bloom and then all those white bolls open up across the fields."

She looked at the land now lying fallow in neglect, seeing the enormous task ahead. She'd hoped to plant a small crop of cotton, enough to gin this fall. If only Frank wasn't fighting in the war, he could help, but then worry for his safety crowded out her selfish thoughts. "When did Uncle Carter stop farming the land?"

"Years back, after Miss Lily die. Things never was the same. Seem like every year we tried to make a good cotton crop, nature just went against us. Now, it's the boll weevil. Nellie and me's holding on though. She takes in a little washin' and ironing, and even though I got the rheumatism, I can still chop wood, hoe, and plow—a little."

She had counted on the farm earning cash, knowing her meager teacher's salary wouldn't nearly cover the cost. They'd need money for seed and fertilizer and the yearly property taxes due in spring. Her father's one-year condition had seemed a reasonable amount of time for her to succeed when the will was read. But now, seeing Alex and the swaybacked mule, worry settled in.

"See that big old oak tree yonder in the middle of the road? The house sits to the right, a ways back from the road. Me and Nellie live in the tenant cottage behind it."

The huge, ancient, oak that divided the road stretched out before them with majestic branches that caught the dappled rays of the late afternoon sun. She could see how over the years man and beast had naturally deferred to the mammoth tree, taking both horse and buggy around it.

The old mule, anticipating the riddance of passengers and harness, quickened his pace, jerking them onto a narrow rutted path.

Anne Aletha shielded her eyes from the setting sun as the modest farmhouse came into view. Had she envisioned it grander or in better repair without a sagging porch and missing roof shingles? She scolded herself for the momentary disappointment and turned to Alex. "I can't believe it's really mine, Alex. I hope to make Uncle Carter proud."

Sulky jostled them until he stopped at the hitching post in front of the house. Moments later, Nellie stepped out on the porch looking just as Anne Aletha had imagined her, hearty and kind faced with stout arms held out in welcome. Anne Aletha waved, grateful for her good fortune.

2

ON HER FIRST SUNDAY in Ray's Mill, Anne Aletha knew she should be in church, sitting next to Neville on a hard pew and listening to a preacher drone. Instead, she hurried down the millpond's rutted lane toward town, stepping over mule dung, and praying for a long-winded sermon. Neville would soon chide, saying that she must get out and meet people, especially the parents of potential pupils. But she could do that later. Today, after a week of scrubbing, she wanted to explore Ray's Mill in the deserted quiet of the mid May morning.

In the tall pines across from her, mourning doves cooed as squirrels chattered and fussed, chasing each other round and round the trunk of a loblolly pine. Alongside in the ditch, a black swallowtail butterfly flitted among the Queen Anne's lace, and up ahead, a plump robin darted out from the weeds, intent upon something in the middle of the road. She paused, but the bird ignored her, hopping first forward in pursuit, then backwards in retreat. Creeping closer, she saw the bird's dilemma as a small baby snake sat basking in the warm dirt. And though neither bird nor snake took notice, she skirted their periphery.

Further ahead, she stopped to re-pin the hot heavy hair off the nape of her neck. Propping up her aunt's old broken parasol against a tree—brought in case of nipping dogs—she tucked as much hair as possible beneath the rim of her straw hat. And though the new raised hemlines allowed more air to circulate around her ankles, it didn't help cool her today. She rolled up the sleeves of her high-collared blouse and decided to keep to the shade. Perhaps see where Neville lived.

At the corner, she turned right, walking past Miss Effie's front yard, admiring her small war garden, fenced, she assumed, to keep out the goats. Everywhere, vegetables grew in mass profusion. Along the picket fence and up the front walk, young sweet potato vines trailed, pole beans climbed, and squash plants blossomed. Even onions spilled out of her flower boxes, sprouting like daffodils. In fact, it appeared that President Wilson's war-gardening campaign had struck a patriotic chord with the whole country. He'd rallied everyone by asking each American to add to the nation's food supply so that essential labor and freight trains could be released for the war effort. All spring, posters lined the train depots and store windows advertising the campaign with catchy phrases like: *Can Vegetables, Fruit and the Kaiser too*, and *Every garden a Munitions Plant*. She liked *Sow the seeds of Victory* the best, but as always, thought of Frank, knowing that the trenches of France loomed ahead for him soon. Maybe tomorrow she'd receive a letter. Just this week she'd read that the Huns had let loose a storm of mustard gas on General Pershing's men, and now she felt even more dread.

She walked a little further and stopped in front of a large white house with a wraparound porch. She gazed at the unusual cupola perched on top of its gabled roof. Perfect for cloud watching and a book, she thought, except in summer when it would be hot as Hades. As she stood wondering if anyone ever went up there, a horse and rider came up so suddenly that she didn't have time to step off the road out of sight. She swore an unladylike profanity beneath her breath.

The horse rode toward her and she continued to walk, hoping the rider wouldn't stop. But the huge bay horse galloped toward her like a colt, halting beside her in a cloud of dust. The large man astride the horse touched the brim of his hat, but did not remove it.

"Good morning," she said, noticing his sawdust-covered boots and the heavy muscled thighs that strained through khaki work pants. Shading her eyes from the sun, she looked up into the face of a square-jawed handsome man.

"Isn't the new school teacher supposed to be in church on Sunday?" he asked. His amused eyes traveled her torso without apology.

She reddened but held his gaze, noting the familiar pale eyes. Bluer in an outdoors face, she decided. And he was leaner in body than Neville too. "Playing hooky and hoping I wouldn't get caught," she replied.

"Well, I'd say you've got about an hour before church lets out. But I wouldn't be caught on this road when it does. You'll just give the ladies of Ray's Mill fodder for their gossip and set tongues to wagging."

"You must be Patten, Neville's twin brother." Without his courtesy and manners, she thought, as she craned her neck to converse.

He nodded. "Neville says you plan to start a school out there on your uncle's old place. Did he tell you we've got a visiting school teacher? Had her for years. An ornery old maid who lives in Hahira and splits her boarding time among families. She'll be none too happy."

"Well, hopefully the parents will be, since they'll no longer have to board her." She ignored his remarks about spinsterhood, liking her own just fine.

"Keep on going and you'll dead end into the lumber mill, about a mile down the road. Shut down with boiler problems right now. But if the war ends too soon and the banks won't extend our credit, it'll be permanent." Patten Clements tipped his hat, gave the reins of his horse a light slap, and with the same abruptness in which he arrived, rode off toward town.

She watched the dust swirl in his wake wondering how twins could be so opposite. Though she admired forthrightness, no Odum boy had ever acted as ill-mannered or stared with such boldness. Still, she wished all of her hair wasn't tucked up under her hat.

THE NEXT MORNING, Anne Aletha pushed open the kitchen screen door with her shoulder and stepped out to the backyard. She carried a greasy dishpan full of meat scraps, pork skins and fat trimmings—leftovers saved for soap making. While Alex and Nellie picked up Monday's washing from the well-to-do white families in Ray's Mill, she had a hot kindling fire going beneath the big three-legged kettle in the backyard. Fragrant wood smoke filled the air and the buckets of water she'd hauled from the well on the back porch bubbled to a boil. First, she carefully added the lye rendered from all the fireplace ashes, and then scraped the fatty meat trimmings into the boiling black kettle. She would check it in an hour, and, as Nellie instructed, test it with the feather of a chicken wing to see if the lye had dissolved the grease. If the chicken feather dissolved, leaving only the stem, the portion of lye was correct. But if part of the feather remained, she'd have to add more lye. "Folks don't want no meat skins and scraps in their soap," Nellie warned.

She hated the whole disgusting mess, especially the smell. But the lye soap would bleach the floors a creamy white and scour all the winter's soot from the lace curtains and bed linens. Even shampoo her hair to a shiny sheen, if afterward she rinsed it with vinegar.

The screen door slammed behind her and she turned to see Nellie coming down the porch steps, her brow wrinkled in a frown.

"Y'all are home early, Nellie. I thought I'd get the soap started so we can scrub floors this week."

Cicero, her uncle's old orange tabby followed behind, walking stiff-legged with rheumatism like Nellie. "We got done early, Miss Aletha, but you's got company on the front porch. I told 'em to just have a seat while I fetched you." Nellie whispered as she neared, "It's Miz Idabelle Perry and Mr. Ralph Attaway come to call. Come to snoop and gossip's more like it."

Anne Aletha shook her head as she wiped greasy hands down the front of her apron and pushed up the sleeves of her old, brown calico dress. How did anyone get a thing done in a small town? Growing up on her family's large farm out in the country with its endless chores and cooking, there was little time for visiting, except on Sundays. And that suited her just fine. Didn't women in Ray's Mill have anything better to do than put on a damn corset and go calling? And they never talked about anything of interest to her. Mostly, how many jars of watermelon rinds they'd pickled and who was feeling poorly. Lately, it seemed, all anyone was talking about was the *Birth of A Nation*. An outrageous and fictitious moving picture based on a book that portrayed the Ku Klux Klan as chivalrous and heroic. And what angered her the most was that the three-hour epic was playing in Atlanta to cheering record crowds. Fortunately, Ray's Mill didn't have a moving picture house.

Nellie interrupted her thoughts. "Miss Aletha, you want to run go change into something else? I'll go offer 'em some cool water. We don't got no ice left."

"Oh, thank you Nellie. No, I think I'll go just like I am. Maybe they'll see we're busy and go home."

"HOW NICE OF YOU BOTH TO COME," she said, greeting her visitors with a smile and handshake. "I'm

Anne Aletha O'Quinn. Won't you have a seat? I'm sorry I can't offer y'all something besides water."

Introducing themselves, Idabelle Perry looked at Anne Aletha's soiled apron and exchanged glances with Ralph Attaway. "Oh dear, it looks like we've come at a bad time. I told Brother Attaway you're probably still getting settled in, and that's why you didn't come to church yesterday." Sweet faced, without a hair out of place, she dabbed at her perspiring nose and forehead, careful not to disturb the face powder caked into the creases of her wrinkles.

Anne Aletha nodded. "Oh yes, there's so much to do. It's hard to know where to start. We're scrubbing the house from the inside out. And hoping to get the fields cleared before next spring. Y'all know my Uncle Carter couldn't do much these last few years."

"Lord a mercy, girl, you ain't no field hand. But you sure are pretty. Folks thought you might be kinda plain … I mean not being married and all." Idabelle giggled, bringing her hand to her mouth, though not in time to hide the mule-sized teeth.

The effeminate little man rushed to speak, sputtering in a high-pitched voice.

"What Miz Idabelle means is we knew you were a young lady school teacher and all. Your uncle was real proud. But aren't you scared staying out here by yourself? Being a white woman and all … I mean with the colored situation, that is."

Anne Aletha didn't know what he meant about the colored situation and she had no intention of asking. "Why no, Mr. Attaway, I'm not a bit afraid. I have Alex and Nellie behind me in the tenant cottage, and they're already like family to me." She stepped back slightly from his spittle and the smell of mothballs that assailed her nostrils. How strange that he wore a wool suit in summertime. But surprisingly, the only evidence of sweat was one long wet strand of hair he'd combed over his balding scalp.

"Well, Miss O'Quinn, Brother Attaway and I won't keep you. We just stopped by to introduce ourselves and to invite you to Wednesday night prayer meeting. New Ramah Primitive Baptist has a fine new preacher. If you haven't taken Jesus as your savior, Brother Elrod will sure make you want to step forward to the pulpit."

She forced a smile. "Y'all are so kind. Mr. Neville has already invited me to his church and I've promised to come with him soon." This was a lie, but she'd stomached enough sermons on sin and perdition to last a lifetime. In fact, she might not ever go back to church. "I do so appreciate y'all coming out here though, and I hope you'll come again when I'm settled. We'll have some lemonade on the porch." She turned, pointing to the steps. "Be real careful on that next to last step. It's rotten. Alex and I need to replace it."

Ralph Attaway hesitated. "Oh, and Miss O'Quinn, we almost forgot. Miz Idabelle and I are on the Liberty Bond Committee. We were wondering if you've made a pledge yet for the third Liberty Bond. If you haven't, you only have to pay two fifty today, and then the next ten- dollar installments are not due till July eighteenth."

"Thank you Mr. Attaway, but I pledged at home before I left." This too was a lie, but one she regretted because she was financially unable to make another pledge. With school still months away, she struggled weekly with her first fifty dollar Liberty Bond pledge. And no matter how often she tallied the column of figures, her debt and the prospects of paying it off anytime soon remained unchanged.

THE NEXT EVENING in the fading daylight of the front parlor, Neville Clements rose from her uncle's favorite chair and adjusted the wick of the kerosene lamp to better illuminate the room. Across from him on the horsehair settee, Anne Aletha plumped up the crocheted pillow behind her back, wishing she could prop her feet up on the ottoman in front of her. Instead, she crossed them ladylike at the ankles, delighted that Neville had brought a book of poetry to read.

"Thank you for coming, Neville. Nellie says you came by and read to Uncle Carter every evening while he was sick. I know you were good friends and that you miss him." She paused a moment before smiling. "Nellie says you talked wars a lot."

He grinned. "Well, you know your uncle loved history. And his recall was quite amazing, especially the long passages of prose he could quote. One of his favorites was Shakespeare's *Henry the Fifth at Agincourt*. I'm sure Nellie heard his recitation many times. 'We few, we happy few, we band of brothers, for he today that sheds his blood with me.'" Neville stopped, and she suspected that he too knew the long speech by heart.

"But this evening, I brought the poem your uncle requested on his last night."

"Really? You read this to him on the night he died?"

"Yes, Matthew Arnold's 'Dover Beach.' As you may know, Arnold died at the end of the last century, long before our great war began. But your uncle found the corollary to our war today quite interesting."

She nodded as Neville began the poem in a deep baritone whisper:

> The sea is calm tonight
> The tide is full, the moon less fair
> Upon the straits, on the French coast, the light
> Gleams, and is gone; the cliffs of England stand,
> Glimmering and vast, out in the tranquil bay.
> Come to the window, sweet is the night air!
> Only, from the long line of spray
> Where the ebb meets the moon-blanched sand,
> Listen! you hear the grating roar
> Of pebbles which the waves draw back, and fling,
> At their return, up the high strand,
> Begin, and cease, and then again begin,

With tremulous cadence slow, and bring
The eternal note of sadness in.

Sophocles long ago
Heard it on the Aegean, and it brought
Into his mind the turbid ebb and flow
Of human misery; we
Find also in the sound a thought,
Hearing it by this distant northern sea.

Neville paused, glancing over at Anne Aletha before continuing. His voice now less subdued.

The Sea of Faith
Was once, too, at the full, and round earth's shore
Lay like the folds of a bright girdle furled;
But now I only hear
Its melancholy, long, withdrawing roar,
Retreating to the breath
Of the night-wind down the vast edges drear
And naked shingles of the world.

Ah, love, let us be true
To one another! for the world, which seems
To lie before us like a land of dreams,
So various, so beautiful, so new,
Hath really neither joy, nor love, nor light,
Nor certitude, nor peace, nor help for pain;
And we are here as on a darkling plain
Swept with confused alarms of struggle and fight,
Where ignorant armies clash by night!

Neither of them spoke as Neville closed the small leather-bound volume of poetry and removed his reading spectacles. Outside the open window, a bobwhite called from the stubble of the fallow cotton field and the evening breeze rippled the parlor curtains.

"It's beautiful, Neville. But so sad and desolate. I'm glad you were with him that last night. That he didn't die alone." Her voice broke with unexpected tears as she whispered, "I shall miss him."

Neville struggled to his feet. "I'm sorry Anne Aletha. I didn't mean to upset you. You know he was so proud of you, your teaching and your intellect. I think you reminded him of the daughter they lost so long ago."

She stood and reached for his hand. "Thank you, Neville. I'm glad you came, and I hope you'll come again soon. I look forward to sharing the great literature together, like you and Uncle Carter." She withdrew her hand, aware of the wide expanse of his chest and her sudden need for the comfort of a brotherly embrace.

"Yes, I would like that too," said Neville. "And on my next visit, we'll discuss your school teaching plans. Perhaps you'll allow me a few suggestions for meeting the parents of potential pupils."

"Thank you, and also, I wanted to ask you about the visiting school teacher—"

"Let's speak first with families who have previously boarded Miss Perkins and I think introductions can best be made after Sunday church."

Anne Aletha nodded, trying not to frown or show her reticence. But she had not realized solicitation of pupils would be necessary.

THE ROBIN COCKED HER HEAD to the ground as if listening for worms. All morning the bird had eyed each spadeful of overturned dirt as Anne Aletha planted her mother's zinnia seeds by the back porch. The robin's first brood of the season snuggled in a cup-shaped nest, smoothed and lined with mud in the tea olive tree by the side of the house. Fortunately, Cicero showed little interest in them other than their chirping during feeding time. Too old to climb the high flimsy branches, he napped beneath the house, opening one eye occasionally as she shoveled manure into the newly dug flowerbed. But mainly he waited for Nellie's return and his breakfast leftovers.

Sweat dripped from her nose and she tried not to smear dirt across her face as she opened the envelope with her mother's prize seeds. Zinnia seeds in red, yellow and pink, her favorite summer flower. At home, nothing would grow from the side porch. This was because all the boys peed off the porch, including their father, though her mother forbade it. As she gathered the tiny seeds in the palm of her hand and scattered them, covering them with a thin layer of dirt, she thought of home, suddenly wistful. The old home place was always quiet in the heat of the early afternoon. Soon, everyone would be napping. After the noonday meal, her mother and sisters would go upstairs to stretch out on top of the big feather beds. There they would lie in hopeful anticipation of any breeze that would stir the languorous air. But mostly, they just tossed and turned trying to reposition themselves on a fresh cool place on the bed as the heat from their body rose up to meet them. Downstairs, her brothers headed to the cool of the springhouse in summer while her father settled into his favorite rocker on the porch. He would prop his feet on the banister, take a few puffs of his pipe and within minutes hold the whole household captive with his loud snores.

She smiled and lifted the heavy watering can, gently watering in the tiny seeds and noticing a big juicy worm slither toward her. Using the shovel, she tossed it to the robin. As she wondered if the bird would take it, she heard Sulky's fast-paced trot and Nellie's excited voice: "Miss Aletha, you's got a letter from Mr. Frank! "

Somewhere in France
April 19, 1918

Dear Anne Aletha,

The mail still hasn't caught up with us yet, but I'm hopeful it'll get here soon. Today, we started our move to the front and the rain and mud sure aren't helping. We walked 21 kilometers in heavy hobnailed boots with the rain pounding down our helmets and backs. Tonight, every soldier has blisters and a headache.

I don't know how far we are from the front but when we get there, we'll be installing radio antenna stations. This keeps the artillery and infantry divisions in touch with each other so we don't bomb our own men as they advance. We go into the battle site first with the infantry, install the radio set, and then advise the artillery division behind us. After the battle, we stay and take down the set. But remember, it's the doughboys that do the real fighting, so try not to worry.

(A few days later)
We're closer now. Last night we began night walks to the front in the pitch dark. The sounds of guns are loud and our orders are given in whispers. You can see silvery light in the distance as German artillery shells pierce the blackness.
The captain says tonight's a good one for a gas attack. The air is moist and heavy and if the breeze lessens, he thinks Fritz'll probably try it. They say it looks like a yellowish brown fog whirling along the ground. We carry a gas mask at all times and have only seconds to get the contraption on. The mask has two glass eyes with a fabric tube that is attached to a metal canister. The mouthpiece uses peach pits as a filter and the filter is supposed to neutralize the mustard gas. I just hope it works.
I think Mama could use one for her beekeeping.

(The next day)
This morning orders came down for us to report to infantry brigade headquarters. A grim sight since we're only a short distance from the front lines. There are lots of tanks in the region and loads of aeroplanes. Dead Germans and Americans lying around terribly mangled. I try not to look.
The food kitchens aren't up this far so it's a question of living on hard tack and corn willy. You wouldn't think you could

eat with all the carnage, but they say the belly rules the mind. Occasionally, the rationing mule carts come by destined for the doughboys.

(A week later)
I am enclosing a few violets from outside our dugout. Even with all the trees destroyed by shells and mustard gas, the war still hasn't prevented these little flowers from blooming, offering their hope and beauty.
Our dugout is quite roomy with a three legged chair, a sandbag table and fragments of a gilded mirror from a nearby demolished house. Along with our straw pallets, mess tins, shaving material, and sputtering candles. In addition, we have several large rats that are watching me as I write you. They are really quite harmless and friendly. Not only do we rely on them for companionship, but you can depend on them to give the first alarm in case of gas long before it harms you. I know you wouldn't mind them, but Thelma and Gussie would alert the whole German army with their squeals.

(The next day)
We have full view of the German lines to the North and the Americans to the South. Today the Germans shot down 3 of our observation balloons. Men jumped out of them with parachutes and then the planes came back and shot them on the way down. I hope every damn Hun rots in hell.

Your loving brother,
Frank

Heartsick with worry, Anne Aletha folded his letter, carefully preserving the delicate lavender violets dried to the paper. Though the Kaiser hinted every day in the newspapers about peace, Theodore Roosevelt was warning the country against the ruse, saying, "We must gird up our loins, build our ships and prepare our military. The only way to win a lasting peace."

She hoped he was right. Now, all she could think about was Frank crawling on his belly like a worm every time he left the dugout with dirt splintering explosions all around him and the unrelenting possibility of death each day.

3

HER UNCLE'S POCKET WATCH said midnight. Either she dreamed it, or men on horses had just ridden by the farmhouse. She didn't know which. Who would be coming back from the millpond this time of night? But as she looked out the open window, crickets were the only night sounds.

She crawled back into the middle of the big feather bed and watched the shadows of the kerosene lamp flicker across the ceiling, thinking about the shadows of Plato's cave. A cave where prisoners were chained to their ignorance, living in a world of appearances and opinion, but not of knowledge. Her uncle said that in life one must be sure to make the distinctions. "Is it opinion or is it knowledge?"

She leaned over the bedside table and blew softly down the glass chimney, smelling the pungency of the snuffed-out wick. Wide awake, she thought about all the tasks for the day ahead, compiling a mental list of everything she hoped to get done. First thing in the morning, they'd bring out the old hollowed-out cypress troughs from the barn and start the water and lye soap to boil in the yard's tripod kettle. She'd go through the house and strip the rooms, gathering up all the washables: quilts, lace curtains, mantel scarves, doilies and bed linens. And just like they'd done at home with each new season, they'd sweep the floors, beat the rugs and sun the feather mattresses. And she mustn't forget her aunt's table linens packed away in the old sugar chest.

She enjoyed the ritual of spring-cleaning, the catharsis of bringing forth order to her world, like nature bringing forth its new spring growth. Drifting off to sleep, she hoped for a cloudless blue sky.

"WHEW, THAT'S STRONG AMMONIA," said Nellie, holding her nose and stirring the sudsy pail of water between them.

"Just hang your head out the window," teased Anne Aletha. While the morning's laundry soaked in the big cypress tubs outside in the yard, she and Nellie washed the tall wavy panes of glass in the front parlor, drying them with old *Valdosta Tribune* newspapers stacked between them. Nellie made her windows squeak the loudest.

As they worked, Anne Aletha envisioned the parlor put back together with fresh lacy white curtains at the windows, scrubbed pine floors beneath the old worn Persian carpet, and her uncle's roll top desk and mahogany bookcases polished and smelling of beeswax. The room reminded her of both her aunt and uncle. Her aunt's love of beauty and her uncle's love of wisdom. "Function and beauty," her uncle would say. "Things must serve both."

As they wiped and dried the last of the windowpanes, she felt the warmth of the sunlight on her cheeks and saw her reflection in the glass. Outside, the sun's rays caught the underneath side of the magnolia leaves making them transparent. They were the young green of spring. Momentarily, a small cloud passed, dimming the sunlight and then a movement in the yard caught her eye. Someone was approaching the house.

"Oh damnation, Nellie. Look who's coming. Again."

Both rolled their eyes as they watched Ralph Attaway scurry across the yard, baggy clothes and turned-down mouth reminding her of a sad-faced clown, except when he smiled and scrunched up his nose, raising his bushy mustache. Then he looked just like a rodent.

"You hoo, you hooo, Miss O'Quinn," he called, his voice high pitched and excited. He stomped across the floorboards of the porch.

She stuck her head out the open window. "Hello, Mr. Attaway." Then held up her hands blackened with newsprint. "Washing windows today." Hoping that refreshments would not be expected, she added, "I'll be with you in a minute."

Nellie slunk into the corner out of sight giving her a conspiring smile as Anne Aletha went to the door. This time Anne Aletha intended to set him in a rocking chair, remembering the last visit when he'd nearly backed her off the porch into the camellia bushes with his errant spit and smell of mothballs.

Breathless, he smacked his lips. "I thought I'd better come out and warn you Miss O'Quinn, you being a white woman out here alone and all."

"What is it, Mr. Attaway?" she asked, grateful she no longer had younger brothers eavesdropping beneath the porch who would snicker and call him a sissy within earshot.

"You best stay inside tonight. And have those two nigras of yours stay put too."

She heard the edge in her voice. "What is it you've come to tell me, Mr. Attaway?"

"There's gonna be trouble. Folks say the Klan's riding tonight."

Her jaw tightened. "What do you mean? Why are Klansmen coming to Ray's Mill?"

He fumbled with his spectacles hooking the gold wire over his ears and then opened the newspaper with a flourish. "It says here:

Hampton Smith, a prominent young farmer living near Valdosta was shot and killed last night through the open window of his home after supper. His wife, Mrs. Smith, escaped and ran through the field to a small branch where she remained in hiding two hours. Mrs. Smith said it was a colored man and thought it might be a young man named Sidney Johnson who had been working for her husband a few weeks. The motive is not known. Mr. and Mrs. Smith have been married only a short while. She is a very pretty woman."

"When did this happen, Mr. Attaway?"

"Night before last. People say he didn't act alone. They're searching for the other farmhands that worked on the Smith place. Says here:

At 5 o'clock this evening Sheriff Dix and a posse from Berrien County with track dogs reached Valdosta to assist the officers and a posse from Lowndes County. At 6:30 this evening a message from Sheriff Dix said that his dogs have run the negro to cover in a swamp several miles northeast near Ray's Mill."

Ralph Attaway rustled the newspaper importantly. "The Klan'll get him, Miss O'Quinn. Sheriff Dix doesn't have to worry. Those fellas won't let him get away."

She felt her anger rise. "So the people in this community condone secret vigilantes that hide behind white sheets and take the law into their own hands?"

"Well now, Miss O'Quinn," he said, sputtering. "Some folks think they do a service in our communities."

"And what would that service be, Mr. Attaway? Spreading hatred and narrow-minded ideas about Negroes and Jews? Tar and feathering people, maiming them or hanging them from the nearest tree? Then having the audacity to promote themselves as decent Christian men who are protecting America?"

His eyes narrowed and she stopped, realizing the futility of her words. "Mr. Attaway, thank you for coming all the way out here, but I have windows to wash." Turning, she marched through the screen door, letting it slam hard against its frame, not caring that the glass transoms shook above her head.

She found Nellie in the backyard leaning over the long-footed wash trough, as serene and unruffled as her prize Rhode Island Reds that pecked the ground around her. Anne Aletha was still taking deep breaths.

"Lord, Nellie, did you hear him? I know he's nothing but an old gossip but are there Klansmen in Ray's Mill?"

Nellie didn't look up as she swished the strong lye soap through the lace curtains, as gently as she kneaded her biscuit dough. "I heard him, Miss Aletha."

Nellie said nothing further and Anne Aletha moved to the trough of quilts across from Nellie, staring at the soap scum that floated on top of the brown dirty water. The air smelled rank and she could almost taste the lye soap. "Nellie, I heard horses coming back from the millpond last night. I thought I dreamed it. But now I know it was the Klan." With an angry thrust, she plunged the quilts down into the trough sending a foul backlash of water up over her. "Oh damn, Nellie, now look what I've done."

"Careful you don't splash no lye water in your eyes, Miss Aletha." She untied her gingham apron from around her waist and brought it to her. "Here now, dry your face good with this."

Anne Aletha blotted her eyes carefully, remembering the little boy in Odum blinded in one eye by his playmates innocently throwing lye powder they'd found in the barn. In the distance, she heard the noonday mill whistle blow. They'd be three o'clock getting the wash rinsed and on the lines, but the hot sun would dry it in a couple of hours. They could still get everything folded and sorted into the large hickory slatted baskets before dusk. "Thank you, Nellie. Let's go sit under the shade trees for a few minutes."

As they walked, Cicero weaved in and out between them. Nellie lowered herself stiffly down on the old bench nearest the woodpile and Anne Aletha reached down to pick up the large ginger-colored tomcat, cradling him in her arms like a baby, scratching behind his tattered ears.

"He's sure taken with you," said Nellie.

She uprighted him, placing him on the worktable between them. "I know he misses Uncle Carter." They were silent a few moments, while Cicero purred and washed his face. In the branches above their heads, a blue jay squawked at the intrusion of the orange tabby. "Nellie, are there Klansmen in Ray's Mill?"

Nellie sighed with barely a nod. "Course it's all hush, hush. Nobody knows for sure, but Alex thinks so."

"Why?"

"Last spring a colored man was hung from Cat Creek Bridge."

Goosebumps prickled Anne Aletha's forearms. "What happened?"

"A white man by the name of Tippin came over here from Adel. Had a turpentine still there. He went over to Mr. Lonnie's still out on Cat Creek. Said the wife of one of his colored workers ran off with one of Mr. Lonnie's men. Said he came to take her back. That Tippin fella went over to the turpentine worker's shack and stood in the open doorway talking to him. Folks said all of a sudden a pistol shot rang out and Tippin was shot dead. The turpentine worker took off running to the woods but later we heard the Klan brought their dogs to find him. They hung him from Cat Creek Bridge and then riddled his body with bullets."

"What did people say?"

"Nobody much minded since folks knew he was guilty. Nobody but us colored."

"Well, I'd like you and Alex to stay close tonight. I want to talk to Neville. I'm going over there late this afternoon."

ANNE ALETHA STOOD NAKED in front of the chifforobe, her damp work clothes piled in a heap on the floor, trying to decide what she would wear, what time she would leave to walk over to the Clements' and if a sponge bath and talcum powder would suffice. If she left too early, Neville might not be home and if she left too late, she might interrupt their supper. Unfortunately, Patten Clements would probably be there too.

From the corner washstand, she lifted the flower-sprigged china pitcher and poured tepid water into its matching bowl. A slight cross breeze between the bedroom windows stirred the warm air as she considered washing her hair. She could take the galvanized hip tub out on the back porch behind the well, draw up water to fill the wash tub and hang a sheet up for privacy but then she probably wouldn't have enough time for her hair to dry. That's another reason to bob it, she thought. On the mottled mirror of her aunt's dressing table, she'd saved a snapshot from this month's edition of *Ladies' Home Journal*, showing three young Red Cross nurses with their arms encircling each other's waists, looking brave and modern with their hair in new bobs. Nellie would require coaxing though. But the war had changed everything, even wearing corsets. Just last spring, when President Wilson declared war, corset manufacturers immediately began to convert steel from women's corsets into ammunition, and now both the endowed and unendowed were finally freed from the dictates of fashion. If women considered giving up their metal corsets to be patriotic, like buying a Liberty Bond, bobbing one's hair should be considered just another practicality of war.

THE FADING AFTERNOON SUN cast lengthening shadows as Anne Aletha hurried down the millpond road. It was her favorite time of day, just before dusk, with its soft, filtered light. Somewhere from the hardwoods, a whippoorwill whistled. Though late, she paused to pluck a delicate pink flower from a blooming mimosa, inhaling the sweetness of the powder-puff blossom, its stamens tickling her nose.

She wondered what Neville would say about the Klan and tried to recollect what she'd read about its recent revitalization, remembering that a Colonel Simmons had taken a small group of followers to the top of Stone Mountain in Atlanta on Thanksgiving Day a few years back. They'd built an altar, doused a pine cross with kerosene and lit up the night sky. Later on, a scandal broke out about Colonel Simmons because he turned out to be only a private from the Spanish-American War. But this had not dampened the fervor and growth of the secret fraternal organization.

At the end of the road, she stopped to shake the grit and sand out of her shoes, balancing one legged on each foot, wondering why she'd worn her best pumps to walk a mile down a dirt road, then thought of Patten's stare and blushed. She didn't see Miss Effie, but the goats were sleeping in the shade of the barn and a small bantam rooster strutted on top of the hen house, his red wattle and comb shaking while his beady yellow eyes followed her.

She turned and soon the widow's walk of the Clements' house came into view. Breezy ferns hung from the wide front porch and old-fashioned red roses spilled over the white picket fence. She lifted the gate latch and walked up the path, hesitating at the screen door to listen before knocking. Silverware clanged from the dining room. Damn, she thought, they were eating. Before turning to flee, she heard a chair push back from the table.

"Sons, I think there's a visitor at the door."

Forced to wait, she watched as the tall, slightly stooped Mrs. Clements came graciously to greet her. She was lovely with wispy white hair pulled back in a bun and crinkly blue eyes. "Do come in, Miss O'Quinn. I'm Roena Clements and it's so nice to meet you. In fact, I was going to send Neville around with an invitation this week."

"Thank you, but I'm so sorry to interrupt your supper. I had a matter to discuss with Neville, but I can come back."

"Heavens no, we're finished and there's plenty left. Queenie cooked some early summer squash and pole beans with hoecakes. Come on in and let me fix you a plate." She beckoned her inside.

"I'm afraid I've already eaten, but it sounds wonderful," she said following the older lady into a large parlor with high ceilings. A tall silver vase of magnolia blossoms sat on the hall table and she could smell their lemony fragrance. They entered the dining room and Neville's smiling face greeted her as he held out a chair.

"What a pleasure, Anne Aletha," he said. "Come sit down here beside Jincy, Patten's daughter, and you must have a slice of mother's superb pound cake. I believe you've met Patten?"

"Hello, yes, and forgive me for interrupting." She sat down, giving Jincy's arm a small pat before glancing quickly at Patten at the end of the table. As he stood at half stance waiting for her to be seated, she felt pink splotches of embarrassment blossom on her neck.

Mrs. Clements returned from the sideboard with a slice of pound cake. "How about some sweet cream on it? Sarah Sweeney has the best dairy cows in Berrien County. Or a glass of buttermilk? My husband always enjoyed buttermilk with his desserts. Drank it out of a big goblet with ice chips in it, when we had a block of ice."

"My father does too, but no, I'll have mine just plain."

"Miss O'Quinn," said Jincy, "grandmother and I were going to invite you to church next Sunday. It's our sacrament foot washing service and there's dinner on the grounds afterward. It'll be just us though because Uncle Neville goes to Beaverdam Baptist and daddy doesn't go to church."

She felt the stare of both men as they awaited her reply. Patten, probably curious to see if she had the gumption to decline, and Neville to see if she intended to get out and meet the parents of potential pupils. It was the last thing she wanted to do. "Why yes, I'd love to."

"Very well then," said Mrs. Clements. "Jincy and I will pick you up in the surrey around nine thirty next Sunday. You don't need to bring a thing. Queenie's coming over early to fry up a chicken. But I'm afraid Jincy and I have to leave in a few minutes for my Missionary Society meeting. We're trying to complete our allotment of surgical dressings for the Red Cross. She turned to Patten. "Son, who was it that said they were having to rinse out and reuse old bandages in the field hospitals?"

Patten placed the damask napkin beside his plate and slid his chair back, indicating his departure. "A doctor from Emory who served in an English hospital. He said they saw bandages and gauze hanging out to dry like the week's wash."

Neville nodded in agreement. "Field Marshall Haig says the new German advance is formidable. Their spring offensive has thus far been a triumph, and they're further south now than since the trench war began in 1914. But with our troops landing now, the Allies should soon be coming into action."

"Let's hope General Foch will be able to turn the tables," Patten replied.

Mrs. Clements interrupted, "Dears, Jincy and I will clear the table. I think Miss O'Quinn has something to discuss with you, Neville, and I know Patten needs to return to the mill."

"Let's see if we can catch a little evening breeze on the porch," said Neville, escorting her down the darkening hallway to the front parlor. "There's usually a bit of a breeze this time of night on the side porch."

As they entered the large pretty parlor, she stopped at the sight of an ebony grand piano in the far corner. "Oh, I didn't see the piano when I came in. It's beautiful. I must have walked right by it. I've never played one before, just uprights and spinets." She hesitated before asking. "May I play it sometime?"

He smiled. "We're hoping you will. Your uncle said he enjoyed hearing you play. Father gave it to mother as a surprise wedding anniversary present."

"How lovely." She crossed the room, touching its satiny finish, tracing the gold script lettering with her finger. "An Ivers and Pond from Boston?"

"Yes, Father was there on business just before the war in France broke out. He happened to be walking past their showroom on Boylston Street and saw it in the window— 'tied up with a big white bow,' he told mother. He asked the dealer if they could ship it—and the bow—in time for an anniversary. They made all the rail and freight arrangements for it to arrive on the eve of their anniversary. As you might imagine, it went off without a hitch until it came in at the train depot and the crate was unloaded. Within an hour, everyone in Ray's Mill knew of its arrival and its contents."

She laughed, imagining the great flurry of activity that news and gossip generated in a small town. "And did your mother know?"

"She says she didn't—at least she feigned surprise. But please play something. In fact, mother will probably mention piano lessons to you. She'd like you to teach Jincy."

"Really. Does your mother not play?"

"She plays by ear, but doesn't read music and—"

"Miss O'Quinn." Mrs. Clements stood in the doorway with her arm around Jincy's shoulder. "It's a fine instrument and deserves Chopin or Mozart, not my church hymns. No offense to the good Lord. My husband would be pleased, and so would all of us, if you'd consider taking Jincy as your pupil when you get settled."

"Oh yes, I'd be delighted." She slid the needlepoint bench closer to the piano and sat down patting the seat beside her. "Come sit beside me, Jincy, and we'll play something short."

Beaming with pleasure, Jincy perched just barely on the edge of the bench, careful not to crowd her.

Pensive for a moment, Anne Aletha spoke softly to Jincy. "Robert Schumann was a great nineteenth century German composer who wrote a collection of piano pieces called *Scenes from Childhood*. He composed them for his young daughters so that they could learn to play the piano. This piece is called 'Traumerei.' It means dreaming. If you like, after we've mastered the basics, we'll begin to work on it."

"Thank you," Jincy said, rising to stand behind her.

Gently, Anne Aletha depressed the first solo key, counting the full beat of the next chord, reminding herself not to rush the simple but expressive piece. Something she did when nervous. She closed her eyes, visualizing the rhythmic breathing of someone dreaming, the slow rise and fall of their chest, the imagery relaxing her. Years of muscular memory overtook her fingers and her body swayed with the music. She could hear the ethereal melody rise somewhere in the recesses of the tall ceiling and then dissipate, the ivory keys springing back effortlessly to her touch until with regret she neared the music's completion. Slowing, she rolled the last arpeggiated chord, playing the final cadence and leaving the room in whisper.

She opened her eyes and glanced at Neville, knowing by his nod and solemnity that he understood the music and her reverence for it.

"Lovely, Miss O'Quinn," said Mrs. Clements. "Now promise us you'll come back and play often. Jincy will work real hard, won't you dear?"

"Yes, ma'am. When can we start?"

"We'll talk about that with Miss O'Quinn next Sunday. I'm afraid we have to rush off. I hope that's not true about the field hospitals having to wash out the used and bloody bandages to reuse them. Our quota of bandages are going out on Monday's train to Atlanta."

"Are you sure there's nothing that I can bring?" asked Anne Aletha, pushing back the piano bench.

"Just yourself dear. See you then."

THE LONG TENDRILS of the hanging ferns cascaded listlessly beneath the porch eaves as Neville and Anne Aletha stepped out into the heated evening air. There was no breeze. From the tall shrubs that surrounded the wraparound porch, katydids and crickets conducted a backdrop of roaring pitches so noisily that voices had to be raised as one entered their insect's den.

Abruptly, their sounds ceased. "Listen," Anne Aletha whispered. The porch remained silent. "We've intruded."

Neville smiled. "We're only momentary intruders, I assure you. By the time we've walked to the end of the porch, we'll think we're back in the middle of Thoreau's woods."

"Oh, I love *Walden*. It's my favorite of his journals. Think of spending two whole years there in solitude with nature, contemplating the cosmos, reading and cultivating your mind ... I envy him. I think the cold would be the only hardship for me." She stopped, glancing up at Neville, realizing she had probably said too much and unsure if his expression was one of disapproval.

He completed her thoughts, a slight change of tone in his voice, "And unencumbered with social interaction, like church going and missionary societies. Is that what you would like to eliminate from your life, Anne Aletha?"

She searched his face, wanting to say yes. She craved solitude and didn't enjoy social gatherings but feared disappointing him.

He touched her shoulder lightly. "Let's sit down. I'm afraid I know what brought you here this evening. There is also something else I'd like to discuss with you."

They walked to the far corner of the porch. She stood, unsure if he needed any assistance as he propped his walking cane against the banister and awkwardly pulled two large Brumby rockers beside each other.

She sat down smelling the scent of his starched linen and cologne. "Thank you."

"I'm pleased that you're going with mother and Jincy on Sunday. But I would be doing you and your deceased uncle a disservice if I didn't voice my concerns over your solitary nature. He told me that, like himself, you prefer the company of books. But remember that people can be hard on someone different. However," the playfulness came back in his voice, "I also want to tell you how lovely you look tonight. As lovely as you played the piano. In fact, I know if our young men weren't off to war, I'd have every suitor in town wanting me to arrange an introduction."

"Oh no, couldn't we fib?" she laughed, grateful for the change of topic and pleased with his compliments, if only fraternal.

He chuckled. "Only if you are an adept fibber and decide to make up a sweetheart overseas. But I warn you, the ladies of Ray's Mill will require lengthy embellishments. If the widow Dew and her sister Beulah get ahold of you, you'll wish you'd stuck with the truth."

"Are they the ones who live next door? Nellie says the two feuding sisters haven't spoken in years and divided the house down the middle with bed sheets."

"Well, the bed sheets may be an exaggeration, but not the lack of conversation. What one sister wants the other to know is mainly passed along by Willard at the grocery and our poor mother. Beulah walks to town every morning exactly fifteen minutes ahead of her sister, but both stop back by here on the way home. Mother no sooner gets one out the kitchen door before the other one is coming up the front walk. They can outtalk a preacher and both are half deaf."

She chuckled, regretting to end the evening's pleasantness with the morning's upset. What she'd rehearsed to say walking over, she now forgot and what she did say came out strained and accusatory. "Mr. Attaway came over this morning to tell me that a young farmer had been shot and to keep myself and my two coloreds in the house tonight. Are there really Klansmen in Ray's Mill?"

Neville made no reply as he removed his pipe and tobacco pouch of soft-looking butternut kid from his pockets. Observing him from the periphery, she wondered if this was a guise that all men used to stall unwanted conversation, having watched her father repeat the ritualistic process so many times: pack it, tamp it, light it and then relight before an aromatic gray cloud could be coaxed forth. His sudden voice startled her.

"Anne Aletha, we have a very volatile situation going on here that Governor Dorsey in Atlanta is monitoring closely. Mother and the rest of the town will hear it in the morning. They haven't yet found Sid Johnson, the young Negro accused of killing Hampton Smith, but they captured the two other farmhands who worked on the Smith place. I regret to tell you that they were hung by an angry mob. Even worse, they also hung the wife of one of the men from Folsom's Bridge."

She bolted upright in her chair. "You mean they killed them? Without a trial?" The rising decibels of her voice hushed the noise of the insects once again. "And they hung a woman?"

"Mary Turner was the wife of Hayes Turner. They hung him down by Okapilco Bridge in Brooks County last night. The telegraph said the mob became enraged when she sassed them this afternoon and made unwise remarks about the execution of her husband. I'm sure there were Klansmen among the mob inciting them. I fear it's not going to end there. It would be prudent for Nellie and Alex to stay near the house."

"My God Neville, where's the sheriff? I came to tell you that I heard men coming back from the millpond at midnight last night. I know it was Klansmen. We have to do something to stop them—"

"As I said, Governor Dorsey is monitoring the situation. He'll send in Home Guards to Valdosta if necessary. But these are not men to be reasoned with. They aren't the illiterate backwoodsmen that made up the first Klan in the War between the States. You've seen their advertisements in the newspaper. They're even selling Liberty Bonds. Their motto is 'A Klan in your community is more than a luxury, it's a necessity.'" He sighed. "This new organization is duping an amazing number of men into thinking they're protecting the home front while our young men are fighting overseas."

She stood, her anger and her voice rising. "What are they protecting us from? It's the Negro who needs protection. I can't believe the people in this town are allowing these vigilantes to go around hanging people without a trial. And to hang a woman for sassing them when they murdered her husband!" She stomped to the end of the porch and stared out into the night, crossing her arms against the fear, just like she had as a child when there were things out there in the dark that couldn't be seen. She turned back to Neville. "Did my Uncle Carter know about the Klan?"

"He knew of its revitalization. At first, he thought it was just tribalism, an 'us versus them' mentality. Like the ancients, Hector and Agamemnon in the old Greek city-states. But soon, he realized its pervasiveness and saw that this new Klan was about money and nationwide recruitment. With the world at war, the Klan has found a purpose. People are afraid and this is their rallying point, that the nation has to be defended against our enemies, whether it's strike leaders, Negroes, Jews or foreigners. Unfortunately, their timing couldn't be more propitious."

"But they have to be stopped, Neville. We can't just do nothing. People have to take a stand. My uncle always cited Edmund Burke who said that for evil to exist, good men have to merely do nothing. We must organize a town meeting and tell people what's going on. We can go out there in a mass and tell those hooded cowards they can't take the law into their own hands."

Neville shook his head. "No, Anne Aletha. You mustn't do anything. You don't realize how widespread their influence is. I'm warning you. Their retaliation will bring harm to Alex and Nellie and a torch to your farmhouse."

4

ANNE ALETHA SHOOK HER HEAD in disbelief as she sat at the kitchen table scanning the stack of weekly newspapers. After more than a week, not only had the lynchings not made the headlines or the front pages of any of the newspapers, but they had received no more mention than the daily weather. She read the entries:

May 15, *Valdosta Tribune*, Page 2
Two negroes stole a shotgun from Hampton Smith and killed him in his home. Mrs. Smith fled from the home and was attacked. She awoke the following morning in the creek and went to a Negro cabin for aid. Those that investigated the story found Smith's body and that all the farm hands had disappeared.

May 16, *Valdosta Tribune*, Page 3
Hampton Smith, a young farmer living near Barney in Brooks County was shot and killed by an assassin firing through the window of his home Wednesday evening. Mrs. Smith was also shot through the shoulder but ran through the field to a small branch and remained in hiding two hours until she went to the home of a negro family and reported the tragedy. She recognized a young negro named Sidney Johnson who had been working for her husband two or three weeks.

May 17, *Valdosta Tribune*, Page 2
Two of the three negroes who killed Hampton Smith

have been captured. The men will be carried before Mrs. Smith for identification, but her condition is such that it is hardly probable that she will be able to look them over. Two of the men were farmhands on the Smith place and were captured late today and it is believed the other one has been located.

May 18, *Valdosta Tribune*, Page 3
Mary Turner, wife of Hayes Turner was hanged this afternoon at Folsom's bridge over Little River. Hayes Turner was hanged at Okapilco river in Brooks county last night. His wife is claimed to have made unwise remarks today about the execution of her husband, and the people in their indignant mood took exception to her remarks as well as her attitude and without waiting for nightfall took her to the river where she was hanged and her body riddled with bullets. It is also claimed that a gold watch belonging to the murdered man, Hampton Smith, was found in her possession and that the plot to kill him had been laid in her house. This makes three persons lynched as a result of the Smith tragedy. All of Sidney Johnson's relatives, including his mother and father, were landed in jail here last night. Beside the chase after Sidney Johnson, posses are looking for other negroes and the feeling among both white and black seems to be growing more intense.

May 20, *Valdosta Tribune*, Page 2
Sidney Johnson, the negro wanted for the murder of Hampton Smith was surrounded in a negro house tonight at 10:30 and shot to death by the officers whom he attempted to kill when they entered the house to arrest him. A large crowd was hurriedly attracted to the scene by the shooting and the negro's body was riddled with probably a hundred shots. The body of Johnson was tied to an automobile and dragged through Patterson Street en route, it is presumed, to the scene of the murder where it is believed it will be burned.

Finally, at the bottom of the page of yesterday's *Valdosta Tribune*, Anne Aletha noticed a small caption:

Governor Asked for Troops

Governor Dorsey was in telephonic communication with Judge Thomas, and the local sheriff said that in the event Johnson was captured, he would be unable to cope with the situation. Later, the announcement was received that the Savannah troops would soon be sent.

Well, the Governor's troops were a little late, she thought, disgusted. How could ordinary people commit such violence? Where was the public outcry? Could people just dismiss the lynchings and remain silent or indifferent? Could she?

She thought of *Birth of a Nation* and its depiction of the Negro as an inferior savage beast. And the Klan's white supremacy belief that racial order must be maintained. And also, the old woman on the train. Such ignorance, like Plato's Cave.

Was the whole world chained to its ignorance?

The mantel clock chimed nine o'clock and she groaned. Mrs. Clements and Jincy would arrive soon. Would the lynchings be mentioned at church this morning? Probably not. It was like the atrocities never happened. But she'd barely slept for a week, listening for nightriders, and Nellie and Alex had not even gone to town to pick up washing. She hurried to the bedroom, slipping into the cotton voile shirtwaist that Nellie had painstakingly starched and pressed. Almost out the door, she remembered her hat and gloves and returned to retrieve them.

"WHOA THERE, BELLA," said Mrs. Clements, reigning in the big freckled mare that had broken into a fast-paced trot once her hoofs crossed the railroad tracks at the edge of town. "We're not going to Uncle Doctor's today," she said, speaking to the animal in a high-pitched voice reserved for critters and children. "His carrot patch won't be ready till fall." The mare snorted and she slackened the reins. "Miss O'Quinn, I don't believe you've met Uncle Doctor yet. He's my husband's brother and practices over in Adel. Lives between here and there."

"No, ma'am," she replied. "But Uncle Carter spoke fondly of him." So far, Mrs. Clements had not mentioned the shameful lynchings, and she doubted she would with Jincy sitting between them.

"I'm afraid we're a little late, Miss O'Quinn," said Jincy. "Queenie had to chase the hen all the way through the cornfield and clear down to the train tracks behind the house."

"Well, this smells wonderful," Anne Aletha said, straddling the picnic hamper between her feet. Queenie's fried chicken and ham biscuits permeated the air. On their laps, she and Jincy held the repository of foot-washing implements. Hers was piled with great mounds of three-yard-long linen towels she was trying not to wrinkle. These would be looped around the waist of each member, one long end to be used for washing and the other for drying. And Jincy's lap held the stack of shiny foot basins. It was a religious sacrament not widely practiced today and her only recollection of it was as a little girl attending her grandmother's church. As the smallest granddaughter at the time, she had been the one most in demand to assist the elderly ladies in removing their stockings—the only one able to squeeze down between the long narrow pews. And though she appreciated the humbleness and symbolism of this holy foot-washing sacrament, the memory remained a malodorous one.

Mrs. Clements slowed the mare and turned onto a narrow rutted road that led out to the little isolated church on the banks of Cat Creek. Melodious singing filled the woods as they neared New Ramah Primitive Baptist Church. Guiding the mare beneath the shade trees alongside the other carriages in front of the church, she turned to Anne Aletha. "Miss O'Quinn, look at our pretty little church."

The tiny brown sanctuary sat box-like in the woods, as charming as a child's unpainted dollhouse. An aged water oak with withered branches and tangled moss framed the small church, partially obscuring the view. Tall ample windows flanked a pair of plain doors, each with a set of wooden steps. She remembered that men and women had separate entrances and seating.

They followed Mrs. Clements through the women's entrance of the sanctuary, stacked the towels and foot basins at the back of the church, and paused for a few moments. Men and women were seated on opposite sides of the pulpit and they rose as the preacher lined out a stanza of "Amazing Grace," emphasizing the words to be sung. On the men's side, a strong tenor began the stanza, singing the slow solo before the other male members picked up the verse, singing in unison. Moments later, across the room, a clear high soprano repeated the stanza. Goosebumps pricked Anne Aletha's forearms. Though no musical instruments were permitted in the primitive church, it reminded her that the human voice was truly the most perfect of instruments.

As the preacher lined out the next stanza, Mrs. Clements, seemingly nonplused at their tardiness, marched down the aisle. Anne Aletha glanced up at the pulpit and the preacher. To Mrs. Clements he gave a slight nod and to her a hard stare. She felt his eyes follow her as they entered the long wooden pew on the front of the women's section and wondered if the next stanza he lined out in the fire and brimstone voice was meant for her. "I once was lost, but now am found, was blind but now can see." She looked away from his unsettling gaze, noticing the empty cordoned-off pews in the men's section across from her.

With a grand sweep of his arms, he motioned the congregation to be seated. She sat down on the flat board bench between Jincy and Mrs. Clements and tried not to stare at the preacher's ears, feeling instant compassion for someone with such great protuberances that stuck out so far from his head. Maybe childhood teasing had caused his dourness.

"Brethren," the preacher began. "The Lord tells us in John, Chapter 13 to call him the Master and the Lord. He tells us that if he then, as your Lord and Master, has washed your feet, ye also ought to wash another's feet. Remember that Jesus rose from his last supper with his disciples, girded himself with a towel and poured water into a basin. He began to wash the disciples' feet and to wipe them with the towel where he was girded. 'Verily, Verily,' he told us, 'the servant is not greater than his Lord.'"

She sat listening to his sermon of scripture reading, hearing the rising decibels of his voice, loathing his tone of self-righteousness. Why did she feel such instant dislike for most preachers—except for old Preacher Burke? He was what a proper servant of the Lord should be: humble, caring and always seeing the good in people. She thought of the years of summer revivals she'd endured—the shouting and showmanship of those dreadful traveling evangelists, stifling as the July heat. But lately she worried about herself because she had become not only a cynic, but worse—a skeptic.

A commotion at the back of the church stopped the preacher's sermon. Curiously, he motioned the congregation to rise. Mrs. Clements looked puzzled. Anne Aletha heard faint singing outside the church and recognized the hymn "Onward Christian Soldiers." She turned as people began murmuring behind her. Mrs. Clements gasped and Anne Aletha stood agape at the apparition of two marching columns of men, hooded and cloaked in white, except for the cutout of their eyes.

Singing in a low chant, they filed into the reserved front row pews, as the lead Klansman stepped forward to the pulpit with an offering. She wondered how much money it took to bribe a preacher.

Again he motioned for the congregation to be seated. Waiting for the mumbling and whispering to subside, the preacher reached over to the cypress water bucket and drank from its long-handled gourd, discarding the waste through the augered hole in the pine floorboards. He cleared his throat. "Brothers," he began, "the Lord said in Romans Chapter 12, 'I beseech you brethren, by the mercies of God, that ye present your bodies a living sacrifice, holy, acceptable unto God, which is your reasonable service. And be not conformed to this world: but be ye transformed by the renewing of your mind, that ye may prove what is that good, and acceptable and the perfect will of God. Be without dissimulation. Abhor that which is evil; cleave to that which is good. Be kindly affectioned one to another, preferring one another.'

"Brothers," he said, turning his head toward the Klansmen. "We have been joined by soldiers this morning, soldiers in our communities, not unlike our young men fighting for us overseas, except these soldiers are needed to fight on our home front. Hamp Smith, a fine young farmer is dead, shot through the window by a nigra he'd given work to. We can't bring Hamp Smith back. What we can do is make our communities safe for the white man again—make our mills safe from outsiders and unions wanting to come in and tell us how to run them—make our womenfolk safe from molestation. Now those dead nigras have still got accomplices out there."

Anne Aletha stood, sickened by the twisted bigotry. The preacher stopped mid-sentence as all eyes turned to her. She looked down at Mrs. Clements and reached out for her hand, grateful that bony fingers encircled her own in a squeeze of understanding. She stepped past Jincy and touched her cheek. Meeting the preacher's stare, she glared at him in disgust as twenty pairs of hooded eyes watched her exit the pew, one pair vaguely familiar.

She walked down the aisle staring straight ahead until she reached the back of the sanctuary. Glancing over at the men's doorway, she hesitated for a moment in defiance. Then remembering Neville's admonitions, she exited through the proper doorway.

Once outside, she strode down the narrow lane toward town, grateful there was no one else on the road. In town, she sat on the old timers' bench outside the corner drugstore, fanning herself to cool off. Though her fury had abated, she felt a growing unease. Her Uncle Carter had believed that men were driven by a moral imperative and that they were capable of reason with the ability to rise above their hatred. But now, after the lynchings and the Klan's bold appearance in church, she wasn't so sure.

Other than a scrawny pup sniffing all the hitching posts, she was the only one in town enjoying main street in repose. Then in the distance, a motor car chugged, and a few minutes later a Model T approached, bouncing and bumping along as the driver maneuvered its thin-spoked wheels down the uneven furrowed road. She watched until it crossed the railroad tracks and then stood to begin the rest of her walk home.

To her dismay, the automobile's horn tooted and the motorcar followed behind her until she turned and stopped. A large man with a full head of white hair swung out of the idling machine and greeted her with a sweep of his straw hat.

"I said to myself, I'd wager that pretty young woman over there is Miss Anne Aletha O'Quinn," he said.

"Oh, yes. Thank you. How did you know?" she asked extending her hand.

"My nephew, Neville, said you were as pretty as the glistening dew on a morning glory blossom."

"You must be Uncle Doctor from Adel. It's so nice to meet you."

"The pleasure's all mine, young lady." He removed a watch from his vest pocket and glanced at it. "And I sure wish I had more time to visit, but Roena sent for me to take a look at that new millworker family that's moved into the colored quarter. Says there's eight of them living in squalor and that the infant and granny are ill. Can I give you a ride home? You look a bit peaked yourself."

"Oh no, I'm fine. Just walked a little further than I'd planned. I hope no one is seriously ill?"

"Roena says the child's got a grayish membrane at the back of the throat. It's likely diphtheria." He turned his attention to his sputtering vehicle. "Miss O'Quinn, I don't want to cut my choke and have to recrank this blasted automobile. Let me give you a ride."

Taking her around to the passenger side, he removed his large black leather satchel from the seat and then a feed mill sack next to it, giving the moving, wiggling bundle to her. "Payment for my last house visit," he explained. "Figured this next family can use some fresh meat."

Two beady eyes and a beak peered out from the hole as she placed it next to her feet. "Nellie and I could make them a big pot of chicken and rice if the family needs help with cooking." She remembered that her mother always planned for ten people to a hen.

"Thank you, Miss O'Quinn. I'll tell them. Diphtheria usually attacks the young and old, but sometimes you can have a small household epidemic if the living conditions are unsanitary."

She held onto the flapping feed sack and the door frame of the coughing and sputtering Model T all the way out to the farmhouse as the chassis hit the ruts and her head hit the roof. Walking seemed much preferable.

5

ANNE ALETHA STOOD on the front porch, barefoot and rumpled in her cotton nightgown, damp from another hot airless night. Someone is burning leaves this morning, she thought, inhaling the strong pungent air and looking up at another cloudless blue sky. Now, it seemed that after the murder and lynchings a few weeks ago, the heat held everything in abeyance.

Curiously, people no longer talked about the martial law or the one hundred and twenty-five Home Guards Governor Dorsey finally sent to Valdosta to quell the county's lawlessness. Nor had the midnight horsemen ridden past the farmhouse again.

Folks were back to talking crops and war. In town, the edentulous and stubby whiskered old men on the bench outside the drugstore greeted everyone with: "Can you believe the heat! It's just mid-June and the mercury's already reached ninety-four degrees. Can't remember when it last rained. Why, the corn's gonna wither in the fields."

She decided that people cared more about the price of corn than the lives of the three Negro men and a woman who were lynched. Behind her, she heard the soft slam of the kitchen screen door and Nellie calling her name.

"Out here on the porch, Nellie. Come sit with me." She scooted over to make room for Nellie on the step, fanning herself with the hem of her nightgown. Tiny beads of sweat freckled her nose, and her new bob frizzed around her head.

Nellie eased herself down on the step. "Look at you, Miss Aletha. You sick?"

"No, just sleepless. About the time it cools down enough so I can drift off to sleep, the mosquitoes find me. I don't know which is worse, smelling that awful concoction of mosquito repellant you made up or swatting them all night. You think it will rain soon?"

"Everything's needing water real bad. We saw Miz Sarah when we was delivering laundry and she say her cows ain't giving much milk. Say it takes some real coaxing to get them out of that clump of shade trees in her pasture." Nellie dabbed at the nape of her neck with one of Alex's handkerchiefs, casting another watchful glance at her. Reaching over, she felt Anne Aletha's forehead. "You still hearing that tree frog croaking?"

She nodded. "I think he's just looking for a mate. I can't believe you can sleep through him. Every time I come out on the porch to hush him up, I see Alex come out on your porch doing the same thing."

Nellie laughed. "He'll sound different when he finds her. He'll be singing. Appreciate you starting my starch water boiling outside and puttin' the irons on the stove to heat. If Miz Idabelle comes calling again and sees you ironing my take-in laundry, she'll have something else to gossip about."

"Well, it's the least I can do since I can't afford to pay you and Alex wages. I just sprinkled those banquet tablecloths of Mrs. Terry's and I figure I can do the flat ironing while you do the fancy ruffles and lace. We should be finished by early afternoon and I promised Jincy we'd go to the millpond."

"I'm glad that child's taken such a liken to you. Mr. Patten should have found hisself a wife a long time ago. He courted a widow woman for a while, but nothing ever come of it. And course lots of ladies in town be sweet on Mr. Neville. Guess he ain't met the right one. But I think he's taken a fancy to you with all them books he bring over every other day."

Anne Aletha grinned, hugging her knees. "He's just seeing that I get settled and that Uncle Carter's wishes are carried out."

Nellie rose stiffly. "Well, I better gets to work."

"I'll be out in a few minutes." Anne Aletha remained on the steps, thinking about the small pang of jealousy she'd felt when Nellie mentioned Patten courting another woman. Was it possible for one brother to stir her passion and the other her intellect? She thought of the Greek gods, Apollo and Dionysius. Apollo, the god of reason, discipline and calm aloofness. And Dionysius, the god of wine, music and passion. The brothers were such opposites and she found herself attracted to both.

THAT AFTERNOON, Jincy skipped with excitement, tossing her pigtails over her shoulder. "Oh Miss O'Quinn, I'm so glad we're going to the millpond today and not having a lesson. I mean … I enjoy my piano lessons, and I have been practicing, but I just don't want to today."

"Me too. It's too hot, even for Bach. Your Uncle Neville told me that you've promised him a recital when he gets back from Washington, D.C." She gave Jincy's shoulder a quick hug.

They walked down the deserted sandy road toward the gristmill. With the war on and labor and rains sparse, farmers would be limited and likely delayed in bringing their corn to the gristmill for grinding. Alex had planted a small corn patch, but they would still need to supplement it with store-bought cornmeal. Anne Aletha sighed. Another staple she'd not planned on for which she would need money.

As they approached the pond, Jincy pointed out the three Sirmans brothers playing on the bank of the inlet. Neville had said that if she could get the Sirmans children as pupils, other families would follow. However, she feared that she'd jeopardized her prospects by walking out of New Ramah. As they stopped to watch the boys play, she tried to push the disquieting thoughts from her mind. Would she fail for want of students?

The oldest brother hiked up his overalls over knobby, skinned knees and waded out among the lily pads and cattails of the black freshwater pond. All the frogs went quiet. Throwing bits of bread from his pockets, he waited until the head of a large snapping turtle bobbed to the surface. On the bank, his two younger brothers jumped up and down with glee at the prospects of catching a turtle while slapping wildly at the late afternoon mosquitoes that covered their pudgy bare legs. Soon their glee turned to squeals as the oldest boy catapulted out of the pond with the giant snapping turtle, chasing his younger brothers down the rutted lane toward home.

Anne Aletha and Jincy laughed as they walked past the wooden rowboats and the bait house toward the loud foaming noises of the gristmill. When they reached the mill, they turned down the side path where the churning waters narrowed to a quiet creek.

"This is where grandmother and I come to swim because nobody ever comes down this far," Jincy said. "See the clear shallow part where the sandy bottom is? That's where we go in. The dark part gets squishy and slimy. Grandmother won't skinny dip. She wears her camisole and bloomers. Then the rest of the afternoon she complains about sand in her drawers."

Anne Aletha glanced up at the ancient cypress branches above their heads. They looked like a giant octopus. "It's lovely here, Jincy. I'm glad you brought me. Let's unlace our shoes and wade over to that big rock in the middle. We can dangle our feet."

Holding their skirts above their knees, they waded into the warm shallow water, their feet sinking into the sand that oozed up between their toes. Jincy scooted close to her on the rock.

"Sometime soon, Grandmother says we're going to have a fish fry out here for you. Daddy and Uncle Neville know where all the best bream and perch are. We bring frying pans and everything out here. Grandmother makes the best hushpuppies. We have grits and bread and butter pickles, and sometimes, she scrambles a big skillet of eggs just before we serve up the fish."

"Sounds wonderful." Anne Aletha noticed that like a puppy, Jincy would soon be growing into her oversized feet. She wondered about Jincy's mother and if she had been pretty. Dragonflies skimmed the pond's surface with their iridescent blue wings, and quiet settled around them.

Jincy broke the silence. "Miss O'Quinn, I wanted to ask you something." She paused, twirling a strand of hair around her finger. "Do you believe in predestination? Grandmother says the difference between Primitive Baptists and other Baptists isn't just their foot-washing sacrament. She says Primitive Baptists believe in predestination and that people call them 'hard-shells' because they believe the Bible word for word."

Anne Aletha smiled at the pretty, young girl, her generous mouth and her face full of freckles. "What do your father and uncle say?" She was uncomfortable with the topic of conversation and her own skepticism.

"Well, Daddy says man is master of his own universe. I heard him tell Uncle Neville one time that he thought it was all just myth. Uncle Neville says what's really important is not the differences in the religions, but the teachings that underlie them all."

"Yes, I think that's true, like the golden rule. If we treat people the way we want to be treated, then despite our differences—Jincy, is that thunder in the distance?"

Jincy frowned, listening and looking up into the trees. "Maybe so. The wind's picked up. Grandmother says it sounds like the ocean when the wind starts coming through the pine trees."

They sat quietly on the rocks, straining to hear the low rumblings of thunder again. They needed the rain, but Anne Aletha didn't want them to get caught in a storm.

Jincy sat motionless, letting tadpoles skitter around her toes. Then hoisting her skirt, she waded out a little ways. When the hem of her skirt submerged into the knee-deep water, she giggled. "Whoops—"

Anne Aletha's concern was momentarily banished by the young girl's joy. Nellie said that people who remembered Jincy's great grandfather thought she resembled him. Her auburn hair and fair skin, but not his fiery temperament. It wouldn't be long before this shy prepubescent girl would attract lots of suitors with her easy grace and smile.

"Listen—it sounds like thunder again, Jincy. Let's see if it's headed our way."

Jincy wrung out the bottom of her gingham dress and followed her back to the embankment. They sat down on the wide-bladed grass to wipe grit and sand from their feet before putting on their cotton hose and oxfords.

Anne Aletha saw the black sky as they walked out from beneath the thick canopy of water oak and cypress. "I think we're going to have a storm. We better head back home. Poor Nellie. She's scared to death of thunder and always keeps her eye on the sky. They're probably in the wagon right now delivering laundry."

"Maybe it's already gone by, Miss O'Quinn."

"No, the wind's coming from behind us." It funneled down the lane, blowing Jincy's sailor collar up against the back of her head.

"All the crickets and frogs have gone quiet, Miss O'Quinn."

As they hurried the quarter mile toward the house, they tried to brush away the hair blowing into their eyes and mouth. The sultry air swirled with debris in the darkened sky. Clumps of Spanish moss somersaulted out of the trees and the tall pines swayed in the wind, shaking loose the needles and pinecones.

A bolt of lightning struck and then thunder. *Bam—*

"Oooooh!" Jincy squealed, clasping both hands over her ears. She stopped in the middle of the road.

"That's close. Let's make a run for it. We don't have far." Anne Aletha grabbed Jincy's hand, the intensity of the winds alarming her. Now the wind was coming toward them, almost pushing them backward. Should they turn back to the gristmill? Crackling and crashing sounds filled the forest beside them.

"Are those trees?" yelled Jincy.

"I think the winds are toppling them. We need to get clear of the trees." An ear-splitting crackle followed by a thunderous boom drowned out her voice.

Jincy flew into Anne Aletha's arms, burying her head. "Was that a tree?" she screamed.

"Yes, sweetie. Come on. Let's run to the pasture."

The winds pelted their skin with pine needles as bolts of lightning lit up the landscape.

"Ouch!" cried Jincy. "They feel like darts."

Anne Aletha searched for a low-lying place in the field, breathless with fright and exertion. Seeing no gullies, she stopped and dropped to the ground pulling Jincy down beside her. "Lie down and cover your head. I'll be on top."

Shielding Jincy with her body, she felt debris pelt her like buckshot. "The rain's coming now, sweetie. It'll pass over soon," she said, trying to sooth her. Something sharp pierced her scalp and she jerked with a groan.

Jincy cried out in alarm. "Are you all right, Miss O'Quinn?"

She reached up to feel the back of her head as the hissing, spitting rain came down in torrents. "Yes, I think so. The lightning and thunder are moving away. Just a little while longer."

Minutes later, a voice called out from the road. "Jincy!"

Jincy screamed. "It's daddy!" Scrambling out from beneath Anne Aletha, she took off running as Patten, sodden in the downpour, strained to see across the pasture.

Recognizing his daughter's flailing form running toward him, Patten crossed the field like an eagle, scooping up its fledgling to the warmth and safety of its wings. Anne Aletha sat upright in the deluge of rain trying to locate the pulsating throb on her scalp, the clinging wet clothes stinging her back. She tried to stand as Jincy and Patten approached.

He reached to steady her. "Are you all right?" The rain streamed off his hat, obscuring the penetrating blue eyes.

"I'm fine, just a bit wobbly." She knew she looked like a wet, bedraggled cat and hated that she cared.

"Daddy, look, she's bleeding!"

She looked down at her white blouse soaked to a rosy pink across her shoulders and front. "I'm all right," she said, touching the sticky place of her scalp.

"Daddy, look, her whole back is bloody! She shielded me with her body."

Patten lifted her effortlessly and hastened toward the house. "Put your arms around my neck, Miss O'Quinn," he directed. "You'll stay a little drier."

She doubted that since rivulets of cold rainwater streamed off the rim of his fedora down the front of her. "I really can walk," she protested.

"Let's see where you're hurt first. Anyway, you're an easy armful, just like Jincy."

The rain slackened as the lightning and thunder moved away. Patten's chest heaved against her with exertion as he carried her across the side yard of the farmhouse.

She gasped when she saw the storm's havoc. "Oh my God." Large tree limbs littered the yard, and the remains of the chicken coop were strewn in all directions. Baby biddies floundered everywhere in deep puddles.

"Jincy, will you run get my apron and scoop them up? They'll drown. We need to get them warm and dry."

"Let's tend to you first," said Patten, his voice winded as he climbed the back porch steps. "Jincy, hold open the screen door. Let's sit her down at the kitchen table."

"Don't worry, Miss O'Quinn, I'll get them. Queenie always puts ours in a warm oven to fluff them up."

As Patten eased her into the kitchen chair, she called to Jincy over her shoulder. "Thank you, sweetie. Go look in my chifforobe for something dry to put on."

Patten carefully parted her thick wet hair. "Lean over the table and rest your head on your arms," he instructed.

"Here," she said, placing her finger on the throbbing part of her scalp.

His fingers probed gently. "It's still bleeding, but it's a small gash. Head wounds are copious bleeders. I want you to apply pressure with this handkerchief while I see if you're cut on your back."

She complied. "It might have been a pinecone."

"Could be. Anything sharp in that kind of wind would do it. Let's get a look, Anne Aletha," he said softly, calling her by her given name for the first time.

She held the compress to her scalp as he struggled with the wet cloth-covered metal buttons on the back of her blouse.

Gently, he unfastened the blood-soaked buttons.

"Scissors might make it easier." She laughed, nervous at the intimacy. "They're hard enough to unbutton dry."

He eased away the blouse. "Lean forward again."

Her breath caught at his touch, its tenderness almost a caress as he slid her camisole down and gently explored for puncture wounds of her back. His hands felt smooth, not rough like she expected, and he smelled woodsy, like wet pine from the sawmill.

"I don't see anything else embedded or cut. Those were deadly winds. I want to thank you for protecting Jincy."

She heard the catch in his voice.

"Keep that head compress on awhile longer. Jincy can help you into dry clothes."

She stood, straightening her blouse. Then steadying herself, she looked out the kitchen window and chuckled. "Look, here she comes across the yard with an apron full of biddies."

Patten grinned at the sight. "I'll leave her here for a while. You need to lie down till the bleeding stops."

"Thank you. I'll be fine. You must go check on the mill. Nellie and Alex will be back soon. Jincy and the baby chicks can dry out in the kitchen till Alex brings her home."

Suddenly, she couldn't wait for him to leave, longing for the solitude that would allow her to think about the touch of his hands.

That night the tree frog sang.

6

THE NEXT DAY, Sulky plodded down the millpond's muddy lane strewn with the storm's debris. "Do you think Nellie suspects anything, Alex?" Anne Aletha smoothed out the wrinkles of her flowered print dress and adjusted the band of her summer straw around her tender head wound. "We didn't really need anything in town but lemons."

"No, ma'am. She probably don't even remember it's her birthday. But she'll be mighty pleased to have some ice cold lemonade this afternoon." He loosened the mule's reins, brushing dried mud from the bib of his overalls.

"I hid a little rationed sugar she doesn't know about, and we'll stop back by the ice house on the way home. Did you hear they're rationing ice consumption in Atlanta to refrigerate the peach crops?"

"That so?"

"The paper said no ice cream or soda fountain drinks till further notice and they said to expect more shortages this summer because of diminished ammonia supplies. It's used in war munitions."

"Well, city folks gonna sure feel this heat without it."

They rode in silence until Alex chuckled a deep, tickled laugh that delighted her every time. "Don't guess Nellie told you 'bout that old tomcat bringing her a green snake this morning. Brought it right up to the house with it dangling and wiggling out of both sides of his mouth."

She giggled. "Oh no—"

"Yes'um. Done scairt the living daylights out of her. You know she don't take kindly to snakes. But he put it down real gentle like and let it slither off. Most times he don't kill things, you know. Seem to just like catchin 'em."

"That's because Nellie feeds him so good." Alex was right. Most critters the cat brought home were captured for praise and then released. Like the chipmunk she'd discovered in the covers at the foot of her bed last week. But fortunately for his prey, Cicero took no further interest in recapturing them once he'd brought them inside, allowing Nellie and Anne Aletha to open the nearest window or door to let the grateful critters escape.

At the end of the road, they waved to Miss Effie sweeping the front porch, her wash already drying out back in the morning sun. The nanny goat bleated from the side yard and her two baby goats raced to her, all three grazing perilously close to the war garden's picket fence.

Sulky's pace quickened when they turned and headed toward town. Since Anne Aletha's discovery of the mule's fondness for syrup and biscuits, he proceeded without complaint. Now, it was only when he dozed beneath the shade of the sweet gum tree in the late afternoons that he balked at being harnessed. That, and if Uncle Doctor's Model T was anywhere within earshot.

Alex reined in the mule at the corner bank, waving to a young Negro woman crossing the road. "There goes Willa Mae and her two poor youngins. She got a hard row to hoe with a husband that's bad to drink. Works a turpentine still, but if she don't get his wages first, ain't nothin' left."

Anne Aletha waved too, feeling for the young woman wearing a dress of faded flour sacks, holding an infant in one arm and the hand of a little tear-streaked girl in the other. Even if suffrage passed, the life of a rural Negro woman without education would remain unchanged. Alex said it had been two years since anyone had come to teach the colored children, and even though the General Assembly had passed the Compulsory Education bill in 1916, it was full of loopholes. Children between eight and fourteen had to attend four months a year till they completed the fourth grade, but children in rural areas were mostly exempt, even white children. She wished she could teach both Negro and white, but there would never be acceptance of the children attending a school together.

"Yep, I was right," said Alex as they passed the barbershop. "There goes Elmore Jenkins, the turpentine foreman. Hangs around Mr. Willard's grocery on Saturday when his nephew Blalock clerks the store. You ain't met Blalock yet, but they's both mean ones. I try to stay clear of them."

"People like Mr. Willard though, don't they?"

"Yes'um. He trade fair with folks, coloreds too. If you ever needin' a little help, he swap out cornmeal and flour for some fresh caught bream. And if you got a little cash, he can dress a chicken from his hen coop out back for you quicker than Nellie can ring its neck and singe the feathers. Had to take in the nephew when his brother died and ain't had nothin' but trouble since."

Alex brought Sulky to a halt in front of the grocery just as two well-dressed ladies stepped out of the dry goods store next door. As they glanced up, she smiled and waved, though neither woman returned her greeting. Their snub caused her renewed concern of being accepted.

"You want me to wait here for you, Miss Aletha?"

She shook her head and climbed down. "You go on to the blacksmith. I'll meet you back here in a few minutes."

The bell of the door jingled as she stepped from the bright sunshine into the cool dark interior of the store. She let her eyes adjust to the dimness for a moment, breathing in the rich earthy smells of Willard's. It carried everything but dry goods, and even then, on occasion, a bolt of cotton muslin or calico could be found among the farm implements and produce. Above her head, plows and harnesses hung suspended from the ceiling. Pitchforks, rakes, and washboards lined the wall in haphazard fashion. The aisles bulged with wooden barrels of dried beans, coffee, tea, and sugar, oftentimes necessitating the more portly customers to squeeze sideways to pass. The floorboards creaked as she walked back to an old wooden cabinet with pullout drawers. She paused to check the contents: flower seed packets in the top bins, gladiola bulbs in the bottom. Above the cabinet, an advertising display hawked Jacobs Liver Salts for toning the liver, Swamp Root for kidney ailments, and Coopers New Quick Relief for rheumatism.

She moved past a large hoop of cheese, a bucket of fly swatters, and then on to the fruits and vegetables at the back of the store. Men's laughter and a child's fretful cry interrupted her musings, and as she turned the corner of a display a disheartening sight greeted her. Elmore Jenkins, the turpentine foreman, leaned forward against the cash register counter, snickering with Mr. Willard's nephew while Willa Mae and her children stood off to the side. Anne Aletha frowned. Were they ignoring the young mother? She turned to inspect the lemons, disappointed at their shriveled appearance. Squeezing one, she turned to the clerk at the counter.

"Excuse me. Do you have any fresh lemons?"

Neither man looked her way, the nephew sorting a box of shotgun shells, his round, boyish face belying a malevolent disposition.

Perhaps they had not heard her. "Excuse me."

"What you see is what we got," said the nephew. He did not glance up.

Laughing, Elmore Jenkins turned around and stared, his heavy reddish beard and light-green eyes oddly attractive. As he took a drink from the wooden dipper in the water bucket on the counter, she noticed the pinned up shirtsleeve of a missing arm. Perhaps this was cause for his malice, though she knew a farmer in Odum with only one arm who could clear fields, split wood, hitch a mule, and pull fodder as well as any able-bodied man.

"Well, I guess these will have to do," she said, taking the lemons to the counter. "I think this young woman was here before me."

"She ain't a customer," replied the nephew.

Jenkins sniggered again while she purchased the lemons in silence. When she moved away from the counter, Elmore Jenkins returned, resuming his conversation with the surly clerk.

Willa Mae edged closer to the counter, her little girl clinging to the hem of her dress. "Please Mr. Jenkins," she whispered. "My babies is hungry. We needin' milk and cornmeal. I ain't got nothin' for them if you don't give me his wages. Please."

Elmore Jenkins stopped his conversation and turned to Willa Mae. Without hesitation, he yanked the wooden dipper out of the water bucket and brought it crashing down upon the poor woman's forehead.

"Don't you ever butt in on a white man's discussion again," he shouted. "Do you hear me?"

Anne Aletha watched in disbelief, horrified as Willa Mae cried out in pain and sank to her knees, still cradling her infant child. Blood seeped from a large gash above her eyebrow while her little girl shrieked, burying her head into the folds of her mother's dress.

She rushed to the woman's side, enraged, cursing Jenkins with every one of her brother's forbidden profanities. "God damn your hide, you sorry son of a bitch. You should be horse whipped for doing that." She dropped to her knees in front of Willa Mae, shaking with fury as she searched her purse for a handkerchief to staunch the blood. "Willa Mae, hold this to your head and give me the baby. I'll go get help and some bandages."

Behind her a soft, breathy voice spoke. "Oh dear, what's happened? Is Willa Mae hurt?"

Anne Aletha turned and stood, grateful for the kind-faced woman before her. "Yes," she answered, her voice shrill with anger. "This man just assaulted this poor innocent woman for asking for her husband's wages. We need bandages and the sheriff. I want him arrested."

"Oh no, ma'am," moaned Willa Mae. "I'll be all right. We can't eat without no job."

Jenkins sneered. "You mind your own business, lady. Her old man's done worse to her."

"Miss O'Quinn, I'm Maidee Findley. I'll get our druggist and some bandages. Willa Mae, it's going to be all right. I'll be right back." She turned to the foreman and drew herself erect. "Elmore, you give Willa Mae her husband's wages right this minute. I intend to tell my cousin Henry about this incident. I know he doesn't want the children of his workers going hungry."

As Maidee Findley turned to leave, a brown arc of tobacco juice hit the brass spittoon next to Willa Mae and a wad of dollar bills and coins were hurled to the floor.

ANNE ALETHA SET THE ICY pitcher of lemonade in the center of the picnic table, welcoming the late afternoon breeze that fluttered the edges of her aunt's lacy tablecloth and cooled the sweat on the back of her neck. Though the storm's aftermath still littered the yard, the table looked pretty. Water droplets beaded the sides of the pressed-glass pitcher with lemon slices decorating the top. Nellie would be surprised.

When they returned from town that morning, Alex had hidden the large block of ice wrapped in a croker sack and newspaper behind the well on the back porch, and that afternoon Anne Aletha insisted that Nellie go back to their cabin to prop up her legs and rest. Now, as she arranged a crocheted linen napkin next to each matching glass, she heard Alex and Nellie coming across the yard from their cabin with Nellie grumbling.

"What you got to show me so important? I ain't even changed out of my house robe."

Anne Aletha suppressed a chuckle, not wanting to betray their surprise. Alex ambled ahead of Nellie, hands in his overall pockets, whistling. Just before reaching the picnic table, he took off his old slouch hat and pointed. "Now look-a-there."

Nellie's face broke into a smile.

"You done forgot your birthday be today," said Alex.

"I sure did. Mercy me, Miss Aletha. I ain't never seen nothin' prettier," she said, gesturing with her hands. "And y'all done gone by the ice house too. I wondered what took you so long."

Anne Aletha glanced at Alex, knowing he would not have mentioned the incident at Willard's.

Nellie lowered herself onto the bench and Alex perched on top of the empty flour barrel as Anne Aletha poured the lemonade into three tall glasses. She served Nellie's first along with a small dainty tea napkin. Alex seemed not to know what to do with his napkin and surreptitiously placed it back on the table.

Anne Aletha raised her glass. "Happy Birthday, dear Nellie. And many, many more."

Nellie's black eyes danced as she took a long sip, smacking her lips with pleasure. "That 'bout the best I ever tasted."

Alex drank his in long thirsty gulps. "Sure is," he declared, chomping on a chunk of treasured ice.

"Mother boils the rinds after squeezing the lemons and then adds the liquid to the sugar water. Let's finish it up," Anne Aletha said, and poured him another glass. "That block of ice will melt quickly in this heat, so y'all take some back to the cabin tonight to have with your buttermilk."

"Yes'um, that be real fine." Rummaging in his overalls, he withdrew a pocketknife and a small block of wood to whittle. "I be lookin' over that old cotton house in the morning. Probably ain't got too many rotten boards so we's can make it over into a schoolroom."

"Thank you, Alex." Anne Aletha was pleased with the possibility of the schoolhouse. She smiled at Nellie as she settled herself in contentment and crunched a chip of ice, savoring it. Plump bumblebees gorged noisily in the blossoms of the hawthorn bushes beside them and Nellie turned to watch.

"Them bees is 'bout as fat as Miz Sarah's baby bull," said Nellie.

Alex grinned. "That bull is as big as his mama. Still out there nursing in the pasture."

A large fly landed next to Nellie on the picnic table and she reached for the fly swatter. "Now shoo!"

"Watch out, Alex!" Anne Aletha teased. "Nellie's got the swatter. Hold your lemonade glass!"

"Huumph," said Nellie, grinning.

Laughter filled the air. Nellie would swat anything that moved. As the afternoon light grew soft and the birds began their late day twittering, Anne Aletha regarded these two special people in her life with love, wishing only for her Uncle Carter's presence to make her happiness complete.

A FEW DAYS LATER, Alex held the ladder as Anne Aletha climbed it. "Be real careful now, Miss Aletha. I got the ladder steady, but I wish I was up there instead of you. My legs ain't that wobbly."

"You just hold the ladder," she said, raking her work gloves over all the wooden shingles that she could reach, hoping the missing shingles blown off from the storm were near the roof line. "The parlor leak must be further in, Alex. These shingles look intact."

"Now don't you go crawling up there no further. I gonna get John Henry to do it. He was by here yesterday lookin' for work. Say he work for some of Nellie's cooking and a little book learnin' if you willing to teach him. What we gonna do if you fall off and break all your bones?"

Alex was right. They did need help, and Nellie spoke often of the bright young orphan boy from the quarter who worked odd jobs. She glanced down. It was further to the ground than she expected. "All right, Alex. I'm coming down." From her vantage point, the movement of a fringed buggy top caught her eye before she heard the clomp of horse hoofs. "We've got company, Alex. I can't tell who it is."

She put her hammer and nails back into the deep pockets of her old divided skirt, handed down the cypress shingles Alex had hewn, and climbed down the ladder just as the horse and buggy pulled up to the house. She groaned at the thought of more visitors witnessing her unladylike behavior.

An elderly, large-bosomed lady in widow's black peered back at her from the buggy, the gold knob of her cane glinting in the sunlight.

"That be Miss Maidee and her mama, Miz Findley," said Alex, lifting the wooden ladder away from the house to carry it back to the barn.

Maidee Findley waved. "Miss O'Quinn, forgive us for calling at an inopportune time. Cora's just put up the mail and said you'd given permission for it to be brought to you. She said there's nothing from overseas."

The kind woman who had come to Willa Mae's aid on Saturday stepped down from the buggy. Even in the heat she still looked fresh and starched, each pleat and tuck of her blue pique dress expertly sewn concealing ample bust and hips, the color complementing the blue gray of her eyes and her translucent skin.

Anne Aletha smiled and waved back, taking off her work gloves as she went to greet them. "How nice of y'all to come all the way out here. And please call me Anne Aletha."

Maidee nodded and smiled, handing her a letter and a penny postcard. "Anne Aletha, I'd like you to meet my mother, Mildred Findley."

She felt the older woman's scrutiny and regretted her appearance of a hired field hand. "So nice to meet you, Mrs. Findley. Can y'all come sit on the porch for a few minutes?"

"Thank you, Anne Aletha, but mother's feeling a bit poorly today. Hopefully another time real soon. I wanted to thank you for intervening on Willa Mae's behalf."

"Oh, it's you who came to my assistance," she said, before turning to Maidee's mother, noticing her still youthful skin, pale and delicate like Maidee's. "Your daughter helped me after a most unfortunate incident at Willard's groc—"

"Yes, and I told Maidee I don't have any use for that Mr. Jenkins either," Maidee's mother interrupted. "But you do have to keep the coloreds in their place."

Anne Aletha's smile tightened as she repressed a reply. The elderly lady continued.

"You young ladies don't realize that the darkies get uppity if you don't keep a firm hand. Why, when I was a young girl in Memphis after the War of Rebellion, the white ladies had to step off the sidewalks into the muddy streets to let the nigra soldiers pass. They'd walk three abreast because they knew there wasn't a thing the Southern whites could do about it." She stabbed the buggy's floorboard with her cane, her lower lip protruding, then added, "The Klan was our salvation."

Anne Aletha frowned, hoping Alex and Nellie couldn't hear. Maidee's cheeks flushed. "Mother, those were difficult times for the South and we were under martial law."

"Well, my friend Matilda in Atlanta," the older woman was waving and pointing to the letter in her hand, "saw *Birth of a Nation* just last week at the Rialto Theater and said everything in the movie is exactly true. People don't realize what it was like for the whites. My daddy and all those brave Confederate soldiers, who fought so valiantly in the war, couldn't even vote or hold office. Our bleeding Southland was turned over to those old carpetbaggers, scalawags, and ignorant nigras. Why, the conditions were more horrible than the war itself. And it was the Klan that restored law and order."

"Yes, Mother, that's true. The Klan was born out of the social upheaval of reconstruction. At first they did mean only to scare the superstitious Negroes away from the voting polls. But soon they became violent, and you know that dreadful wrongs were committed."

"And the Klan is reemerging," said Anne Aletha. "Look at the horrible lynchings that just occurred here in our own community. It's murder to hang people without trials."

"Well, I want you girls to appreciate what they did for us after the war. I'm proud that I sewed my father's flowing white garments and hood." She paused and grinned. "They called themselves the ghostly empire and even the horses wore bedsheets!"

Maidee and Anne Aletha exchanged glances. "Well Mother, we need to get you home to rest and I'm sure Anne Aletha has work to do."

Anne Aletha waited till their carriage rounded the oak tree before taking the letters to the porch step to read.

June 15, 1918

Dear Daughter,

I hope this letter finds you well. We too anxiously await another letter from Frank and pray for him daily. Never is a letter more gladly received. Your father and siblings send their love and everyone missed your presence on Saturday, especially Thelma. She made a lovely bride. Now three of your sisters have exchanged their vows at sunrise beneath the old walnut tree. Did you receive rain last week? Everything here is just ruining for want of it.

Miller continues to ask about you whenever I see him and Preacher Burke's wife says he would have proposed if you'd shown him the least bit of interest. However, I do agree that he was not entirely suitable for you. I think an older gentleman, perhaps a widower, would be a preferable suitor. Your father asks how many prospective pupils you have thus far? Remember that you must avail yourself to the townspeople in order to succeed.

Mrs. Wilkins's daughter mentioned that you have yet to attend church in Ray's Mill. I am aware that you do not accept the validity of the church dogmas, Anne Aletha, and that you've had religious doubts for some time. But remember that the Bible does have great moral truths. I fear our summers of tent revivals and evangelical preachers have prejudiced you against the church. Dear daughter, you must be discreet in order not to estrange yourself from the community, and you must attend church because people will notice if you don't.

Your loving mother

Anne Aletha sighed, folding the letter. Her mother was right. Except for Preacher Burke, she did have a distaste for preachers, especially the shouting, self-righteous ones who traveled the revival circuit. Tennyson had best described her sentiment for preachers as "a rogue in grain, veneered with sanctimonious theory."

She'd spent her childhood summers in stifling makeshift tents, enduring an endless progression of sweating, pacing preachers, most with little schooling beyond a calling. Adept only at stirring a frenzied crowd to come forward and get saved. Though all of her siblings had complied, she alone refused, sitting stone-faced, seething at the fire and brimstone sermons that made her mad enough to spit.

No, she would never rid herself of religious doubt. Oftentimes it seemed the world would be a better place without religion. But now, she only wondered how long it would take the news of her stomping out of New Ramah to reach her mother.

She picked up Toog's penny postcard written front, back and all around in her small rounded script and smiled. She missed her exuberant little sister, and regretted not being there for Thelma's wedding. Sunrise weddings had always been practical for country life in the summertime. Most chores could be put off for a few hours, and mainly, it was just too darn hot to dress up later in the day. Minnie, the eldest, had been the first to marry beneath the walnut tree with family and friends gathered around, holding hands while straddling the old tree's sprawling roots. Gussie followed, and now Thelma. And always after each sunrise wedding, she and her mother and sisters would set out a huge country breakfast of ham, eggs, grits, biscuits, pound cakes and pies on trestle tables beneath the yard oaks before the newlyweds were seen off at the depot.

Dear Sister,

> *I picked violets for Thelma's hair from our Secret Place. The mockingbird dived at Preacher Burke's head while he married them. Mama says if the daddy bird doesn't quit trying to run*

everything off—they won't have any babies to put in their nest. Preacher Burke's wife said you liked books better than boys, and Preacher Burke said if he were the prettiest girl in Wayne County, he wouldn't settle for that Miller boy either. When can I come visit you?

Your loving sister Toog.

7

ANNE ALETHA WATCHED from the kitchen table as Nellie mixed the powdered starch to a thin consistency of paste and then gradually added boiling water. After almost two months, Anne Aletha still failed to make the starch the right consistency.

"You's got to keep stirring," said Nellie. "That the secret to starch making. Otherwise, it be a big, lumpy mess."

Next, Nellie poured the starchy liquid into a dishpan of cold water. In a few minutes they would dip the freshly washed damask napkins into the starchy mixture and hang them out to dry.

"I stir while you keep reading," said Nellie.

She smiled. Nellie favored the *Atlanta Constitution* over the *Valdosta Tribune* and especially liked wartime hints for the housekeeper, recipes that saved time and money, and the price of women's store-bought clothing from both newspapers. Alex preferred crop news and pictures of newfangled farming equipment. Though John Henry had just begun his reading lessons, he liked to study on the words and was fascinated by any kind of machinery, especially automobiles. And everyone relished war news. "It says it's probable that soldiers seen daily on our Atlanta streets a few months ago have now taken part in the great battle raging overseas and have helped stem the drive of the Germans forces toward Paris."

Nellie paused in her stirring. "Yes'um. We gonna beat the stuffing out of them Huns."

Anne Aletha grinned and continued to read the wartime housekeeper hints:

> Do you pay fifteen or twenty cents a yard for crash cloth to make cup towels and other kitchen cloths? Many housekeepers find the soft loosely woven sacks that flour and sugar come in far more satisfactory than coarser cloth. The soft muslin of the sacks absorb moisture more readily and is more easily washed and kept white and sweet smelling because it dries so quickly.
>
> It is believed that a sour-smelling dishcloth can cause fevers—

Anne Aletha stopped. A loud incessant banging on the front door roused even Cicero from his nap in Nellie's scrap basket. "Coming, just a minute," she called. The knocking continued. Who in the world, she thought, opening the door.

Jincy fell into her arms, sobbing.

"Miss O'Quinn, Grandmother's sick! Can you please come? Mrs. Sarah brought me over. She's waiting for us."

Anne Aletha hugged the crying child. "Of course I will, sweetie. Go tell Sarah I'll be right there."

She dashed back into the kitchen to tell Nellie, threw off her apron, grabbed her straw bonnet and ran down the front steps to the wagon.

Sarah, her housedress and white hair disheveled, flicked the reins and they circled the oak at a trot. "Patten's gone to Adel to get Uncle Doctor but Neville's still in Washington trying to get war loans for the mill. Roena started yesterday with a headache and sore throat. Said she was having a little trouble swallowing."

Anne Aletha put her arm around Jincy.

Sarah continued. "After that new millworker family took sick with diphtheria last month, she's been going back and forth to the colored quarter every day taking food and nursing somebody new with it."

"My sister Toog had diphtheria last summer," said Anne Aletha. "Just a mild case. And none of the rest of us became ill. So maybe she'll be better by evening." She squeezed Jincy's shoulders. But she felt sick with dread because the elderly and infants often died from it.

ANNE ALETHA'S STOMACH heaved as she entered the sickroom filled with the warm fetid odors of retching, simmering in the morning's sunshine. She couldn't help bringing her hand to her nose. Discreetly, as if warding off a sneeze, she pressed her fingers against her nostrils, allowing in only tiny gasps of air until the nausea passed.

Mrs. Clements appeared to be sleeping. She lay curled on her side at the edge of the bedstead, so near to it that Anne Aletha feared she might roll off. A crumpled washcloth with rusty sputum lay pressed beneath her chin and noisy labored breathing came from her open mouth.

Quietly, Anne Aletha crossed the creaking heart pine floors, carefully overstepping an assortment of chamber pots surrounding the bed. From the dressing table between the two double beds, she brought a small cane chair alongside Mrs. Clements. Gently, she touched her, feeling her febrile forehead and brushing back strands of damp white hair loosened from its bun.

Mrs. Clements smiled back in recognition, her blue eyes glassy and reddened with fever. Her smile faded into a painful grimace as she coughed and whispered. "You mustn't endanger yourself, my dear."

"Shhh …" Anne Aletha said. "Try not to talk. I'm so sorry you've taken ill." She patted her bony hand, searching for the small cleft inside the wrist. She pressed lightly on the artery's channel, feeling the wild pulse beat much too rapidly against her fingertips.

"Jincy asked me to come. Patten's gone for Uncle Doctor. They should be back in a little while. I'm wondering if you could tolerate a cool bath? It might help bring down the fever."

She nodded, closing her eyes.

Anne Aletha glanced around the room, alarmed at the gravity of her friend's condition, unsure what to do next. She noticed a blue enamel pan on the washstand. "Mrs. Clements, I'm going to put a basin in the chair beside you. If you need to cough into it, just lean your head over, all right? I'll be back in a few minutes."

She found Queenie in tears on the back porch, frantically stabbing an ice pick into a fifty-pound block of ice. "I done sent Miss Jincy to town for more aspirin and rubbing alcohol. Figured we'd be needin' some ice to cool her too."

"Oh Queenie," she said, patting her shoulder. "Yes. Let's give her a cool bath first and see if we can get her temperature down. Then we'll put on fresh dry sheets."

Queenie nodded filling an old galvanized foot tub with chipped ice. "There's towels and an oil cloth on the kitchen table. I know she's done got sick from that new millworker family. It spreading through the quarter and she been trying to help folks."

Anne Aletha struggled down the hallway carrying the foot tub of ice and entered the bedroom. Mrs. Clements had not moved. Spreading the red-checkered oilcloth over the feather mattress to protect it, she gently rolled Mrs. Clements onto her back. The elderly lady was too weakened to lift her head. Anne Aletha worked silently to quickly slip the damp gown over Mrs. Clement's head.

Applying the cold compresses to the areas she thought would help lower the body's temperature, she placed one on her friend's forehead, then another beneath her neck, working her way down the torso and limbs, remembering the pulse points of the forearms, wrists and knees. She poured tepid water into the china wash bowl and gently sponged Mrs. Clement's face and hands, noticing how frail with age and sickness she was, her skin as thin as tissue paper and her breasts withered and hanging like socks at her side.

She squeezed out the remaining icy towels, layering and tucking them over her fevered body. Suddenly she was struck with the image of Egyptian mummies and the pictures she'd seen in *The Mentor*, the bodies of the Pharaoh Kings swathed and encased in multi-layerings of cloth before they were buried and entombed for eternity. Quickly, she chased away any thoughts of burying.

Mrs. Clements spasmed with the first shivers of cold as Anne Aletha removed the compresses. "I know you're chilled. Queenie and I will have you a nice clean bed and fresh nightgown in just a moment. Do you think you can suck on a couple of ice chips and take in a little liquid? It might soothe your throat and cough."

Mrs. Clements nodded as Queenie came in balancing an armful of folded laundry along with the rinsed out chamber pots. She slid the china bowls under the bed and went around to the other side, leaning over Mrs. Clements and patting her arm. "I know this done tuckered you out Miz Roena, but you's gonna feel better after we get you cooled off. And Miss Jincy gonna bake you some teacakes this afternoon in case you get hungry a little later on."

Mrs. Clement's smiled at the mention of Jincy's name, reaching out for Queenie's hand as she sucked on the ice chips Anne Aletha placed on her tongue.

Queenie covered Mrs. Clements with a soft cotton blanket. "Yes'um, she acting real tired yesterday. Said she just had a dull headache and some shivering fits. Then this morning the coughing and fever started."

Gently, they turned her on her hip, sliding her toward Queenie's side of the bed as Anne Aletha worked quickly, rolling up the soiled linens to the middle of the bed and tucking them up against Mrs. Clements as she put on a fresh bottom sheet.

"Not much more Mrs. Clements," said Anne Aletha. "We're going to roll you back over the mound one last time toward me so Queenie can make up her side of the bed."

Queenie snugged her bottom sheet giving it a final tug before walking over to the mahogany dresser. "Miz Roena, let's put on one of those pretty new nightgowns you and Jincy sewed up last week, and we put on some sweet smelling lilac powder too."

As she watched Queenie's black gnarled hands powdering the pale shoulders, Anne Aletha thought of all the baby bottoms of both households that Queenie had dusted and diapered over the years. She'd been with the Clements forever. Anne Aletha guessed they'd shared nearly a lifetime together. Close in age, they'd born and raised children and grandchildren together, buried husbands, and for most mornings of their adult lives, Queenie had crossed the train tracks from the colored quarter and cut across the backyard to greet Mrs. Clements in the kitchen before starting her second breakfast of the morning.

"You've been with her a long time haven't you, Queenie?"

"Yes'um. We go way back, don't we Miz Roena? Her and me's known each other since we was girls. Ever since her daddy got killed up North in the war. Left her mama with all them girls, not a single boy in the bunch."

Anne Aletha looked up as Queenie hesitated. She saw the quivering mouth and the tears glistening on her dark cheeks, then felt the beginning of her own.

PATTEN AND UNCLE DOCTOR arrived early afternoon, haggard and grave as they entered the bedroom. Patten barely acknowledged Anne Aletha's presence, and once again, she felt the familiar discomfort. Averting her eyes, she heard the self-justification in her voice. "Jincy and Sarah came for me this morning."

Uncle Doctor crossed the room to his sister-in-law's bedside, the floor groaning beneath his weight. "Anne Aletha," he said in his gruff, bellowing voice, "you're a kind young woman to come over and help out, but I'm afraid you've been exposed to diphtheria." He sat down on the bed beside Mrs. Clements, his large frame causing a concavity in the goose feather mattress as he lovingly caressed her cheek, taking her slender hand in his. She opened her exhausted eyes and neither of them spoke. For a fleeting moment, Anne Aletha wondered about the past between them.

Patten stood at the foot of his mother's bed while Uncle Doctor began his examination. The room hushed to a tense silence as he placed his stethoscope and massive hands on her frail chest. "Now breath in. Now out. Now in ..."

Anne Aletha felt her own chest rise and fall with his instructions, feeling each percussive thump that he made with his fingertips.

"Roena, I know it's painful to cough. Are you having sharp pains?"

She nodded, pointing to the left side of her chest.

"Can you tolerate anything on your stomach?"

She shook her head. "Ice chips. Anne Aletha gave me ice chips."

"Good girl, now you rest. We're going out to the kitchen to see what Queenie's left us on the stove."

No one spoke as they followed Patten back to the kitchen. Uncle Doctor went over to the large wood-burning stove, lifting up all the pot lids, calling out their contents: "Field peas with snaps and ham hock, okra and a little corn in this one."

Patten remained in the doorway of the kitchen. "I told Queenie to put out the word in the quarter that I'd pay the asking price for someone to come in and nurse mother. They'll be hesitant when they hear it's diphtheria."

Anne Aletha spoke quietly. "I'll stay till you find someone."

Patten looked at her, his expression indiscernible. After a long silence he said, "Thank you."

"Daddy! Uncle Doctor!" Jincy called, running into the kitchen and seeking the arms of both men. "Grandmother isn't going to die is she?" Her eyes were wild and swollen in her tear-stained face.

All three of them looked to Uncle Doctor. "She's very ill, Jincy. It's diphtheria pneumonia, the worst kind. But your grandmother's a strong lady, and that's hopeful for us. However, young lady, you are not to enter her bedroom until we're sure the contagion has passed. Is that understood?"

"Can I sit in a rocking chair on the front porch and talk to her and Miss O'Quinn through the bedroom window?"

"Yes," he said, leaning down to kiss the top of her head. "You can do that, and you can help Queenie with the cooking, and you can also make your daddy and me some of your teacakes for my next visit."

"Jincy," said Anne Aletha, "would you like to show me the new kittens you told me about? I bet Queenie left that plate of table scraps by the backdoor for you to feed mama cat with." She looked at the two men and winked in conspiracy. "Let's let your father and uncle sit down and have their dinner." As she and Jincy picked up the plate of scraps and some cream off the kitchen table, she turned back to Uncle Doctor. "May I speak with you before you leave about instructions for her care?"

"Certainly, Anne Aletha, but the most important thing for you to remember is that the body fluids and excretions, especially the sputum, are the causes of the contagion. You and Queenie be real careful."

Jincy raced down the back steps with the plate of table scraps and saucer of milk, placing them just under the porch. She returned to the top step beside Anne Aletha and tucked her skirt and petticoat beneath her, hugging her knees.

"What's the mama cat's name?"

"Prettything, but grandmother calls every cat we've ever had Prettything."

Anne Aletha smiled. "That seems like a good name." She looked out to Mrs. Clements' well-tended flower and vegetable garden, enjoying the sweetpeas trailing up among her pole beans, wishing she'd brought some of her mother's sweetpea seeds as well.

They both saw the movement—

"Look," she said, pointing to the array of black and white kittens, all identical to their mother, encircling the bowls of food and milk. "I see four … no five kittens, Jincy, and your grandmother is right, they're all prettythings."

Jincy grinned, nudging closer to Anne Aletha as the mama cat ate. The kittens, full from nursing, frolicked around her. The plumpest and largest kitten in the litter swatted and batted at his mother's tail, trying to make it wiggle. Then in frustration, he went over and pounced on top of one of his smaller siblings.

Both laughed at his antics as Anne Aletha put her arm around Jincy and gave her a small squeeze. Nature was like that, she thought, able to offset life's pain and sorrow with innocence and joy. Always assuaging the bitter with the sweet.

DESPITE THE ICE AND ALCOHOL baths, the fever steadily climbed and the painful coughing increased. By nighttime, Mrs. Clements was slipping in and out of lucidity.

Patten said little except to tell Anne Aletha that he'd telegraphed Neville to return home as soon as possible, even though he'd not yet met with all the potential bankers. With train schedules and the Georgia and Florida Shortline running only one train a day from Augusta, they estimated his soonest possible return would be day after tomorrow.

The rest of the evening Patten sat brooding by his mother's bedside. Anne Aletha longed to console him, feeling his torment for his mother and the added burden of the failing lumber mill. But she knew her words of comfort would not be welcome.

Later that evening, Patten and Jincy retired to bed, leaving Anne Aletha alone in the darkened front bedroom with Mrs. Clements. Although her elderly friend slept, Anne Aletha was too tired and worried to light the lamp and read. She slipped out of her dress, glad that Nellie had sent fresh clothes, and felt cooler in her camisole as she stretched out on the other double bed. Luxury was having a whole bed you didn't have to share with sisters. As always before bedtime, her thoughts went to Frank, hoping for his safe return home. For a long time, she watched the moonlight glinting across the foot of her bed, patterning her legs with lacy designs from the curtains. She closed her eyes, drifting but staying on the surface of sleep. A few minutes after midnight, she heard the forlorn sound of the last train pass behind the house and felt the floor tremble beneath the iron bedsteads.

Sometime in the middle of the night, a bone-chilling scream stopped her heart. She sat up in the strange room, unsure for a moment where she was. Then she recognized the whimpering and flew out of bed. "I'm here Mrs. Clements, it's me, Anne Aletha. Are you all right?"

"Spiders! Big spiders … Oh, oh, they're on the ceiling!" She struggled to breathe. "One just dropped down off the ceiling. It's in the bed with me!"

Horror filled Anne Aletha. She hated spiders. She looked up, knowing that Mrs. Clements was hallucinating or having a nightmare, but in the darkness she wasn't certain. As she held her friend, heavy footsteps stomped down the hall.

Patten stood in silhouette, barefooted and shirtless, the suspenders of his pants pulled up hastily over his broad bare chest.

"Your mother thinks there are spiders on the ceiling, Patten. I think she's hallucinating. Can you find the matches and light the lamp?"

She felt him moving behind her in the dark, and heard the match strike as he lit the lamp's wick. It suffused the bedside in a glare of light and she stood squinting up into his drawn face, stubbled with a day's growth of beard.

"I'll get her a cool washcloth." She brushed past him to reach the basin.

Patten leaned over his mother. "See Mother, no spiders anywhere, just bad dreams from the fever." She nodded and lay back, sprawling sideways in the bed. Gently, he lifted her in his arms, repositioning her more comfortably.

Anne Aletha turned and watched him, noticing his well-defined musculature, the straining muscles of his arms and upper torso that were as well-honed as any of his millworkers. It didn't surprise her that he cut and loaded planks of lumber alongside his men. Unlike Neville, he was too restless for ledgers and books. He would feel caged behind a desk, like the elusive black panthers that roamed the swamps of South Georgia, powerful, wary, and solitary.

"Mother, we'll keep the lamp burning for you tonight. See if you can rest some." He turned to Anne Aletha. "Can you sleep with the lamp burning?"

She nodded, watching as his eyes swept over her camisole and down her body. She found his scrutiny unsettling and yet strangely flattering in his awareness of her as a woman. If only Nellie had sent one of her prettier camisoles, and if only she had bosom to fill it out.

At daybreak, Anne Aletha lay in bed listening to the distinctive clucking of a red cardinal outside the bedroom window before realizing a new sound filled the room. Dread clutched her heart as she recognized the rattle that came from Mrs. Clements' chest. Uncle Doctor had explained the stages of pneumonia and its progression. Her lungs had filled in the night and now she labored to breathe. Uncle Doctor called it the death rattle. He said the lips and nail beds would become blue when the lungs were involved and unable to get enough oxygen into the bloodstream. Anne Aletha crawled out of bed and a loud sob escaped from her when she saw the darkened lips.

ANNE ALETHA CRINGED when she heard the wrenching wail from Jincy's room … a high pitched yelping sound like animals made when they were wounded.

"Patten has told her," said Uncle Doctor quietly.

She stood behind his slumped shoulders, shielding herself from looking at the motionless form on the bed beneath the sheets.

"We'll go in to see Jincy in a moment, Anne Aletha. Roena said the child's taken such a fancy to you." His voice cracked when he said her name.

Anne Aletha wished he would cry. Tears constricted her own throat so tightly that no words could pass through. She watched him wearily rub his forehead, sighing as he turned away from the bed, staring at the dressing table and the large array of brown bottled medicinals. She'd never seen such a large assortment of tinctures and powders and tonics, enough remedies it seemed to cure all the maladies of mankind. Each bottle was labeled with fancy gold block lettering, most with undecipherable contents such as Tincture of Myrrh and Ipecac. Some she recognized, like Tincture of Foxglove; its digitalis extract had relieved her grandmother's heart spells. "Eases my flutterings," her grandmother would say. And her mother's summer cutting garden wouldn't have been complete without the tall purple backdrop of foxgloves, known as deadly night shade.

The loud crash of glass startled her. Bottles jarred against each other as Uncle Doctor stood with his open satchel angrily sweeping the contents of the dressing table off into his bag, as if every bottle had been as useless to him as the leeches and bloodletting of a century ago.

She knelt down. "Nothing broke, Uncle Doctor. The stopper just fell out of this one; none of the powder spilled."

She handed it back to him noticing the palsied tremor of his right hand.

"Thank you, child," he said, struggling to buckle the leather fasteners of his medicine bag.

She reached over to help him guide the metal prongs into the small holes. "Anne Aletha, would you be able to stay and help lay out the body? I think Patten'll have trouble getting anyone to come in because of the contagion. Have you ever prepared someone for burial before?"

She hesitated. "Yes," meaning to say that she could stay, not that she'd ever helped with someone dead—but she couldn't think how to say it delicately. Her grandmother had died when she was Jincy's age. But her only duty had been to run take the fanciest bedspread off the visitor's bed and bring it to the parlor while her two eldest brothers brought in the sawhorses from the smokehouse. They had helped her father lift one of the heavy walnut doors off its hinges and place it across the sawhorses, while she and her mother draped the brightly colored cross-stitched spread over the door. It was too small and did little to hide the ugly sawhorse legs. When her father brought their grandmother into the parlor, everyone cried. That whole day and night friends and neighbors came by to pay their respects and no one spoke above a whisper. The next morning, a pine coffin was brought out from town and her seven brothers carried their grandmother down the front steps, out through the pecan orchard to the wagon. The whole family had walked in procession behind the coffin down the little lane to Friendship Baptist Church.

Uncle Doctor turned to her as he picked up his straw fedora and satchel. "Patten is going to the lumber mill to see about her coffin. I might as well warn you, he's insistent that no one stay tonight and sit up with the body. Plans to sit up with her himself. You'll probably have a devil of a time getting folks not to stay and sit with him. But I imagine he'll stay away until they've all gone home tonight … and probably just as well. He'll just ruffle feathers that Neville will have to unruffle when he returns."

She nodded, planning to stay with Jincy as long as she needed her, until all the people went home. Neville said that Patten never bothered with the cordialities of life. But grieving should be more private anyway. Nowadays, it seemed that death was more an occasion for visiting and feasting than it was for the bereaved.

"Will you be going back home to Adel this afternoon?"

"Yes, for a difficult birth, but I'll be back tomorrow. I asked Sarah to come over and help you. She can stay with Jincy today. I want you to go home and rest. Roena's Missionary Society will bring food late this afternoon."

"Patten thinks Neville will arrive home on the morning train."

"Yes, and he wants the burial to take place in the afternoon. But it's Jincy I'm concerned with right now."

"I'll come back late this afternoon and stay with her till Patten gets home. You try to get some rest too."

His soft fleshy palm cupped her chin. "Bless you child."

She sadly closed the door behind him. Could it really be only yesterday morning that Jincy had come for her? How could a day seem like a week?

8

'**WE'RE READY WHEN YOU IS,** Miss Aletha," Alex called from the side yard as he brushed Sulky's flanks and then down his long back legs. The mule liked to be brushed.

"The shortcakes are just coming out of the oven. Nellie's bringing the basket."

"I thought we done used up our flour rations this week—"

"We have." Anne Aletha interrupted. "She's trying a new shortcake recipe with cornmeal."

Alex shook his head and walked around the mule to brush the other side.

Patriotism was at a fervent pitch now, and few people complained about the rationing. The maximum monthly allowance of sugar for household purposes had been cut from three pounds to two pounds, and every grocer was compelled to keep a record. Several people in town had given up their weekly pound and a half of flour rations for the troops, and most everyone had a war garden to see them through the winter. The newest slogan for a war garden was "*Every weed killed helps drive a nail into the Kaiser's coffin.*"

She reviewed the contents of her aunt's floral sewing bag that she'd gathered for Jincy. That afternoon, she'd gone through her aunt's chifforobe, rummaging for silk ribbons, a colorful hankie, and small trinkets of jewelry. Anything to brighten a nine year old's sorrow.

"They still got to cool," said Nellie, bringing the picnic basket. "Tell Queenie there's a jar of fig preserves for her on the bottom of the basket. And tell her how sorry we is." She called to Alex. "Y'all better be on your way. Folk'll be getting there pretty soon." She turned back to Anne Aletha. "You got everything you need, Miss Aletha? You sure look pretty. What time you want him to come back around for you?"

"I don't want Alex out at night, Nellie. I promised Uncle Doctor I'd stay with Jincy till she goes to sleep and Patten gets home. I'll get a ride home with somebody."

"Well, you don't need to be over there by yourself, sittin' up with the dead and waitin' on Mr. Patten. Especially with Mr. Neville away. Bring Miss Jincy back over here and I'll make her a nice bed in your room."

She gave Nellie a quick hug and took the basket. "Don't you worry. Go get off those feet for a while."

She handed the basket to Alex and climbed up beside him. Sulky responded to the first jiggle of the reins. "Well, he rarin' to go this evenin'," Alex said.

The late afternoon sun beat down hot and she reached up to adjust her summer straw, tilting it to cover her chin. "Do you think a lot of people will come this afternoon?"

"Yes'um. Everyone from around these parts will come pay their respects. She was a mighty fine lady."

She swiped her perspiring palms across her skirt worrying that people would snub her. If only Neville were here by her side. But it was her own fault that she hardly knew anyone besides the Clementses and Maidee Findley. Maybe Queenie would need help in the kitchen.

Alex turned Sulky onto the main road. Buggies lined both sides of it, almost up to Miss Effie's.

"Oh Lord, Alex, look at all these people."

Squaring her shoulders, Anne Altha stepped down from the buggy, struck by the unexpected silence. Mourners, sweltering in the late afternoon sunshine, crowded both front and side porches, spilling out into the yard. Ladies clustered together, shading themselves beneath their parasols, handkerchiefs dabbing at both tears and perspiration. No one spoke above a whisper, as though the front parlor held a napping child they didn't want to awaken, instead of a coffin with the dead.

Custom dictated viewing the body first, and the line of mourners extended down the flagstone walkway. Townspeople waited courteously at the open doorway, allowing the person in front of them to step inside and over to the coffin for a moment of private farewell. Most held an engraved card from their calling card case, some scribbling a few personal words of comfort. She hoped Jincy was seated on the parlor couch, in the far corner behind her grandmother's coffin, surrounded by hovering church ladies. Although people came expecting to stay for food and visiting, she wished that with the absence of Neville and Uncle Doctor, they'd soon eat and go home. Jincy had endured enough.

Anne Aletha paused at the gate and took a deep breath. Just as she reached down to unlatch the ball and chain gate, Ralph Attaway rushed up behind her.

"I declare Miss O'Quinn, it's such a tragedy." He stomped sand from his shoes and removed his hat. Hair oil plastered his head and dandruff dusted his shoulders.

"Yes, good afternoon, Mr. Attaway." Since learning that he was a boarder of Maidee and her mother, she tried to be nicer.

"Miz Clements was just trying to help that millworker family and them living in squalor."

She held the gate open. "Mr. Attaway, you go ahead. I see Maidee coming down the road."

Maidee walked toward them with unhurried ease. Anne Aletha had felt an instant friendship with her, drawn to Maidee's calm, serene nature. But after having met her cantankerous mother and boarders like Ralph Attaway, she wondered if Maidee's patience had been born of necessity.

"Oh Anne Aletha, what a dreadful two days it's been for you," said Maidee, her soft breathy voice soothing and kind. "You were so good to stay and nurse Roena." She lifted the rim of her wide-brim hat and searched Anne Aletha's face, genuine concern clouding her smile.

"Maidee, I'm so glad to see you and I—" Suddenly, unexpected tears smeared her cheeks.

"Here, let me take the food basket. We'll slip around to Queenie in the kitchen and then find a quiet place to talk."

She nodded, blotting her eyes. "Thank you. There's quite a crowd. I didn't expect so many people. Was your mother not feeling well?"

"I just walked her back to the house. 'Healthy as an ox,' Doc Clements tells her. He says she's going to outlive him and that all mother's ailments are in her head. I left her on the porch revising her pallbearers list."

"What?"

Maidee grinned and shook her head. "Mother's been planning her funeral for years. She takes great delight in crossing off the ones on her pallbearers list who make her mad—which is most of them, most of the time. Today, she says Mr. Willard snubbed her while waiting in line to pay his last respects to Roena. I keep telling her if she'll wait a week, she won't be mad anymore and then she won't have to bother reinstating them."

Anne Aletha laughed, cheered by Maidee's humor, and brightened with the prospects of her newfound friend.

Maidee, smelling of Jergens hand lotion, briefly linked her arm through hers as they stepped over the border of liriope leading to the side yard. As the sun continued to set, visitors strolled out into the shady yard. Maidee wove through the crowd, greeting everyone warmly as Anne Aletha followed behind, noticing that conversations paused midsentence as she passed, and though she pretended not to eavesdrop, she couldn't help overhearing snippets of conversation.

"They say she just stomped out."

"I hear she keeps pretty much to herself."

"Well, do you think she ever plans to attend church?"

Anne Aletha's face reddened.

Maidee stopped to speak to a tall willowy young woman twirling a black parasol. "Hello Luella, so nice to see you. It's a terrible tragedy, isn't it?"

"Yes, I can't believe she's gone," the woman replied, rigid in posture but with warm brown eyes.

"Luella, I'd like you to meet Miss O'Quinn. Anne Aletha has her teaching degree and perhaps you've heard that she intends to take pupils in the fall. Anne Aletha, this is Luella Sirmans."

Anne Aletha extended her hand and received a perfunctory handshake. Had she too been at New Ramah?

"Luella has three rambunctious boys that you've probably seen at the millpond," said Maidee.

Anne Aletha nodded. "Yes, I believe Jincy and I saw them recently with a large snapping turtle in their clutches."

Luella chuckled. "Yes, and the little rascals brought it all the way home. Fortunately, their father thwarted their efforts and made them return it."

They laughed and while Anne Aletha wanted to say something more about her plans for a school, she hesitated, feeling it inappropriate for the sad occasion.

Maidee took Anne Aletha's arm again. "We'd better get these teacakes to Queenie so she can set them out."

Behind them a shrill voice called out. Maidee muttered beneath her breath. "Oh no, the widow Dew."

The widow came puffing up to them with a scowl. "I want you to know your mother was just plain rude a little while ago."

Maidee looked stricken but recovered quickly. "Oh, Mrs. Dew, you know how mother is." She turned toward Anne Aletha. "Mrs. Dew, I'd like you to meet—"

"And she broke into the receiving line!"

"Please pay my mother no attention, Mrs. Dew. I apologize," said Maidee. Widow Dew's mouth was open and poised for a new complaint when another elderly lady interrupted with a greeting and came to their rescue.

Finally, as they climbed the steps to the back porch, Anne Aletha's shoulders relaxed.

"The widow Dew is really not as bad as she seems," said Maidee.

Anne Aletha wondered if Maidee had noticed the townspeople's cool reception toward her. While the mourners acknowledged her, no one stopped to speak, and these were the parents of her potential pupils.

Queenie sat at the large kitchen table fanning herself with the top of a corset cover box that had held teacakes. A thumbprint of flour smudged her left nostril and a huge smile appeared on her face as the two younger women came through the backdoor. "Lawdy, Miss Maidee and Miss Aletha. I sure glad to see you. These nice church ladies done made me take off my apron and sit a spell."

Jincy's black and white cat flew through their ankles seconds before the screen door shut. Maidee gave Queenie's shoulders a squeeze and slipped into the chair next to her. "We came to help put food on the table and arrange flowers, if you need us to Queenie."

Anne Aletha handed Queenie the picnic basket, hugged her neck, and wiped the smudge of flour from her face. "Nellie told me to tell you how sorry she is and she wants you to take care of yourself. There's a jar of her fig preserves on the bottom just for you."

Queenie reached out to take Anne Aletha's hand, holding it tightly in the small plump palm of her own. Her eyes teared. "Miss Aletha, I want to tell you how pretty you and Miz Sarah fixed her up ... not too much rouge or face powder, just real natural like. And that dusty rose silk you put her in was her most favorite."

"Jincy told us it was. How is she doing?"

"I wish you'd run see after her, Miss Aletha. She done gone to feed the chickens. Trying to be too grown-up, if you asks me. She needin' to let it out. Ain't too big for crying, that's what I told her."

Anne Aletha stepped out onto the back porch, jarred by the sad reminders that Mrs. Clements would never return. The porch was just as she had left it, as though she'd come from the garden only moments before. Her old gardening oxfords sat at the top of the steps, the ones she'd taken pruning shears to, cutting out holes to ease her bunion toes. She'd lined them up neatly next to her sunbonnet and tucked the worn out cotton lyle stockings that she used to cover her arms against the sun. A half dozen dirt-filled wooden crates, each marked with an empty seed packet, lay scattered beneath the well's water shelf. Tiny seedlings peeped up through the dark loamy soil. She touched the dry soil thinking she must remember to water them.

A slight breeze rustled the yard oaks and dry leaves crunched beneath her feet as she passed the smokehouse and then the privy. Someone coughed inside the privy and she hurried on. Outside the barnyard doors, a dozen Rhode Island Reds pecked at scattered kernels of corn, clucking and scratching in quiet tranquility. She waded through the plump hens as their biddies skirted away from her, darting beneath their mother's tail feathers. From around the corner of the barn, she caught sight of a neighbor puppy watching the chicks, his oversized ears cocked in puzzled wonderment at the small moving objects. "Better go on home, little fellow," she told him. "Or you'll have a pecking in store for you."

She stepped inside the cool barn that smelled of hay and manure. "Jincy?" A horse snorted from one of the stalls, and as her eyes adjusted to the dimness, dark bovine eyes stared at her from the single stall on the left, the cow's tail swishing at flies like a metronome. She saw the unhitched surrey, remembering that she would need a ride home tonight. The last stall that housed Mrs. Clements freckled mare stood open and empty.

"Jincy! It's me—Anne Aletha," she called, walking back toward the loft.

An arm waved at her from halfway up the loft steps. Wiping away her tears, Jincy placed a finger to her lips to silence Anne Aletha and pointed to the contents of her lap.

Quietly, she climbed the narrow steps squeezing in to sit on the step just below Jincy. A nesting hen in a roosting crate on the stairs above them clucked at the intrusion. Anne Aletha petted the two sleeping fluffs in Jincy's lap. "Where's the mama hen?" she whispered.

Jincy pointed to the barnyard. "I lured her out. See the one above us? Her name is Pretty-head. Grandmother puts everybody's eggs under her cause she's such a good sitting hen. Right now she's got seven under her wings and has been on them for ten days. She's not flighty like some—turns her eggs every day. Grandmother says Rhode Island Reds have the richest yolks and the best flavor of all."

Anne Aletha let her chatter, conscious of how young and fragile Jincy looked, her full shapely lips pursed in a childlike pout and her black patent Mary Jane's caked with manure and straw. "I love your pretty ribbons. Did Sarah braid your hair?"

Jincy nodded and picked up a baby chick to cuddle it.

"Miss O'Quinn, Mrs. Sarah says grandmother has passed over now and is in heaven with grandfather. Do you think she has?"

"I hope so, sweetie and I know she'll be worrying about you being sad and lonely without her. You know your father and Uncle Neville are going to be real sad too for a while. They're going to need you."

Jincy nestled both sleeping biddies in her lap.

"And the last thing Nellie said to me this afternoon was, 'Ask Miss Jincy if she'd like to come stay a few days with us.'"

"Really Miss O'Quinn? Can I come spend the night with you?"

"Yes. But you must ask your father and uncle first. We can use an extra pair of hands right now. Did you know Alex and John Henry are fixing up the old cotton house out in the field? We're going to make it into a nice schoolroom for me."

"Do you have any students yet, Miss O'Quinn?"

"I have John Henry," she said, smiling.

"You're going to teach the coloreds?" asked Jincy in disbelief.

Anne Aletha tried to keep the reprimand out of her voice. "Yes, sweetie, everyone needs to learn to read and write. And the Negroes and sharecroppers haven't had the opportunity. I'll be pleased to teach anyone, young or old, who wants to learn."

Jincy frowned in thought, contemplating her words. "Uncle Neville says it's a shame that people want to bring that Miss Perkins back here to board in everyone's houses when we've got someone like you living right here. I hate her, Miss O'Quinn. She's mean and boring and she'll switch your knuckles at the least little thing. Can I come to your new school?"

Anne Aletha reached up and patted Jincy's knee. "School is a few months off and meanwhile we have our piano lessons together. Just think how much it would please your grandmother for you to sit down and play her beautiful piano."

THE HALL CLOCK struck ten p.m. and Jincy called from her bedroom. "Miss O'Quinn, will you ask father to come kiss me goodnight when he gets home? Even if I'm asleep?"

Anne Aletha put her head in the door. "I promise, sweetie. Now try to go to sleep." She closed Jincy's door at the end of the long hallway. Where in damnation was Patten?

At last, the mourners had gone, though she'd feared they'd never leave. Especially the two old-timers who considered themselves to be the town's official body sitters. From the way they smelled, she suspected their all-night duties of sitting up with the dead were more conducive to imbibing corn liquor unsupervised by their wives than their Christian duty of not leaving a body unattended.

She paused in the wide hallway, marveling at the glass-enclosed oak bookcases that lined both sides of the walls. Neville's, she presumed. She thought of the philosopher Cicero and his quote that if you have a library and a garden, you have everything. But this library collection far surpassed her uncle's. She turned up the kerosene lamp on the seat of the hall tree, perusing the many shelves of fine leather books, awed by the vast range of literature and philosophy, appreciating even more the closeness and special friendship her uncle and Neville had shared. His death left an emptiness in both of their lives.

The first bookcase held law books. She glanced at them briefly, remembering that Neville had read law with the Honorable Judge Pendergrast. She knew little of the years he'd spent away from Ray's Mill. She moved to the next bookcase, noticing that he'd devoted it entirely to the subject of philosophy. And curiously, he hadn't grouped the philosophers alphabetically, nor had he divided them chronologically into the epochs of Renaissance or Enlightenment the way her uncle had categorized and taught them. It appeared he grouped them as to thought. The top shelf held the political philosophers: Adam Smith, De Tocqueville, Machiavelli and then the more recent ones with whom she was unfamiliar. On the next shelf he'd placed the theists. The well-known writings of St. Augustine, Aquinas and Kant. The last shelf he'd devoted solely to the works of Hobbes, Darwin, Schopenhauer, Spinoza and Voltaire. Perhaps some who were freethinkers or skeptics like herself? As though separating the secularists and nonbelievers from the believers, consciously delineating the age-old and unresolved inquiry of faith versus reason.

The next bookcase contained almost the complete history of Greek thought. Beautiful antique bindings of Plato's *Dialogues*, the writings of Aristotle, the plays of Aristophanes, Aeschylus and Euripides. The works of Homer. She slid back the glass panel and carefully removed a small marbleized leather volume of Greek mythology. Holding it to the light, she thumbed through the pages, smelling its mustiness as she looked at the fine lithographs depicting the mythical gods created by the pagan Greeks. Her uncle thought the Greeks invented their gods and myths to explain the chaotic world in which they lived— to make themselves brave and strong. She wondered if all religions weren't just myth. That later, men had created God just like the ancient Greeks had created their gods— to ease man's suffering and give him hope for an afterlife. Had Christianity caught on in the Dark Ages to withstand hell on earth because paradise would be waiting for them in heaven? She remembered Jincy's questions in the barn that afternoon about her grandmother's passing and her untruthful answer about heaven. Wasn't it all invention?

She closed the book, easing it back into place and walked into the parlor. Her feet hurt and she realized she'd spent the last hour tidying an already tidy dining room: brushing off a crumb here and there from the sideboard, checking the contents of the pie safe to be sure there would be something sweet if visitors came by after the graveside service tomorrow. All in an effort to avoid entering the parlor with its disquieting and grim reminder of death's finality.

Mrs. Clements rested in the middle of the parlor, her half-opened coffin draped with a simple spray of green magnolia leaves. Tresses of silver moss hung from the shiny leaves. She suspected that Jincy had gathered the simple adornment. Fresh tears stung her eyes.

She set the kerosene lamp on the marble hall table across from the coffin and straightened the voluminous stack of calling cards left by visitors on the silver tray. Preferring to sit behind the coffin, she walked over to the horsehair couch in the far corner of the darkened room and removed her shoes. Yawning, she leaned her head against the lumpy headrest and closed her eyes for just a moment.

She awoke to the sound of Patten's heavy footsteps on the front porch and the toppling of the wicker fern stand by the door. He cursed, attempting to upright the potted fern, then entered and stood in the doorway, staring at his mother's coffin. He reached into his back pocket and took a long swig of clear liquid from the glass flask. The chain of his gold watch fob glimmered in the lamplight and she realized she'd never before seen him in dress clothes. Standing, she stepped from the corner shadows of the parlor.

He turned to her, his shadow towering in the lamp light on the wall behind him. "Where's Sarah? She's suppose to be staying with Jincy."

"She did, but it's late and she's old and tired. I told her I would stay till you returned. Alex is coming back around for me." Why had she lied? But she had never dreamed Patten would be midnight getting home.

"God damn, Anne Aletha. Don't you realize a colored man has no business being out on the road this time of night." He stopped, shaking his head as he glanced again at his mother's coffin. Turning away, he staggered from the parlor.

Please don't go into Jincy's room drunk, she thought. Instead, he entered his own bedroom and shut the door. She sighed, trying to decide whether to take the lantern to the barn and take Bella home. She could return the mare tomorrow.

The crash that followed moments later seemed to shake the house.

"Patten?" she whispered, hesitant to knock but placing her ear against the bedroom door. No sounds came from within. She tapped lightly, hoping not to awaken Jincy at the end of the hall. Should she enter? What if he'd fallen and hurt himself. Perhaps he'd passed out from his drunkenness. She turned the glass door knob.

"Patten?"

The oil lamp on the nightstand illuminated an undisturbed bed, casting dim shadows elsewhere in the corners of the room. A plain four-poster bed faced the fireplace, dominating the sparsely furnished bedroom.

Not a place he spent much time in. She stepped inside, her eyes drawn to the fireplace mantel and to the sepia-colored pictures and daguerreotypes. Was his deceased wife among them? The mantel clock ticked loudly, distracting her, and she wondered how anyone could sleep with such an annoyance. She stepped further inside and almost tripped over the long outstretched legs.

His head rested against the footboard, his eyes open, staring vacantly into the empty hearth. He turned watching her approach him and lifted the flask to give to her.

"Don't want to spill good whiskey."

She placed it on the mantel. "Did you hurt yourself?" She could hear her mother's same impatient voice after one of her father's infrequent drinking bouts.

"Boot caught," he said, indicating the culprit to be the upended boot on the far side of the fireplace.

She kneeled down beside him. "Patten, you don't want Jincy to come in and find you on the floor. Help me to get your other boot off and you over into the bed."

Roused from his lethargy, he wordlessly pushed at the heavy boot as she tugged. "There." She placed the boots beneath the washstand. "Will you be able to use the bedpost to lift yourself?"

He turned and grabbed the post, hoisting up his large frame. "Jincy … need to kiss her goodnight."

"She's asleep Patten. She won't know you didn't come. Let's get you up and into the bed." Quickly, she slipped under his shoulder, pressing herself like a crutch beneath his arm, encircling his sinewy waist, intensely aware of the contoured fit of their bodies. Patten made no motion to move.

"Just walk with me slowly around to the other side of the bed."

He massaged his temple as they walked. "Headache powders … some in the bureau drawer, I think."

"I'll get them in a moment. Now turn around and ease yourself down gently."

He sat down hard and fast catching her off balance. Both toppled back into the feather bed, painfully pinioning her right arm beneath the weight of his body. "Ow!" she cried.

He rolled off her arm toward her, collapsing his head on her shoulder as if any further effort of movement would be too great for him. He sighed and mumbled, "Gone … all gone. Won't have to know now."

She didn't know if he meant the mill was gone or his mother or both. She answered him softly, almost in a whisper. "I'm so very sorry, Patten, so very sorry." She stroked the back of his head, aware of the impropriety, yet unable not to console him.

He lifted his head, gazing down at her intently, as if sobered by her words and touch. She shut her eyes when she saw the square outline of his jaw move toward her. Suddenly, she felt his mouth cover hers, pressing it open. His hand glided over her throat, tilting her chin so that she met him more fully. He tasted like whiskey and kissed like no boy she'd ever known.

Wordlessly, he shifted his weight, drawing her up further beneath him. Apprehension mingled with excitement and curious sensations filled her. She felt her heart hammering against her chest wall and her pelvis jutting somewhere into the softness of his belly. Her breaths quickened and she hoped the loud gasping sounds were Patten's and not her own.

Unexpectedly, he moved to her side and kissed her again. She stiffened with alarm as his hand slid from her throat swiftly and deftly down her body, like fingers playing octave arpeggios on the piano. She froze, holding her breath.

Abruptly, he stopped and sat up quietly on the edge of the bed. Putting his head in his hands, he said nothing.

She tugged at her skirt and petticoat squirming as gracefully as possible out of the middle of the feather mattress. All she could think to say was, "I'll get the headache powders."

"No, I'll go hitch up the wagon."

"No Patten. You stay with Jincy and try to get some sleep. Alex will be waiting for me. Goodnight," she said, almost catching the hem of her skirt in the door in her rush to close it.

9

BALANCING THE PILE of laundry beneath the soft jowls of her chin, Nellie carried the sun-stiff clothes into the bedroom. Anne Aletha lay half awake sprawled on her side, her pale legs twisted in the tangled heap of the top sheet with Cicero curved against the sway of her backside. He opened one eye.

"Like trying to wake the dead," Nellie muttered. She draped the folded muslin sheets across the bed's foot rail. "And you's a worthless old tomcat," she whispered. "How's I 'spose to make up this bed with you both still in it?" She opened the warped door of the chifforobe and it groaned.

Anne Aletha bolted upright, upsetting the sleeping tomcat.

Nellie turned. "Miss Aletha, you ain't taken sick with the diphtheria has you? I done checked for the umpteenth time and even been banging pots and pans around in the kitchen."

"Good Lord, Nellie, what time is it? Have I missed the funeral?"

"No'um, you's all right. It's about nine. I got water heatin' on the stove so you can have a good wash. Miz Sarah say they's gonna wait to see if Mr. Neville come in on the 11:15 this mornin', and then the buryin' will be this afternoon. She say Mr. Patten don't want Preacher Elrod having nothin' to do with his mama's funeral and that Doc

Clements is gonna say words over her at the grave. 'Spose to be just family and near friends."

"Really Nellie?" she asked, rubbing her bleary eyes. "I bet that'll give folks something to talk about." She picked up the disgruntled Cicero, settling the two of them back against the pillows, relieved to be spared another of Preacher Elrod's sermons on sin and perdition.

"Nellie," she said, stroking Cicero. "I know you don't much like Mr. Patten, but at least he's no hypocrite like that preacher. I'm glad he's not going to allow that man to preach about Jesus and his love while we all know he's openly supporting the Klan's hatred. If you could have just seen him that Sunday having the audacity to let those men parade up and down New Ramah's aisle in their white robes. And then having the gall to thank them for their patriotism while he's taking their bribe money."

Nellie shook her head in silence, her back turned as she continued hanging up the laundered garments.

Anne Aletha sighed and leaned her head back against the pillows, closing her tired eyes. At least Patten had taken a stand against the Klan and its bigotry with his rejection of Preacher Elrod. Or had he? She knew of Patten's hatred for unions. And didn't the newspaper say that part of the Klan's new appeal was protectionism against the unions—along with their vendettas against Negroes, Jews and foreigners? No, she decided, he was a contradictory man but his stand against the preacher was probably no more than his own intolerance for his mother's Primitive Baptist sect. Mrs. Clements had told her she'd given up long ago on "bringing Patten any closer to the Lord." But what would Neville say? Wouldn't he think that for their mother's sake and propriety that Preacher Elrod should conduct the service in his own church?

She dreaded the sad day ahead, especially for Jincy and poor Neville, who had been telegraphed of his mother's death. She wondered if Patten would meet his train and if Neville had been able to get the crucial new bank loans for the mill. Still holding Cicero, she swung her legs over the side of the bed, searching for her slippers. With a loud thump, the cat jumped from her arms, indignant at being twice disturbed. Glancing down, she noticed the front of her gown. She'd found her nightgown in the middle of the night, in the pitch black, but it was on backwards—and Nellie would surely notice.

As if reading her thoughts, Nellie turned, the corners of her mouth pursed downward in displeasure. "Alex says we got the Clements' mare keepin' Sulky company in the barn."

Anne Aletha reddened. Heat flushed her face as last night's vivid image flashed through her mind, her body pinioned beneath Patten's, returning his drunken kiss. She feared he'd think her no better than some rouged up tart, like the ones in Jesup her brothers bragged about visiting on Saturday nights.

"You sure you's feelin' all right, Miss Aletha? You look feverish to me."

"I'm fine, really I am." She reached over for her hairbrush, yanking down hard on the dark snarled curls she'd neglected to comb out the night before. Her stomach churned and she did feel queasy, but it wasn't diphtheria that flushed her cheeks filling her with shame. She remembered that Plato said reason quelled a man's passions and desires, gentling their spirited nature. But reason had deserted her.

"Nellie, when y'all delivered laundry this morning, did you hear if anyone else has taken sick?"

"Miss Maidee didn't mention nothing. Just told me not to forget to give you the Honor Roll section of the *Atlanta Constitution*. She done saved it for you. It's yonder on the dressing table. Said she'd see you this afternoon. While you look through it, I got to go get your surprise."

Wondering about the surprise, she winced as Nellie walked by the chair that held last night's crumpled up clothes, praying she wouldn't pick them up. "Don't bother with those Nellie. I didn't get a chance to put them away last night. I'll shake out the wrinkles and hang them up in a minute."

"Humph," Nellie grunted, picking up and inspecting the white batiste blouse and the navy linen skirt, both looking as though they'd been slept in. "I don't think nothin' but a good washin' and ironin' gonna help these." Draping them over her arm, Nellie left the bedroom with a look of concern once more on her face.

Anne Aletha hoped they didn't smell like whiskey and cigarettes. She picked up the newspapers off the dressing table, wondering where Frank was at that moment. She didn't really expect to see his name under "missing in action" or "dead," but still, she felt better checking the paper's Honor Roll section each week. Most likely, if anything happened to him, they'd telegraph Odum and then someone would carry the news out to the house. But the heavy assault had begun.

Flipping through to find the page of dead and wounded, she turned to the alphabetized columns of Privates between the M's and the P's, underneath all the gruesome categories of how they were wounded or killed, searching carefully for the name O'Quinn:

Missing In Action

Privates
McAllister, John S, Albany, Ga.
Matunis, Joseph, Portage, Pa.
MacGillivary, Horace B, Chicago, Illinois
Osher, Harold, New York, N.Y.

Wounded Severely
Privates
Meyer, Amos Herr, Lancaster, Pa.
Mcguire, Edward J, Richland Center, Wis.
Richardson, Henry W, New Albany, Ind.

Died From Accident and other Causes
Privates
Robinson, Charles M, Vincennes, Ind.

Died From Aeroplane Accident
Privates
Nimocks, Robert G, Winston-Salem, N.C.

Next she searched all the categories: lieutenants, sergeants, corporals, wagoners, nurses, and cooks just in case the name Frank O'Quinn had been misplaced. Usually after doing this, she felt some small measure of relief. But today as she read the article by General Pershing about American soldiers holding the fighting line for a distance of thirty-eight miles on the western front, despair surged over her. Before, her fears for Frank had been the smothering tunnels of collapsing earth that he dug beneath the ground for enemy surveillance and the constant threat of artillery fire. Now, even if the soldiers were fortunate enough to escape the shelling and gun bombardments, the threat of mustard gas lurked unseen amongst them, sweeping with abandon across the fields.

NELLIE GROANED with rheumatism as she eased herself gently onto the old tapestry gout stool she used for sewing and hemming. "Walk over there just a little ways and turn around real slow," she instructed. "Let's see if I got it even. I done had to take it in everywhere."

Anne Aletha touched the bodice's delicate lace inserts and pin tucking of her aunt's mourning dress, marveling at Nellie's surprise for her. "You mean it's been packed away in that trunk all these years?" She buried her nose in the dolman sleeves, smelling the lingering scent of lavender.

"Yes'um, after the typhus took Miss Claire, Miz Carter didn't wear nothin' 'cept mourning clothes. Turn around and let me see the back. Yes'um. It's even. And I believe it's hemmed short enough, even though nowadays, you young girls want to show more ankle and leg."

She reached over to help Nellie up, smiling with affection and hugging her. "Nellie, you look after me just like my own mother. Thank you. It's lovely."

Nellie beamed. "Folk's been seeing you in that other outfit so long, they's gonna think you don't got nothin' else to wear. Now, you look like a city lady with a store-bought dress—like one of them fancy china dolls. And after you wash, you eat that sweet potato and biscuit I got warm on the stove and we'll put some curves on you too. Mr. Neville gonna say you's a sight for his sad eyes today when he gets off that train."

She laughed, shaking her head at Nellie as she moved to look in the dresser mirror. It was useless to argue, or to try to change Nellie's mind about the twin brothers. She had missed Neville and looked forward to his return, but it was Patten's admiration she wanted in her new dress.

The face that peered back at her seemed all eyes, with shadows in places she'd not noticed before. She felt sure all she needed was a good night's sleep, but still, you could never tell what might happen. As soon as good manners would permit, she intended to speak with Neville about securing the land deed for Alex and Nellie.

"Oh, and Miss Aletha," said Nellie, sticking her head back inside the door. "I meant to tell you I 'bout tripped over John Henry and his mutt this morning on the back porch. He's done got his alphabet learned and most of the words in those picture books you gave him. He wantin' to spout it off to anybody that'll listen. Even pestering Alex. They gonna start on the makeover of the cotton shed. Gonna make you a nice schoolroom."

"How many pupils do you think will come, Nellie?"

"Oh, I reckon a handful at first. But word'll get around. They'll be seeing how much you taught John Henry."

Yes, she thought, but few would be as eager and bright as John Henry. No white child she'd ever taught could write and recite the alphabet so quickly or sound out new words in the speller with such amazing ease and retention.

"Book learnin," said John Henry. "It's the only hope for a colored boy like me."

She agreed. Education would take him away from chopping cotton and subservience, away from white robes, burning crosses, and men like Elmore Jenkins. And someday, she hoped, to a Negro college in Atlanta.

10

UNCLE DOCTOR'S faltering voice carried out across New Ramah's tiny cemetery, his grief as raw as the shoveled-out earth of his sister-in-law's grave. He stopped, cleared his throat, and started again. "We stand here together this afternoon, stricken by the passing of our beloved Roena. With a swift and merciless blow, a deadly form of diphtheria struck Roena, ravaging her and devastating all of us who loved her …"

Anne Aletha held her breath, praying his voice would steady as he stood hatless under the wizened oak, taking no notice of the scant shade under the two o'clock sun or the pesky black gnats swarming around the sweat on his upper lip. She shut her eyes, longing to shoo them away.

"To all of us who knew and loved Roena, she was a warm and generous woman, with few, if any, pretensions. In all my years of knowing her, I never knew her to be anything but kind and compassionate toward every living person and critter. She loved the Lord, her family and friends, and her church. As you all know, Roena never wanted any fuss or big to-do made over her. And dear family and friends, she wanted none made today. I am here at her request."

Slowly, Uncle Doctor glanced around those clustered before him in the small semicircle. He ran his hand through his white unruly hair and a sad, bemused grin spread across his face as he continued. "And I know it won't come as any surprise to you that Roena told me what to say today."

A tiny release of chuckles rippled through the small gathering as Anne Aletha sighed with relief, hoping the humor would help keep her own tears at bay.

"In fact," he added, in his half-joking tone, "y'all probably thought this unorthodox funeral was Patten's idea, given his predilection for church services."

People smiled at the irony, casting furtive glances at both Patten and Preacher Elrod, while Anne Aletha stared at the back of Patten's thick wide shoulders, unable to see his response.

Uncle Doctor turned to Jincy as his face grew solemn. He reached out for her delicate hands, cupping them inside his own. "You know, sweetpea," he said, his voice gentle and quiet. "Your grandmother knew this would be the hardest on you. You were the light of her pretty blue eyes. 'The best part of my good, long life,' she told me just day before yesterday. 'You tell Jincy to be strong,' she said. 'You tell her that not a day'll go by that I won't be with her, that my love will be a part of her always.'"

Jincy sniffled, nodding her understanding, as Uncle Doctor kissed the top of her bonnet. She stepped back to stand between her father and uncle. Anne Aletha watched the shoulders of both brothers edge closer to Jincy.

"Queenie," Uncle Doctor bellowed, waving his arm and beckoning her forward from the rear. "Roena said you were to come up here and take credit for raising all three of these youngins."

"Ah Lawd," Queenie called out. She shuffled to the front toward his outstretched arm, her heaving shoulders and streaming cheeks dispelling any hope of dry eyes for Anne Aletha.

Uncle Doctor reached out for Queenie's hand, struggling for composure. "Lord knows, Queenie, how long you've been a part of this family. Roena always said she couldn't have done without you. She wanted me to thank you, not only for all those years of devotion, but for your friendship." He sighed, the quiver of his lower lip unmistakable. "And she's told me that every time I come by the house, I'm to remind you to take your heart medicine."

"Lord a mercy, Doc Clements," Queenie cried. "What we gonna do down here without her?"

Anne Aletha's face crumpled in tears as she watched Uncle Doctor tenderly hug Queenie. From the corner of her eyes, she noticed men fidgeting with their spectacles and heard noses blow all around her. She froze when Uncle Doctor called her name.

"Anne Aletha?" he said, looking back at her with a smile. "As everyone here knows, we've got a fine new schoolteacher who has moved to our community. What you folks may not know is that Anne Aletha came at Jincy's request, and risked herself to nurse Roena." He paused. "Anne Aletha, our family will be forever indebted."

She felt the stares of people looking at her and flushed. Quickly, she glanced at Neville as he turned around and smiled, the gratitude unmistakable in his eyes.

Patten's back remained to her.

"I promised Roena two things this afternoon." Uncle Doctor continued. "First, that I would make her eulogy short, and second, that I would not be morose. So I will simply say to her family and friends gathered here today, how grateful she was for the many years she shared with you. And to her sons, Patten and Neville, her last words were of you, how proud you'd both made her and how much she loved you."

No one moved as Uncle Doctor bowed his head in silence. A horse snorted from the lane as birdsong from the woods heightened the awareness of life's fragility and finality. With a trembling hand, Uncle Doctor removed his handkerchief, wiping the sweat from his brow before turning to face the coffin behind him. In a soft whispering voice he said, "Roena, you were the very best amongst us, and my brother was a fortunate man that you found favor in him. You will be sorely missed."

As if on cue, Preacher Elrod stepped forward, his large ears bright red from the heat and sun. As he nodded to Uncle Doctor, he exchanged a brief glance with Neville and once again, Anne Aletha recognized Neville's hand of diplomacy, how smoothly he'd averted the preacher's wrath and any slight to his dignity.

Clutching a worn oversize bible to his chest, Preacher Elrod said, "The family has asked me to lead us in prayer for their mother's crossover. Let us bow our heads and pray."

As everyone bowed their heads, Anne Aletha raised hers, wondering at her own irreverence. Glaring at the preacher for whom she had so little regard, she braced herself for his loud, sing song beseechings. But to her surprise, in a low, soft voice he began recitation of the Lord's Prayer, asking everyone to join him.

As the peaceful prayer flowed from her lips, Anne Aletha bowed her head, pondering the rote religion that had once given her such solace and certitude in life. She opened her eyes and felt the large droplets pool on the fringe of her lashes, knowing she was helpless in letting them spill.

As the mourners took their leave, Anne Aletha walked to the far side of the cemetery, allowing the family the privacy of a last goodbye. Her heart lurched at the sound of Jincy's muffled sobs and the sight of Uncle Doctor reaching out to enfold her into his arms, patting her tawny braids and soothing her with inaudible words of comfort.

At the adjacent grave, Patten and Neville stood side by side before their father's headstone, even their stances reminding her of how opposite their natures. Patten, stiff and erect, gazed up at the tops of the rustling loblolly pines, his posture as unbending as the lumber he harvested. And Neville, weary from travel, leaning heavily against his cane, unabashedly wiping tears from his cheeks.

She didn't want to intrude and walked along the edge of the cemetery toward the older graves at the back of the graveyard thinking that the monuments were the only tangible proof of someone's existence, a permanent engraving of a lifetime. She paused in front of a child's grave: Suzy, 1900–1907, with a lamb and the trunk of an oak tree that signified a child's life cut short. These always touched her heart. Though cemeteries made her sad, they heightened her awareness of mortality and the sweetness of life and she found peace in the quiet surroundings.

She meandered further, reading more of the quaint inscriptions on the headstones. Nettles crunched beneath her feet and she leaned over to inspect the cockleburs embedded in her shoelaces. Extracting a half dozen spurs, she noticed the nineteenth-century epitaph on the gravestone before her:

The Sweet Remembrances of the Just
Shall Flourish While They Sleep In Dust.

She paused, contemplating the noble sentiment that memories of the just would flourish. But justice seemed so nebulous with the world at war now, armies clashing with other armies for reasons that each deemed just. And even in Ray's Mill, decent God-fearing people were allowing themselves to be deceived by hate-filled men who portrayed themselves and their cause as just.

She remembered sitting on the riverbank of the Altamaha with her uncle one warm Christmas afternoon. He'd read the ancient passages from Plato's *Republic* when Socrates had posed the same question. "What is Justice?" he had asked his fellow Athenians. She'd read Polemarchus' reply to Socrates first: "Justice is doing good to your friends and harm to your enemies."

Her uncle, scholarly but dramatic, shook his head in exaggerated argument and read the reply of the other

Athenian, Thrasymachus. "No, no. Justice is the advantage of the stronger over the weak."

Then her uncle assumed the wise counsel voice of Socrates, asking both men if justice could be separated from morality. "Doesn't justice come," he said, "not from private good and private interests, but common good and common interests?"

Though Anne Aletha pondered the ancient question of justice, she realized that twenty-five centuries later, the world appeared no closer to the answer.

Walking back toward the tiny brown clapboard church, she passed a modest grave with the surname Jenkins crudely carved into the white wooden cross. She wondered if Elmore Jenkins was any kin to them. If justice was moral goodness, as Socrates said, and injustice was moral ignorance, why didn't the good people of Ray's Mill stand up to men like Jenkins and Elrod?

Movement across the cemetery interrupted her thoughts. Uncle Doctor, Neville and Jincy started back toward the church, leaving Patten behind. Signaling to two men squatting with ropes and shovels beneath the sycamore, Patten took off his hat and coat. Laying them across the top of his father's headstone, he untied his necktie and removed the stiff detachable collar. Frowning, he looked at his pocket watch. It didn't surprise her that he'd remain to bury his mother. She watched him roll up his shirtsleeves, staring at the sight of the thick sinewy muscles of his forearms, feeling again the touch of his hands and the racing of her heart. Unexpectedly, he turned and she hurried on, hoping she'd not been seen.

Jincy, Neville, and Uncle Doctor remained in the churchyard. While Uncle Doctor cranked the Model T, Neville helped Jincy up into the buggy. He called to Anne Aletha in his deep pleasing voice.

"Come ride out to the mill with me in the morning. I've got company books and ledgers to pick up and I'd sure appreciate the company."

She smiled into his careworn face as Uncle Doctor held the door to the Model T open for her. "Yes, I'd like that. You and Jincy rest up and I'll see you in the morning."

THE NEXT MORNING, she waited for Neville beneath the old oak in the forked road, perched upon the roots of its elephant-like trunk, her skirt and petticoat tucked securely around her legs and ankles barricading herself from chiggers and ants. Nearby, a loquacious grackle, having a one-bird conversation with himself, uttered low guttural sounds. A yellow sulfur butterfly careened among the roadside milkweed while a bumblebee sucked nectar from a morning glory blossom. But today, Jincy's grief occupied her thoughts, allowing nature to bring her little joy. Though neighbors would visit and Queenie would hover, the shattered heart of a nine year old squeezed her own.

Carriage wheels clattered over the deeply rutted road down the lane. She stood brushing lichen from her navy blue pique and straightening the grosgrain ribbon of her summer straw. Would Patten be at the mill? She blushed. Moments later, Mrs. Clements' old freckled mare plodded toward her, Bella's drooping head as sorrowful as any mourner at yesterday's funeral.

Neville called out a greeting and guided the surrey alongside her. "Morning, Anne Aletha. I'm glad you could accompany me. I've missed you."

"Me too," she said, seeing the sad exhaustion in his eyes and the sorrow etched in his face. Though shaven, he still wore yesterday's weskit and galluses. "Did y'all get some sleep?"

"Patten slept in a chair by Jincy's bed all night. But the first thing she told us when she awoke is that you invited her to stay overnight and to help with the new schoolhouse." He grinned. "She wants to know when she can come."

"You tell her anytime. We look forward to her visit." She reached up to stroke the gentle creature she'd ridden home two nights ago in the dark, caressing the mare's velvety muzzle and feeling the warm air from her nostrils on the palm of her hand. "Animals really do sense loss and grieve, don't they?"

"She didn't eat her oats this morning," he said, extending his hand to Anne Aletha as she climbed up into the buggy. "Mother's had her since she was a filly. But it's you I'm worried about. Uncle Doctor says the incubation period can be two to five days. I fear mother exposed you to something deadly."

"I'm fine, really I am. My sister Toog had a mild case last summer and no one else in the family took ill. Uncle Doctor instructed me on taking precautions. How is Queenie?"

"Worn out, I'm afraid. But Sarah came over this morning to help Queenie deliver leftovers to the quarter while Jincy tends to household chores. You saw all the food people brought, even with rationing." He circled the wide oak, guiding the mare back down the lane.

"I'm glad. That will keep Jincy busy today." She gave him a sidelong glance. Though proper manners would not allow her to ask about the financial success of his trip, her impatience demanded she inquire. "Were you able to take care of your business in Washington?"

He shook his head. "Banks aren't willing to extend credit for land options now that contracts with the War Department might soon expire. Unfortunately, when Uncle Sam came begging for lumber to build army barracks last summer, Patten and I bought more land options. Everyone thought the Allied offensive would take at least a year to succeed once we got our troops overseas. But if the Allies can launch a large offensive this fall, some think Germany will be brought to her knees by next spring."

Though elated at the prospect of an end to the war, his family's tragic losses dampened her joy. Would creditors call in their loan and would they have to sell? She didn't ask. "I wish there was something I could do to help."

"You have already, Anne Aletha, more than we had a right to ask of you. I only pray that mother did not infect you."

He said no more, clearly grief stricken for his mother and worried about the mill's survival. She wanted to mention deeding the land to Alex and Nellie, but decided against it. "Patience, child," her uncle would say. "You must learn patience." They rode in comfortable silence as the horse lumbered down the road kicking up clods of dirt. Like her uncle, Neville made her feel special. She loved his delight in pursuits of the mind and their easy companionship felt like the tonic chords of music, always drawing her back to its home key. Unlike the dissonant, jarring chords of Patten that so unsettled her.

They passed Miss Effie's once resplendent war garden in her front yard noticing that the runner beans on the side fence were nibbled to nubs. The bantam rooster straddled the roof of the chicken house, but the goats and Miss Effie were nowhere in sight.

The buggies and wagons that had lined both sides of the main road yesterday were gone and the only evidence of death at the Clements' house were the browning magnolia leaves in the pair of wicker flower stands by the front door and the white satin bow of mourning tied to the gate of the picket fence.

Soon the road to the lumber mill gave way to a land ravaged by logging. Felled trees and stumps stretched as far as she could see. The desolate sight of a lumber mill, with the ruined earth that seemed like a sin against nature, never failed to disturb her.

As always, Neville sensed her thoughts.

"You know, we've considered our forests an inexhaustible resource for far too long. Many think the South is on the verge of logging out her trees because of the destructive cutting practices. I think Teddy Roosevelt is correct about conservation and reforestation. We must begin to put back what we take."

"Yes. My father says we're cutting ourselves right out of our own livelihood. He says we're depleting our forests with no heed to the future." She sighed. "I don't remember a year he didn't have to hire men and oxen to come harvest timber off our land for extra cash. It sickened me to see those century old-cypress trees felled, as though we have a right to decimate nature's best." She shook her head. "My brothers were the only happy ones. They got to help my father and the hired men raft the timber down the Altamaha to Darien. It was an adventure for them. But all the girls got to do was cook for a week in order to feed all those hungry men."

"No Aristotle and Plato," he teased.

She smiled, squinting in the harsh sunlight and fanning gnats from her face, trying to imagine the blighted wasteland before them when it was once a forest. A hawk circled above and the air hung heavy with the scent of pine resin. In the distance, she heard the first squeal of the planing mill. Few people complained about the roar from the bandsaw of a lumber mill, but none could forget the ear piercing sound of the planing mill, its machinery working at high-pitched speeds, carving wood into shape.

She cringed. It sounded like wood shrieking.

Neville reined in the mare as they entered the lumber yard, a mountain of uncut logs, sawdust piles, and open-sided wood sheds. Several millworkers approached them, and, except for a short bandy-legged man with a large bushy white mustache, the men looked thin and gaunt. It was hard work. Six days a week, ten hour days, sun up till sundown. And she knew accidents were common among lumbermen. Many lost fingers, limbs and life to the bandsaws and axes, and few companies helped with anything more than doctor bills.

The little bandy-legged man spoke first, taking the reins from Neville. "Me and the men are real sorry about

Miz Clements. She was a fine lady, always helping folks that needed it." He removed his hat, wiping sweat from his brow. "I know the Lord has his plan, but it sure don't seem right taking the best amongst us."

"Thank you, Clyde. We sure appreciated the fine coffin you and the men built."

She heard the quaver in his voice.

Using his cane, he climbed down and walked around to assist her, taking her elbow as he steered her toward his crew. "I'd like you to meet some of our men, Anne Aletha. You know good lumbermen are hard to find. We couldn't run the mill without them, and fortunately Uncle Sam knows that too. The draft board makes exceptions for millworkers and designates them as essential war workers."

The men moved forward.

"Clyde, I want you and your boys to meet Miss O'Quinn, Carter Irving's niece from Odum. We've got us a fine diploma-trained schoolteacher now. She'll be signing up pupils for fall, so y'all pass the word."

They touched the brims of their hats.

"Clyde here is an old mule skinner from way back. He and my daddy cleared the land together in the early days. This man can pick a fly off a mule's back with a whip and come just close enough to flick it, but never touch the animal's hide."

She smiled and extended her hand. "That takes real prowess with a whip." Clyde had the pale blue eyes of a billy goat, and she felt his affection for Neville. Two towering boys stood next to him with the same light eyes, dimpled chins and thumbs thrust into their suspenders.

"Ned here is Clyde's oldest boy. He's a tree feller. You know some folks call them flatheads. He and another man work a two-handled cross saw and do a fine job." Neville turned to the other son. "And Jeremy is Clyde's middle boy. He's our saw filer and an expert at keeping all the saws sharp and clean. These trees can dull a saw's teeth in just a few hours."

She nodded, exchanging handshakes with both boys, wondering if they were minus any fingers.

Neville waved to other crewmen as they walked back across the mill yard. They lifted their hats to her. "Tim over there is a scaler. He can calculate the board feet in a single tree or estimate a whole cypress tract with amazing accuracy."

As they approached the towering stacks of drying lumber, Neville stopped among a group of Negroes and embraced an elderly gray-headed man. Though neither spoke, both wiped tears from their eyes before turning back to her.

"Anne Aletha, Stanley here and his men are stackers. You know there's an art to stacking and these fellas make all that hard work look effortless." He patted Stanley on the back. "He's kept Patten and me out of trouble since we were knee high."

Stanley grinned. "Yes'um. I's had to chase after them youngins playing hide and seek in all these sawdust piles and then they'd sneak behind my back and try to climb up those big stacks of lumber."

She laughed. "I grew up with seven brothers, Stanley, and they were always into mischief." Touched by the closeness of the millworkers, she felt the burden of responsibility that Patten and Neville would feel if the mill closed.

They continued walking, passing long narrow rows of wooden hangars. Neville pointed to them. "Our best wood is routed to these dry kilns. Steam pipes bake them till they go to the planing shed."

She nodded as the sun slid behind a cloud for a few blessed moments.

Soon, the noise increased as they neared the saw sheds and Neville leaned close to her ear. "We're going in that first shed. It houses the carriage and sliding log holder, and presses the log against the bandsaw. The rough outer bark is sawed off first and we use that to fire the boiler. Then the inner wood is sawed into planks and stacked outside to dry or baked in the kilns till it goes to the planing shed. It'll be too loud to talk once we're inside."

She nodded and then grimaced as they stepped inside. A huge log entered into the log holder, shaking the walls of the wooden shed. As the saw cut into the behemoth log, she covered her ears to the noise. Bark spewed in all directions and Patten stood behind the carriage watching her.

She looked away quickly before turning back to his knowing eyes. She could read nothing in his face.

11

STANDING IN THE DOORWAY, Anne Aletha watched Jincy back out of the dirt-swept schoolyard, raking a gallberry bush broom across the path of her footprints and squinting against the mid-July sun. The young girl paused, looking back at the made-over cotton house, and Anne Aletha wondered if she was remembering past outings with her grandmother to the millpond. Jincy had told her that as a little girl, when the fields blossomed into white and the tiny one-room house bulged to its rafters with giant bales of cotton, she and her grandmother would often stop back by from the millpond when the distance to home and privy seemed too far. Mrs. Clements would rein in the old mare and tell her, "Hop down here, child, and run; squat, yonder, over there behind the cotton house."

Jincy lifted her pigtails off the nape of her neck, surveying her morning's efforts. Not even a prickly ball from the nearby sweet gum tree marred the neat appearance of the swept schoolyard. She'd raked the whole yard clean of debris, and then gone over it a second time to sweep the sandy brown dirt into a pattern of large fanciful swirls. Her design looked like a sky of puffy clouds reflected in the millpond on a summer's afternoon. Now, Jincy hesitated. If she stepped back across, she'd make footprints.

Anne Aletha stepped onto the porch.

"Miss O'Quinn?" called Jincy. "Can you come look?"

"Be right there, sweetie." She was relieved to see a smile on Jincy's face after weeks of mournful frowns. Lugging a pail of dirty lye water to the porch railing, Anne Aletha emptied its contents between the railings with a loud splat and then hurried down the uneven porch steps. Brushing the remnants of dirt dauber nests from her hair, she slapped at the fine white lint that dusted her from head to toe. "Phew!" She laughed and snorted mule-like at the cotton fuzz tickling both nostrils.

Jincy waited, shading her expectant eyes from the sun, as Anne Aletha admired the meticulously swept yard with its pretty swirls and design. She even studied a game of hopscotch drawn in the sand beneath the sycamores. She gathered Jincy into her arms. "It looks so pretty and you've worked so hard. Let me see those hands. No blisters?"

Grinning, the girl extended her hands, palms up for inspection. "No, ma'am, Miss O'Quinn. Grandmother says I'm a real good worker."

Anne Aletha snugged the bow of Jincy's sunbonnet, noting the first mention of her grandmother and the slight tremble of her lip. "I know you miss her, sweetie. She'd be very proud of you."

They turned back toward the schoolhouse. A column of gray smoke billowed up from the huge brush pile behind the old cotton house. The pungent smell of wood smoke and John Henry's easy laughter drifted in their direction. "By the way, have you told Peety he's not allowed to dig any holes in our pretty new schoolyard?"

At mention of his name, Peety whined beneath the porch. Giggling, they looked back at the doleful eyes of John Henry's mutt, one ear drooping, the other pert. He lay half-submerged in the cool sandy hole he'd dug beneath the schoolhouse porch.

Beside him lay a growing stash of scavenged booty. Daily he added to his pile. Monday, he brought an old cow bone, bleached by the sun, along with a large shriveled garden squash. Yesterday, a freshly caught catfish, now bloated and malodorous. Today he'd brought a rooster's head that looked disturbingly similar to Miss Effie's prize bantams.

Anne Aletha could only hope that the rooster or his parts had been discarded by Miss Effie and not pilfered by Peety.

The 11:30 mill whistle sounded in the distance and Jincy turned to her. "Miss O'Quinn, did I tell you father's coming to pick me up at noon?"

"Your father? He's coming here?" Her face reddened. "But Alex can take you home anytime, sweetie." She watched Jincy's puzzled expression at her fluster, but could only think of how to freshen her wild curly hair and sweat-stained dress. She eyed the mule's watering trough.

"Father says he has a surprise for me."

"Really? How wonderful. I wonder what it is?" she said, feeling fresh shame at the prospect of seeing Patten. "Let's go find some shade and cool off. We'll see how Alex and John Henry are coming on those school benches."

Peety trotted off ahead of them, sniffing, his curled tail held purposeful as he nosed the ground by the side of the schoolhouse. The charred remains of a yellow-jacket nest detained him. Lingering above ground were a few survivors from the nest that Alex had torched the day before with kerosene. Two bothersome bees flew up alongside them as they walked, hovering with persistence at their exposed skin.

Jincy swatted, making a loud swooshing noise. "Go away," she cried.

"Careful, sweetie. I don't know why they're so pesky this time of year."

"Miss Effie says they send out special sting messages to each other and if one bee gets hurt, they all chase you."

"Well, let's not make them mad," Anne Aletha said, trying with little success to gently wave them aside. She knew that the first frost would kill them, but hated the thought of summer coming to an end. She'd much prefer to live with their annoyance year round if she could just walk out on the porch every morning in her cotton nightgown and bare feet.

As they came around the schoolhouse, Alex stopped hammering and turned a log bench upright for their approval. With pride, he ran his large knuckled hands carefully over the split pine log, checking the top's surface for smoothness.

"Have you already finished one, Alex?" she asked, trying to sound enthusiastic for the crude but functional pine benches that would have to serve as school seats.

"Yes'um. Just had to make sure none of them pegs is comin' out through the top." He wiped the surface with his kerchief. "Have a seat, Miss Jincy. See how it sits. Might be a little wobbly on this uneven ground."

She sat down, tucking the folds of her skirt, making room for Anne Aletha on the bench.

"Thank you, sweetie," she said, picturing her old schoolroom in Odum, the slant fronted wooden desks in graduated sizes with cubbyholes and compartments. Each had storage space for the young children's writing slates and *McGuffey's Reader* along with the pen and ink implements of her older pupils. She looked at Alex's proud face.

"How many more do you think you can get from that log?"

"I reckon two more. 'Course we still got those straight-back chairs in the barn with the busted cow-hide seats. John Henry gonna fix them. And that old worktable inside the smokehouse gonna make you a fine teacher's desk."

Such meager beginnings, Anne Aletha thought, wondering if she would fail for want of students. How foolish she'd been to think that her Normal School diploma would assure her the visiting teacher's position by parents in the community. She'd estimated two hundred and twenty dollars in teaching wages for the school year. Enough to pay the property taxes next year, with leftover money for seed and fertilizer in the spring.

Jincy interrupted her brooding thoughts. "Miss O'Quinn, what are you going to name the school?"

She hesitated, looking at Alex's expectant face, feeling his unvoiced doubt.

"What do you think about calling it Miss O'Quinn's Academy?"

He removed his straw hat, solemn as he mopped the sweat from his brow. "Miss Aletha, it don't make no difference what you call it. 'Cause white folks ain't gonna send their children to a school with no sharecroppers and colored, even if you teach the coloreds out back on the porch. And the colored ain't got no money to pay you with. Seem to me we between a rock and a hard place."

She sighed, folding her arms across her chest, knowing he was right. She'd never have the school she envisioned—a place for learning, without regard to color, age or community standing. "Well, maybe Miss Perkins won't be asked to return this fall and we'll have the schoolhouse all ready, just in case. Who's going to teach the white children? And if they don't come, I'll teach the Negro children. And any of their parents that want to learn too. Maybe we can trade out lessons for help at plowing and harvesting time. We've got the land."

Neither Alex nor Jincy replied as John Henry ambled over from tending the brush pile. Undeterred, she turned to him. "John Henry, what do you think about loading up Aunt Lily's windup Victrola on the wagon and bringing it to the school for an open house? We've got all those phonograph records, not just classical, plenty of spirituals the grown-ups would like, and some Sousa the children can march to."

Alex stood up and dusted wood shavings from his overalls, softening with indulgence, as he often times did with Nellie. "Well, most colored folks ain't never seen a talking machine before."

Jincy clapped her hands. "And Miss O'Quinn, if we finish in time for Halloween, we can decorate the schoolroom with Jack O' Lanterns and paper cutouts." She turned to John Henry. "And since John Henry memorizes so easy, he can recite something and show the parents all that he's learned."

John Henry smiled, shy with Jincy's praise. "I'll be real careful bringing around the Victrola, Miss Aletha."

"Thank you, John Henry."

"Ain't John Henry suppose to be at Mr. Willard's by now?" asked Alex.

"Oh goodness, it's almost noon, John Henry. You run along. I don't want you late on your first day. Mr. Willard's got wood for you to chop. I told him you could do just about any job and that you're real good with figures. I wanted to tell him he needs to put that no-good nephew out back chopping wood and you behind the counter on Saturdays, but I didn't."

"Grandmother said Mr. Willard's nephew's not a bit like him. She said Blalock's sorry to the bone," said Jincy.

John Henry turned to leave.

"You just stay clear of him whenever he's around, son," Alex warned. Don't give him no chance to trouble you."

She remembered Blalock's sneer behind the counter when Willa Mae asked Elmore Jenkins for her husband's wages. Had it been a mistake to recommend John Henry to Mr. Willard? Though the nephew only worked Saturdays, had she placed John Henry in jeopardy?

Suddenly, Jincy shouted, waved. "Uncle Neville, we're back here. Did you come for me instead of Father? Do you know what my surprise is?"

Relief swept over Anne Aletha at the sight of Neville instead of Patten. She waved too, watching as he approached and pleased that he looked less weary.

Neville took Anne Aletha's hand, greeting her warmly, then turned to Alex and John Henry, saying hello and shaking their hands. Patten would never do such a thing, she thought. Probably not even acknowledge their presence.

Neville tousled Jincy's pigtails but gave no reply to her question. "Looks to me like y'all have done a heap of work in a short time. How soon till it's finished?"

"Reckon we'll be done in a few weeks," said Alex. "Thanks to your Miss Jincy here. She 'bout wore herself out with cleaning and raking." He winked at Jincy's beaming face.

Anne Aletha smiled, nodding in agreement, thinking about the start of school, not really worried about the delay. Most rural schools waited until after cotton was picked anyway because of low attendance. She'd start classes the first week of November and teach until spring planting, about March first. Then they'd resume in June for the summer months and the laying by of cotton.

"Uncle Neville, can we go fishing tomorrow? Miss O'Quinn said she'd like to go sometime."

Neville raised an eyebrow.

"Well, I would like to go out in the boat and see the pond, and I did have something to discuss with you." She'd not mention her distaste for baiting a hook and having to spear a poor earthworm three times through. Or worse, putting her fingers down into a tobacco can full of crickets. She'd try not to grimace.

"We'd be delighted, wouldn't we, sweetpea?" said Neville. "Now tell these nice folks goodbye so we can go see who our surprise dinner guest is."

ON THE MILLPOND'S sandy embankment, Neville struggled to heave the small rowboat into the water. Using his cane to balance himself and his foot to shove, he pushed the boat's stern into the lily-covered pond, scattering a school of minnows out into the clear shallows and quieting the croak of a boisterous bullfrog. Steadying the boat's bow, he turned to Jincy and Anne Aletha. "Ladies first," he said, extending his hand to assist them.

Jincy lifted the hem of her green plaid dress and bounded into the swaying boat, heedless of its unsteadiness. Carrying an assortment of fishing equipment—poles, hooks and lines—she grinned back at Anne Aletha and her uncle, motioning them to follow. "All aboard!" she called, flushed with excitement.

Anne Aletha clutched a tobacco tin full of dirt-covered earthworms. She looked down at her dry feet, judging the stepping distance from shore to boat. Reaching for his hand, she stretched one leg over the gunwale, then swung her other leg over into the boat. As she let go of his hand and stepped forward, she lost her footing on a long wooden oar. "Oops," she cried, as she plopped backward and felt her bottom meet the hard plank of the seating board. Gratefully, she was still inside the boat.

"Good girl!" he teased. "You didn't drop the bait." Handing her his walking cane, he hobbled to give the boat a small push from shore. "Hold on tight."

She grasped the sides of the boat and watched as Neville, with practiced success, leapt into the boat like a three-legged dog unaware of its impediment.

Jincy giggled, moving from stern to bow as she traded seating places with her uncle. He took the wooden oars, positioned himself, then whirled them around with great flourish before steering the rowboat out toward the open water of the cypress pond.

Rowing slowly, he guided them out through the massive clumps of lily pads that covered the pond's periphery, barely disturbing the great tangles of their long underwater stalks. Jincy leaned over, dangling fingers in the black water, reaching down to touch the tough leathery green leaves of the lily pads. Anne Aletha peered over into their delicate white blossoms, wondering if they were fragrant.

As they passed the gristmill to their right, they could hear the dark churning waters of the pond spilling over the dam, tumbling noisily into the water wheel of the mill below. Jincy looked back at her and pointed to the partially submerged cypress log with a large array of turtles, all sizes, basking in the sun. She smiled and nodded, not wanting to intrude with human sounds as a pair of turtles glided into the water.

The tall reed grasses and cattails barely rippled in the late afternoon breeze and she turned back to watch the retreating shore. The air hummed with dragonflies flitting their iridescent blue wings. Out of the corner of her eye, she studied Neville, watching how effortlessly he mastered the water, his movements smooth and efficient, so unlike his limitations on land.

Like Patten, he was a handsome man with the same early streaks of gray at his temples, the same broad shoulders. But wider in girth, and softer, she decided, with none of Patten's hardness. A lap made for cuddling.

He slowed his rowing, slipping into an easy rhythm. She settled back too, letting her hand dangle in the water, allowing herself the pleasure of the pond's beauty. She closed her eyes, feeling the paddle meet the water's resistance then feeling its release. But nagging at the pleasure were her rehearsed words. If she could just blurt them out, get them said and over with: *Neville, after careful consideration, I've decided to deed the land—*

She opened her eyes to Neville's smile.

"Not too much further," he said. "Jincy has a favorite spot, a cool shady bank where the bream bite the best, don't you, sweetpea?"

Jincy, leaning out over the boat's bow, turned back to them. "Do you want to fish, Miss O" Quinn? I brought a pole for you."

"No thank you, sweetie. I brought Aunt Lily's binoculars, and I'll enjoy just watching you and the birds." She closed her eyes again, drowsy with the rhythmic movement of the boat, then sat up straight and searched for the sequence of her rehearsed words, stammering. "Neville, I want to deed Nellie and Alex their tenant's cottage and a little land. They're getting old and with their only son dead, I feel it's the right thing to do."

Neville dipped the paddle deeper into the water, his face unreadable and spoke softly. "Have you thought of the repercussions, Anne Aletha? Your uncle turned down good offers for that land. It won't set right with people, especially Elmore Jenkins."

She heard the reproach of caution in his voice. "How would anyone know? If the deed is registered in the county seat—"

"Negroes owning land in Ray's Mill is news, even to county clerks over in the courthouse."

She drew in her breath and let it out slowly. She heard her mother's admonitions about stubbornness and her uncle's about patience, of which she had little. But what about justice. What if everyone cowered to threats. She held his gaze. "Plato said that courage is doing what needs to be done, unafraid of consequences. I think it's what Uncle Carter would want."

He lifted the oar out of the water, bringing a halt to the boat's forward movement. He looked at her for several moments, saying nothing. "Yes, Anne Aletha, justice does require courage, but also moderation and wisdom. True justice is produced when courage, moderation, and wisdom go hand in hand. That is the theme of Plato's *Republic*. Why do you think your uncle never deeded any land to them?"

A great shadow passed over them and she heard the flap of wings.

"Look, Miss O'Quinn," called Jincy. "It's a blue heron!" They raised their heads as the big ungainly bird flew past them, its stick-like legs held out awkwardly behind and its long neck tucked compactly back into its body. The bird landed on the branch of a barren cypress tree.

"He's got something in his mouth," said Jincy. "Is it a fish?"

She handed Jincy her binoculars, grateful for the distraction to Neville's disturbing question. "Here, sweetie, look through these."

He resumed paddling and with a quiet dismissal of their conversation, cautioned her. "Elmore Jenkins and his accomplices are a threatening menace in this community, Anne Aletha. Your uncle had the wisdom to understand that."

SWISHING HER FINGERS in the tub of bathwater on the back porch, Anne Aletha checked to see if the late-afternoon sun had warmed the chilly well water. Tepid, she decided, but not too cold.

Since discovering the luxury of a solitary bath on the porch, she couldn't wait for Alex and Nellie's Wednesday-night prayer meetings. Twice that day she'd asked Nellie if they were going to church until finally Nellie said, "Why you care whether we's going to New Bethel tonight?"

"Just wondering," she answered, reluctant to confide another of her newfound pleasures of independence, a bath by herself, without sisters sharing it and brothers menacing it.

Growing up, she and her sisters bathed outside the springhouse in summertime in a huge hollowed-out cypress log their father had hauled from the riverbed. However, great precautions were necessary in order to shield themselves from the peeping eyes of their brothers. Bed sheets were strung from a makeshift clothesline and each sister took a turn as sentinel.

Frank had posed the worst threat to their girlish modesty. The most adept at sneaking up, giving one hard yank to the wooden clothespins and sending all five of his naked sisters squealing for cover, especially embarrassing since most times the Timothy brothers from the farm next door accompanied him. Even the threat of their father's whipping belt did little to deter him, so that baths for the girls took place mostly when their father and brothers were occupied elsewhere in the fields.

Her heart lurched at the thought of Frank. She'd had no letter since June and knew the Allies were hoping to launch their great offensive in the fall.

Across the barnyard, Nellie's ill-tempered rooster crowed, diverting her thoughts. She watched him strut among the laying hens, scratching in the ruts of the buggy wheels. Glancing at the setting sun, she decided she still had another hour before Alex and Nellie's return. No need for bed sheets this evening.

She brought the milking stool closer to the washtub and arranged her birthday present of toiletries: a cake of sweet smelling soap from Toog, talcum powder from her other sisters, and a bottle of rosewater from her mother. She held the bar of soap to her nose, inhaling it's scented fragrance, and poured two generous capfuls of rosewater into her bath. She pattered barefoot back inside the parlor to wind up the Victrola. Placing the record on the turntable, she counted, winding it twenty times before setting the arm across the record. When the needle caught the first ridge of the black disc, she hurried back outside, submerging herself into the perfumed water just as Chopin's "Fantasy Impromptu" echoed throughout the house. "Ah … heaven," she murmured, sliding down into the scented bath, warmed by the afternoon sun. She closed her eyes feeling the water lap over her breasts and the glorious music wash over her.

When the phonograph ended, she sat submerged listening to the birds chirping in the twilight, calling to each other before roosting for the night. First the whistle of the towhee, then the clucking of a cardinal and finally a chorus of robins. After lathering her hair and body with the perfumed soap, and rinsing herself, she reluctantly stepped out of the bath.

As she wrapped a towel around her head and dried her puckered skin, a cool breeze blew, hardening her nipples. Slipping on her wrapper, she felt the pleasure of soft cotton slide over her scrubbed naked skin. Cicero meandered across the yard and she called to him. He meowed in reply. Most likely, he'd shared Nellie's early supper and was now coming in search of a second. He climbed the porch steps, stopping on every other one to rest his aged haunches.

"Stay there and I'll be right back," she instructed the old tomcat when he reached the top step. "We've got time for one more record. How about a mazurka?"

She brought her comb and brush set and seated herself next to him attempting to comb out the tangled curls that had defeated her efforts of straightening since childhood. A mockingbird perched on the wooden shingles of the smokehouse. Singing loud, vocal protests over Cicero's presence, he flexed and extended himself, flashing his prominent white wing patches in the last light of day.

Cicero ignored it, purring loudly and bathing a paw. Then abruptly, he stopped and raised his ears. Anne Aletha stiffened. She heard it too, a horse nickering? She stood as the large bay gelding with Patten astride rounded the side of the house.

He guided the horse toward the porch and touched the brim of his hat. "Music's too loud for knocking," he said, without apology for his intrusion.

Cicero darted down the steps past the huge beast with its flickering tail as Anne Aletha snugged the wrapper closer to her body, wishing for undergarments.

Dismounting, he tethered his horse to the banister. "You're hell bent for trouble, aren't you Anne Aletha?" As usual, he dispensed all pleasantries.

She made no reply and watched him walk over to the iron boot scraper, his back to her. "What I want to know, Anne Aletha, is where in hell do you get these God damned notions?"

Neville must have told him about the deed. "Notions?" she repeated. Just the word itself riled her. She put her hands on her hips, then remembered her nakedness beneath and crossed her arms over her chest. "Oh, is that what you call it if it comes from a woman? And I bet you call it convictions if it comes from a man." Her face flushed and her voice rose. "You and this whole town are as threatened by a woman with opinions as you are the poor Negroes with rights. No wonder everyone's against suffrage. Even the women in this town, and they should have better sense."

Patten removed his hat, wiping his brow on his shirtsleeve. He shook his head, as though confused, a half grin emerging on his face. "What surprises me, Anne Aletha, is that you didn't take the train up to Atlanta last week. Just think, you could have marched on the state Capitol with all those other suffragettes we read about. We might have even gotten to see your picture in the *Valdosta Tribune.*" He climbed the porch steps. "But then you've been busy here, building a schoolhouse for coloreds."

Patten's amusement angered her further. And why was he climbing the steps? She had no intention of inviting him inside. He walked to the water shelf, helping himself to a dipper of water then turned to take in the aftermath of her bath. Looking up at his towering figure, she regretted that she was no taller than his nine-year-old daughter. With a hard edge to her voice, she turned to go inside. "I owe you no explanations, Patten. We have nothing further to discuss. Goodnight."

She let the screen door slam behind her, and retreated down the darkening hallway. The second slam surprised her. She darted into the parlor, overturning her aunt's wicker sewing stand. "Damn," she said, kneeling on the floor to gather up yarn and knitting needles.

The delicate porcelain figurines on the mantel shook as Patten entered the parlor. "I have more to say to you, Anne Aletha."

Outside the open windows, she heard the mockingbird singing his repertoire, repeating the three-note phrases of the songs he mimicked. Standing rigid in the middle of the parlor, she strained listening for the sounds of Alex and Nellie's buggy.

"There are things you don't understand, Anne Aletha." Patten's tone was now soft and conciliatory. "Before you get yourself and others hurt, I want to tell you about the Klan. This is more than you walking out of New Ramah and showing them your disdain. Deeding that land will rankle deep. Folks don't take kindly to coloreds owning land. Especially prime land."

Patten turned and went out into the hallway to the front door, returning with her uncle's shotgun. He emptied the chambers and handed it to her. "Do you know how to use this? Because harm's going to come to you or something you care about."

She nodded yes, but it was a lie. The muscle in her upper lip quivered and she hoped he didn't notice as she handed the shotgun back to him. She hated guns. Hated the loud explosion, the kickback into the soft flesh of her shoulder, the thud and searing pain its impact made in both man and beast. No, she was an awful shot, the worst of all her sisters, because her hands shook and she shut her eyes when she shouldn't.

For a few quiet moments, he looked at her. Wordlessly, he returned to the hallway. She heard him reload the shotgun and prop it by the front door. Slowly, he walked back into the parlor toward her. She saw the faint sheen of sweat on his upper lip, the tiny nick of a shaving cut in the cleft of his chin. He seemed to be taking in the details of her too.

"Gumption can be a fine thing, Anne Aletha. In fact, I admire it in a woman." He moved closer to her. "But it can be a foolish thing too. You know, Anne Aletha, you certainly have a way of stirring up things in a town … and in a man too."

When he reached for her, she didn't pull away. He ran his hands through her damp hair and cradled her head against his chest.

"What is it you want, Anne Aletha?" he whispered. "Tell me."

She lifted her face, wanting to explain herself. To tell him that she wanted to teach, both white and colored, to make a difference in their lives. She wanted her independence and she didn't want to spend banal afternoons visiting with ladies on the front porch.

His kiss banished her words, scattering her thoughts to faraway places. Breathless, she heard her mother's admonitions not to sully her character. And she saw Preacher Burke's wagging fingers from the pulpit telling her not to give herself to the devil. But her body told her something different.

As with the old wood-burning cook stove in the kitchen, Patten tended the small fires of her body, experienced with all the secrets to which she was not wise. First, adding tiny sticks of kindling and letting the fire burn slowly. Then when the moment was right, opening its damper and letting oxygen ignite the fire.

Only the mule's snort through the open parlor windows saved her. "Oh, my God!" she cried, trying to untangle herself from Patten's embrace. How did Alex and Nellie get almost up to the house without her hearing a sound? "Hurry!" she pleaded. "Go out the kitchen and take your horse around the side. Wait till Alex goes to the barn and *please* make sure Nellie goes inside with him before leaving."

12

ANNE ALETHA SAT cross-legged in the middle of the schoolroom floor, her back propped against the curve of the pot-bellied stove. Surrounding her at arm's length lay an empty wooden orange crate and a meager stack of sorted schoolbooks. Once again, she counted: seven spellers, six arithmetic, three geography, four early readers, two elocutions, one primer and a tattered dictionary missing the pages for 'R.' "Not nearly enough," she muttered and sighed at her dashed hopes of sending a book home with every child. Should she have scrimped on the glass window panes?

Glancing up as the first rays of the morning sun spilled across the scrubbed pine floorboards, she felt pleased. The children would thrive in a bright, sunny schoolroom. Nellie's yellow gingham curtains hung starched and pretty at each window, and Jincy's paper cutouts and alphabet pictures decorated the painted plank blackboard.

Small pleasures even as new worries occupied her thoughts. What if she had advanced pupils? Sporadic schooling was commonplace in rural areas, especially during harvest. She knew that many of the children would attend school no further than the fourth grade. But what if she had pupils in all the grades, with eight subjects to teach for every grade? She sighed at the prospects of teaching sixty-four subjects a day leaving her little time and energy for the Negro children in the late afternoons. Usually, she would leave an older higher achieving student to aid a younger less-talented pupil. If the eighth graders finished their work, she might assign them to give a spelling or reading lesson to the fourth graders while she instructed the fifth grade. Even a sixth grader could teach a third grader multiplication and addition. She chewed on her bitten pencil. So far, she didn't even have pupils.

Her stomach growled noisily in the empty schoolroom, reminding her of her hastiness in leaving the house. In order to avoid Nellie, she'd splashed her face with water and rushed out at daybreak, forgetting to look in the pie safe for any leftover biscuits. Now hunger would force her back to the house, and to Nellie's reckoning. Soon, she'd know if Nellie saw Patten's horse last night. Pursed lips and a furrowed brow would tell her.

She closed her eyes, wishing she could shut out the images in her mind. Visions of her hasty scrambling from his embrace—the pink wrapper that lay puddled at her feet. And the ease with which he had slipped it from her shoulders. She flushed with fresh shame, baffled by a desire that seemed beyond her restraint.

From the open window, she heard John Henry's familiar birdcalls ringing out across the field, his whistles, a summons for Peety to follow him toward the schoolhouse. She paused, listening to his repertoire of bird sounds, recognizing the rattle of the millpond's belted kingfisher, and the haunting *keeerr* of the red-tailed hawk. He, too, loved the natural world. She stood up, shaking out her flowered apron, wondering how long she and Alex could divert Peety's scavenging ways while John Henry worked in town. She went out to greet him, stopping first at the blackboard to tuck both chalkboard erasers into her apron pockets, knowing if she didn't, they'd be absconded and found wet and slobbery in Peety's pile beneath the schoolhouse.

"Morning, John Henry," she called.

Angular and long limbed, he walked with a grace about him, proud in the new hand-me-down clothes that Nellie had altered for him. Though her uncle's serge trousers were a little too heavy for the heat and the arms of the chambray shirt a little too short, Nellie had taken great pains turning both collar and cuffs inside out, giving the garment new wear.

"You look nice today John Henry," she said, bracing herself for Peety as he raced past John Henry and bounded up the steps to her. As he nuzzled her apron pockets, she rubbed his floppy lopsided ears, chiding him softly and plucking cockleburs from his fur. "Are you going to be a good boy and stay here all day with Alex and me ... away from Miss Effie's chickens?"

She smiled at John Henry. "You're early this morning. Are you still cleaning the stockroom?"

"Yes'um. Mr. Willard wants me to clean and rearrange the store shelves next."

She was pleased that he liked his new job, but still fretted. Though he hadn't voiced any complaint about Mr. Willard's surly nephew these past few weeks, she couldn't push away her unsettled feelings. She reminded herself of this opportunity for him, and Mr. Willard did seem like a decent sort of man. In fact, lately she found herself daydreaming about John Henry's future, fantasizing that when Mr. Willard discovered his aptitude with figures, he'd place him behind the counter, instead of Blalock. Before long, he'd be dazzling customers, adding impressive sums in his head and estimating the seed and fertilizer needs of white men with half his intellect.

He interrupted her daydreams. "Reckon I'll be staying till closing time, Miss Aletha. Mr. Willard's cousin took sick and he's supposed to carry her over to Adel this morning."

She frowned. "I hope he won't be too long." Peety pawed her leg to resume his ear scratching. "Do you want to have a lesson when you finish work? Nellie will have leftovers on the stove for you."

He grinned, reaching into his pants pocket to withdraw the small leather-bound book of children's poems she'd given him. "Yes'um, and I hope to do some reciting for you this evening. I 'bout got 'em all memorized."

Peety whimpered from the porch as John Henry turned to leave. "Stay," he said, continuing to walk away. Peety barked once then pleaded with a last pitiful whine before flopping lengthwise across the top of the steps, an obstacle to now be stepped over till Nellie's noonday table scraps arrived. Anne Aletha chuckled at his antics, but her smile quickly faded when she saw Nellie cutting across the fields toward them—too far away to tell if her lips were pursed or her brow furrowed.

Waving her arm, Nellie called to John Henry. "Come get yourself a biscuit and sweet tater. Miss Aletha done left before the rooster crowed and I've brung breakfast."

She grimaced as she watched Nellie limp toward John Henry, favoring her bad hip. Letting him catch up to her, she handed him the food basket and then straightened his shirt collar. After wrapping his warm food in a tea towel, she herded him off toward town.

Peety roused himself as Nellie approached the schoolhouse, wagging his curled tail for the earlier-than-anticipated meal. Nellie rested a few moments on the bottom step, searching Anne Aletha's face.

Anne Aletha held her breath.

"Looks to me like you's done a whole night of frettin' yourself, Miss Aletha." She shook her head in disapproval. "Them dark circles ain't gonna go away less you quit working yourself so hard." Nellie took out Peety's pan of breakfast scraps. "Me and Alex didn't sleep much neither. Somehow, folks has found out and all we heard at meetin' last night is how upset the white people gonna be 'bout you deedin land to us coloreds."

Relief swept over her. Nellie hadn't seen Patten's horse.

"Anyways," Nellie continued, "we want you to tell Mr. Neville there ain't no hurry in deedin' us that land. If we never gets it, we's grateful for the tryin'." She paused to catch her breath. "So, don't go fretting yourself about no deed. Ain't any use in bringing on trouble."

She took Nellie's hand, patting the old misshapen fingers. "You're right, Nellie. Neville, too, says I should hold off. I promise we won't do anything for a while. But I'm not going to let the Klan and people like Elmore Jenkins control us with their hate and bigotry."

"Well, we doesn't want to cut off our nose to spite our faces, but I also needs to tell you that Miz Sarah say there's a letter waitin' at the post office. I told her you and Miss Maidee is going to town this mornin'."

Her heart lurched. "Oh Nellie, is it from Frank?"

"Yes'um, I think so. Let's be getting some breakfast in you and a little meat on them bones. Ain't no man that wants a pole bean."

OUTSIDE THE BEDROOM window, buggy wheels clattered to a stop beneath the shade of the sweet gum tree and a high-pitched man's voice called out from the yard. "Yoo-hoo, Miss O'Quinn. Are you ready?"

Anne Aletha cursed and looked out the window. Though Ralph Attaway was just a boarder with Maidee and her mother, he seemed to weasel a ride with them every time they went to town. "Coming, Mr. Attaway," she called from the window, hearing the false friendliness in her voice and resenting him even more. He was as distasteful as the bitter part of a pecan.

She fastened the tiny hooks of her good blouse, quickly pinning on her yellow silk rose. She hoped Maidee would wear her rose today so they could show their support for women's suffrage to all the ladies in town. President Wilson was in support and said he hoped the suffrage bill would soon pass, even though the bill had lost by a margin of one vote in May.

Maidee greeted her with a knowing smile. "Morning, Anne Aletha. Hope you don't mind if Mr. Attaway goes to town with us." She tucked aside the skirt of her pale-lavender dress, making room for Anne Aletha, and checked the freshly picked yellow rose pinned to her lapel.

"No, of course not," Anne Aletha replied. Politely, she accepted the limp, damp hand that he extended and climbed up on the seat. As he settled himself next to her, the odor of liniment and mothballs made her queasy.

"We like to never got here, Miss O'Quinn," he prattled. "Miz Sarah caught sight of us and wanted to know if we'd heard about Whitaker. You know he's the one courting old man Benson's daughter. Come to find out, he got himself liquored up and beat some turpentine nigra near to death. Landed himself in jail over in Adel."

"The coloreds is all upset." Dabbing his forehead with a handkerchief, he continued. "And you heard about them race riots up in New York City. Stabbed eighteen policeman. So you can't ever tell. With our boys off to war, why any day now we could have us an uprising in Ray's Mill."

She rolled her eyes choking back a retort as Maidee traded a quick glance with her.

"Now Ralph," said Maidee. "All this anti-Negro sentiment does nothing but fan the flames. The whites are the ones stirring up trouble. Don't forget those shameful lynchings just a few miles from here and Preacher Elrod letting Klansmen parade down New Ramah's aisle—taking their bribe money too."

Undaunted, he turned to Anne Aletha. "Miz Sarah says you're doing a fine job fixing over that cotton house. Says if you can't get the white children to come, you're going to teach the coloreds and sharecroppers. Is that really true?"

Maidee sighed. "Ralph, I think Anne Aletha is to be commended. You know in the past people haven't thought sharecroppers and Negroes needed an education, but thank goodness that is changing."

"Yes, thank goodness," said Anne Aletha. "My Uncle Carter always said it's a shame that ignorance is stronger than wisdom. I don't understand how people can still insist that the Negro is inferior when scientists have proven the only difference between us is the climate in which we originate."

Ralph tugged on an earlobe, re-crossed his legs, and sat back in a huff.

"I think some people just have to feel superior to other people," said Maidee. "It gives them a reason to hate." She brought the mare to a hitching post in front of the post office. "Ralph, will you hitch the mare and meet us back here in an hour?"

Outside the tiny redbrick bank next to the post office, a gentleman tilted his hat to each passerby, his strong voice ringing out. "Ladies and Gentlemen! Our Allies are crying for food. Uncle Sam needs your help to win this Great War of Liberty. This is the greatest war ever waged on the face of the earth. And it's being fought to defend our liberties, our democracy, and our right to live as free men and women."

Those gathered around him murmured in agreement.

"Who is that?" Anne Aletha whispered, recognizing the heavily jowled man with the walrus mustache from the train depot on the day she arrived.

"Russell Burkhalter," said Maidee. "He's our self-appointed mayor."

He continued. "Our government doesn't have enough money to carry on this war alone and Uncle Sam is using his debt to borrow. He expects you to do the same. Only by obligating yourself to the fourth Liberty Bond will you assume your full share of responsibility. The Bank of Ray's Mill is here to assist you."

He glanced across to them and gave a brief bow. "And ladies, remember that every new frock or fancy millinery hat takes food away from our fighting boys. Put that money into a Liberty Bond today."

"Oh no," whispered Anne Aletha. "Can we go around him?"

He turned back to a group of men. "And gentlemen, what can you do to help? Can you further cut your personal expenses and dig deeper for Uncle Sam? What about that daily shave or shoe shine?"

"Now! Let's go," said Maidee, darting toward the post office.

Anne Aletha hurried behind her, trying to stifle her laughter. Giggling like school-girls, they dashed into the post office, shutting the door behind them.

Cora Lee called out a greeting from the mailroom. "Be out in a moment. I'm almost done sorting."

"No hurry, Cora," called Maidee. "Cora has two school-age girls," she whispered. "Hopefully, you can meet them soon."

Anne Aletha nodded and turned to the bulletin board in the corner noticing a large poster. She walked over to read it.

A KLAN IN YOUR COMMUNITY IS MORE THAN A
LUXURY,
IT'S A NECESSITY. OUR MESSAGE:
BUY A LIBERTY BOND
STAND BEHIND UNCLE SAM

Below the poster was a smaller newspaper announcement:

August 12—Knights of Ku Klux Klan to hold a big conclave in Atlanta.

10,000 Klansmen from Georgia will be present. On the night of August 11, a great street parade is planned in which eight thousand will participate in their weird costumes of white. Every principal street in the city will be traversed by the march.

"Maidee, look at this."
Maidee read it, shaking her head.
Neville was right, Anne Aletha thought. The Klan had cleverly wrapped itself in the American flag and were

presenting themselves as patriotic red-blooded Americans fighting on the home front.

Cora Lee bustled out, retying her mailroom apron and smoothing her bun of copper hair rolled back like a halo around her head. "I see Russell has got himself quite a crowd this morning. You were lucky to escape him."

"Fortunately, he was distracted for a moment," said Anne Aletha, grinning. She liked the cordial postmistress and realized that she and Maidee were the only women in town who were friendly toward her now that Mrs. Clements was gone.

"I do feel sorry for him, Cora," said Maidee.

Cora turned to Anne Aletha. "His poor wife stepped on a nail and died of lockjaw a few years back. He's not got over it yet." She withdrew the letter from her apron. "It's from France. Has the word "Censure" written across the envelope. Guess they've got to make sure our boys don't blab anything to the Germans."

"Thank you for sending word," said Anne Aletha. "Also, I'd like to invite you and your girls for a visit when Alex and John Henry finish making over the old cotton house into a schoolroom. I would be honored to have your children as pupils."

The bell jangled and the door opened to more customers. "Why yes, Anne Aletha, thank you for the invitation," said Cora.

As two ladies entered, Cora and Maidee turned to chat with them and Anne Aletha stepped back into the corner of the tiny post office.

His letter trembled in her hand. "Please be all right," she whispered seeing Frank's small slanted handwriting scrawled across the front of the bulky envelope, the postmark dated July 1, 1918, and in the lower left-hand corner "Passed As Censored" stamped with a seal. Below that 2nd Lt. L.P. Maier had signed the letter and written "O.K." as a precautionary measure in case a soldier innocently divulged maneuvers or location and the mail fell into enemy hands. She tore open the letter, wincing as the edge of the envelope nicked her. Sucking her salty tasting thumb, she read.

Somewhere in France

Dear Anne Aletha,

The mail finally caught up with us and it's the best day I've had since I left home. Many thanks for the letters and packages, and especially thank you, dear Sis, for the cigarettes. Keep the smokes coming if at all possible.

Yesterday, we arrived in the village of H—[censored] after a heavy barrage of artillery fire. The shells burst several hundred feet ahead of us and the rockets throw off a greenish light. They call it Baptism by Fire and even though I find myself with the shivers afterward, I'm getting used to the constant pup, pup, pup of Fritz's machine guns.

What I can't get used to is these damn cooties and the torment of their itching. They say where there is straw, there are cooties and no amount of bathing or change of underwear seem to help. Some men hang their underwear over sandbags at night and use the butt of their rifle like a battling stick to try to bludgeon the varmints to death. Others try to pick them out of the folds, and creases of their clothes. I've attempted to drown them by wading into a creek, but cooties like to swim. Most of the soldiers just scratch and seem to accept body lice as their fate.

You'll think this is a tall tale, but last week we were on a scouting and wiring mission on the outskirts of a small hamlet, about ten miles from our billets. Me and another signal corpsmen missed our lorry ride back to the village and a nice farmer and his wife offered us lodging for the night. They live in a very old one room stone house with a thatched roof. Because of the remoteness, the Huns never shelled the house and it's one of the few undamaged cottages that I've seen. That night, we bedded down on one side of the fireplace and the old couple on the other side. At dark, in came the cow, the pig, and all the chickens. No one had to call them.

And they knew exactly where to go—right in front of the big stone fireplace. They were all housebroken and congenial. At sunrise, the cock crowed, the farmer opened the door, and all the animals quietly left. Quite amazing.

But this Great War is like hell has been let loose on earth and I've come to realize that Providence and Luck are my only saviors.

Your loving brother,
Frank

13

ALEX STOOPED OVER the cracked dry earth of the sweet potato patch. "Look like we gonna have a right good crop of taters this fall, Miss Aletha. My pappy used to say if we had corn in the crib, taters in the bank, and meat in the smokehouse we'd be set for winter. You think we's set for winter?"

She followed behind him with a hoe, stabbing half-heartedly at weeds, thinking they'd be eating little else. Would there be enough food on the table this winter? Fortunately, John Henry's fishing helped conserve their meat. But it was only August and each day her small cash reserve seemed to dwindle. How mistaken she'd been in the amount of money she would need before the start of school. "Didn't Mr. Sirmans offer to trade out meat with us if we can help him at hog killing time?"

"Yes 'um and I's mighty thankful. In a few more months, when we gets that first little cool spell, we gonna be having us a big ole pot of collards, crackling bread and some good fresh pork meat."

She was grateful, too, but hated the thought of hog killing, dreading the dirty work of slaughtering and smelling its horrible stench. She didn't know which was worse, scalding the hog's carcass with boiling water and scraping the bristly hair or slitting the belly open to release its steaming entrails into the tub below with blood up to her elbows. She felt queasy at the thought.

"Maybe Frank will make it home in time for spring planting next year and can help us."

"Yes'um. The good Lord's gonna look after him. And we gonna make us a good cotton crop next year. Course, it's mighty hard work. One time, my pappy helped this sharecropper hoe twenty acres. Him and all of us youngins picked every last boll. By the time the farmer took out what was owed for the planting and growing, my pa didn't bring back a cent. We hauled a dozen bales to the gin and Ma never got so much as two yards of ten-cent gingham."

Suddenly, Nellie hollered from the kitchen porch. "Y'all come quick! We done got us a heap of trouble! "

"MISS ALETHA, I didn't steal that money. I swear to you on a stack of Bibles," said John Henry, his face and hands bloodied from a scramble through the blackberry thicket and his voice ragged with fear.

"I know you didn't, John Henry," she said placing her hand on his shoulder and guiding him to the kitchen table. "Let's get you cleaned up. Then you can tell us everything that happened."

Alex took off his old felt hat ringed with salty sweat and mopped his forehead. "I'll draw up a bucket of water."

Nellie went to the wood stove and poured warm water from its side compartment into a blue enamel pan. At the table, she moved aside the piles of dampened laundry and gently washed John Henry's cuts with a dishcloth.

Peety whined at the screen door.

"We might as well let him in," said Anne Aletha, sliding from the chair beside John Henry. Peety dashed in and settled between John Henry's legs.

"I'll make up a little salve to put on them cuts later," said Nellie.

John Henry buried his face into the mutt's scruffy fur, his long lashes wet with tears when he raised his head.

"When did it happen?" Anne Aletha asked, quietly.

"Just after closing time, Mr. Blalock come out to the woodpile and told me to go back inside and sweep behind the counter. I said, 'Yes, sir, but I done just swept it out.' When I went back inside, he had the cash box on the table. It was empty. Said I stole it."

"Oh, help us, Lord," said Nellie.

Alex frowned, rubbing his jaw.

"I told him I didn't take it, Miss Aletha, but he said I was a lying nigger. Said I just been waiting for a chance to steal it."

"Did he go for the Sheriff?"

"No, ma'am. Said that Sheriff Dix is away till tomorrow and as soon as his uncle and the Sheriff get back, they's gonna be coming to get me."

Peety's ears cocked as he scrambled to his feet and growled.

They all looked at each other in alarm as the sound of horse hooves grew louder.

In the front hallway, Peety barked and everyone shushed him hurrying to peer out the narrow paned windows by the front door. Nellie wedged herself between the umbrella stand and the hall tree while John Henry kneeled beside her to quiet Peety. Anne Aletha and Alex took the other window as he spoke to her in a low whisper.

"I bolted the backdoor, Miss Aletha. Ain't gonna stop nobody, but at least we'll hear 'em coming." He gave out a low whistle as the men on horseback rode into the front yard. "Looks like Jenkins brought him some company. That tall one's Wade Madry. Mean as a snake. The others are Hiram and Culpepper. They's all in cahoots."

She swallowed hard. "Who's the fourth one?"

"Rutledge. He's Sheriff Dix's old deputy. Been put out to pasture awhile back."

She nodded, wondering if the sheriff's deputies were the same ones that did the lynchings too. Peety scratched at the door. "John Henry, you and Peety go hide in the pantry. Try to keep him quiet. I'm going out to talk to them."

Nellie's eyes widened and she grasped her arm. "Oh, child, be careful."

"I'll go with you, Miss Aletha," said Alex.

She shook her head. "No, Alex. It's better if I go alone." She took a deep breath, pausing to gather her thoughts, then opened the door and walked out on the porch. Her face reddened as some of the men's jeers reached her.

Jenkins, slouched on his horse, urged the large gray gelding nearer to the house while the others remained behind. "Howdy, ma'am. Reckon you know who we've come for."

She glared at him with loathing. The men's horses blew softly in the silence.

"Been some thievery going on." Jenkins took a plug of tobacco, unhurried. "Appreciate it if you'd go get us that colored boy. He's got some questions to answer."

She straightened her shoulders, drew herself up tall and put her hands on her hips. Her heart pounded. "Do you have a warrant, Mr. Jenkins?"

He shifted his wad of tobacco. "Don't need no warrant to question him." He rubbed the bushy side whiskers of his graying red beard.

"You do if you're trespassing on my property."

"Thieving's a serious business, Miss. Got to be dealt with."

"John Henry didn't steal that money, Mr. Jenkins."

"Ain't the way Willard's nephew's telling it."

"Where's Sheriff Dix?"

"He ain't here. We're standing in for him."

"John Henry is not a thief. He's been unjustly accused. If you and your men did not come with a warrant, you're trespassing on my property."

Jenkins nudged his horse forward, leering at her. "Come on now, Miss Schoolteacher. Everybody knows you're a nigger lover. We know he's in there."

Anne Aletha, her face flushed in anger, strode back inside the house, letting the screen door slam loudly behind her.

Nellie stood stock still in the corner. "Lord a mercy, honey, what you gonna do?" she whispered.

She reached for her uncle's shotgun, remembering Patten's warning and vowing to herself, *If I get through this, I'll be a damn better shot next time.* She walked out to the edge of the porch carrying the shotgun.

"You tell Sheriff Dix that John Henry will come to town for questioning any time he says. And you tell him Mr. Neville will be accompanying him for the questioning." She raised the double-barreled shotgun, pointing it at Elmore Jenkins. She felt for its decorative hammers and cocked them hoping he couldn't see her knees shaking beneath her skirt. "Now get off my property."

Clouds crossed the setting sun, darkening the sky. Jenkins rode his horse almost up to the porch with the men muttering curses. He laughed a hollow, skittish laugh. "Miss, you're making a big mistake," he said, turning his horse and men back toward town.

She shut the front door behind her and leaned back against it before handing Alex the shotgun. "They've gone, at least for now. If they come back, it won't be before dark."

"Lord Almighty, Miss Aletha. You done run 'em off," said Alex, propping the shotgun against the door frame.

Nellie embraced her. "Honey, you's shaking all over."

She slumped down on the bench of the hall tree. "I was more frightened than when a wild boar chased me through the swamp at home." She held up her trembling hands as John Henry and Peety crept out into the hallway. "It's alright, John Henry, they've gone. How did you keep him from barking?"

"I knocked over the crock of sausage in the pantry. He ate the drippings."

She nodded with a slight grin. "Y'all, we need to get word to Neville. I'm going to take a note to Miss Effie."

"You want me to go?", asked Alex.

"No Alex. You stay here and fire a warning shot out the back window if they return. I won't be long."

"Son," said Alex. "You think you can make it to Catfish's lean-to in the swamp?"

Anne Aletha shook her head. "He won't have a chance if they set their hounds loose on him, Alex. He's safer here tonight. Without Sheriff Dix and a warrant, they'll be trespassing."

Alex nodded. "I got my pappy's shotgun."

She hugged John Henry. "This is my fault. I don't want you to worry. Neville will know what to do."

"We'll take turns keeping watch tonight, but that old mutt'll bark first," said Alex, rubbing his jaw.

"I'll fry up a little shoulder meat and boil some grits for supper," said Nellie. "Y'all gonna need to eat."

Anne Aletha nodded, watching Alex rub his jaw. He'd been rubbing it for days. "Alex, Nellie says that tooth is acting up again. Let her dab a little carbolic acid on it with a toothpick. It's on the top shelf in the kitchen. That brown bottle with the skull and crossbones. My grandmother used to swear by it."

She hurried to her aunt's writing desk in the parlor, her hands still trembling as she dipped the fountain pen into the glass inkwell and scratched out a frantic scrawl to Neville for help.

SHE FOUGHT THE URGE to run straight to Miss Effie's for help, but caution forced her to circle back around the barn and schoolhouse and cross the road nearest the shelter of trees. Just in case Jenkins and his men were lying in wait. She searched the empty road in both directions, her panicked breathing the only sound she could hear. Stomach acid rose in her throat. If vigilantes could hang an innocent Negro woman for sassing, they could hang a young colored boy on a white man's accusations. She swallowed, and then bolted across the road.

The stand of hardwoods that grew along the creek at the edge of the fields offered cover and she followed the bank of the small branch until she reached the wide-open pasture behind Miss Effie's property. A tattered diminutive scarecrow in Miss Effie's clothes stood sentinel in the middle of the field, its straw-plucked dress long since ignored by the crows. She squatted down to retie her shoelace, took a deep breath, and sprinted across the pasture to the scarecrow. Shielded from the road, she surveyed Miss Effie's fence. Old and splintery, but not too high to climb. At least goats didn't bark.

Making her way past the outhouse, barn, and smokehouse, she stepped cautiously in the dwindling light around the small pellets of fly-infested goat droppings. Beneath the large sycamore, the baby white goats frolicked, and nearby the small bantam rooster pecked, watching her movement. Dirt filled cans of mother-in-law tongue cuttings lined the path to the back porch and she hurried along thinking that even goats must not eat the tall ugly spikes.

Miss Effie stood at a work table on the porch with her back turned. She wore the same old-fashioned bonnet and muslin dress, humming while cleaning an assortment of kerosene lamps, first trimming the wicks and then wiping down the inside of the sooty chimneys with newspaper.

She hesitated, not wanting to startle the elderly lady. Perhaps she should approach from the side. When the rooster crowed, Anne Aletha jumped straight up, but Miss Effie just turned and didn't seem surprised.

"My sakes alive child, you got trouble over yonder? I saw a whole posse ride by here a little while ago."

She waved the note in her hand and dashed up the steps, nearly overturning the spittoon. "Miss Effie, could you take this to Mr. Neville? Mr. Willard's nephew accused John Henry of stealing. Sheriff Dix is out of town and Elmore Jenkins came looking for John Henry." She paused to catch her breath. "He didn't steal that money and we need Neville's help."

Spectacles magnified Miss Effie's rheumy brown eyes. "Course I'll fetch him," she said snatching the note. "Tell

John Henry to sneak over after dark. I got a good hiding place. We don't need no more night riders."

"NOW REMEMBER, Anne Aletha, let me do the talking," said Neville the next morning as he guided the mare and buggy to a stop in front of the hitching post of Willard's General Store. "We'll speak to Willard and his nephew first, then pay Sheriff Dix a visit, if he's back in town. John Henry says Blalock called him back into the store after closing yesterday and told him to sweep behind the same counter he'd swept earlier. Let's see what Blalock has to say."

She nodded in agreement, placing her hand gently on his arm. "Thank you for helping us. I'm so afraid for John Henry. This is all my fault. I recommended him to Mr. Willard. You warned me—" Her voice broke.

Neville patted her hand. "Don't show your fear, just your indignation. Remember that John Henry is innocent." He climbed down from the buggy, shifting weight to his walking cane, and murmuring praise to his mother's old mare as he looped the reins through the iron ring of the hitching post. He reached up for her. "Watch that first step now."

She took his hand. Unlike her chapped and rough hands that were now perspiring, his were soft and dry. She heard Nellie's chiding. "Them ain't no ladies' hands, them is field hands."

He removed his hat and wiped his brow. The morning's early humidity promised another day of sultry heat. "Looks like Willard doesn't have any customers yet." Opening the screen door, he ushered her in ahead of him. The bells on the door jingled loudly. "Willard, you open for business yet?" he called. "We'd like a word with you."

The plank floorboards squeaked beneath them as Neville led the way down the long aisle to the back of the store. Something furry scurried between the rice and flour sacks and she saw a baited mousetrap on top of the cornmeal, not yet sprung.

Willard stepped out from behind the counter to greet them, disheveled, his chin stippled with gray whiskers and his black armbands holding up the sleeves of yesterday's rumpled shirt.

"Good morning, Willard," said Neville. "Miss O'Quinn and I would like to speak with you. We won't keep you long. I think you know what this is about."

He nodded, donning his grocer's apron as he led them back to a small storeroom where a large rolltop desk took up most of one corner. He pulled up two cane-bottomed chairs for them and leaned back wearily in his swivel desk chair.

"Willard, we'd also like to speak with your nephew this morning."

He flushed, seemingly surprised. "Uh, well ... Blalock's not here. He had some business to attend to. He'll be back in a few days."

"Oh? You sent him away?" The gentleness was gone from Neville's voice. "I see." A long, awkward silence followed before Neville cleared his throat. "Willard, John Henry did not steal from your cash box. I'm quite certain that you know that, and I'm sure that your nephew does."

The grocer sighed, tilting back in his oak chair. "Now Neville, Blalock didn't outright accuse that colored boy. It just looked mighty suspicious, him being here after closing and all." He uprighted himself. "But I've decided not to take this matter any further."

"I'm afraid that won't suffice, Willard. Your nephew placed John Henry's life in peril with his allegations. I'm sure you heard that Jenkins and his vigilantes rode out to Miss O'Quinn's house last evening, demanding that John Henry be turned over to them for questioning. And you know what happened just sixteen miles from here a few months ago."

Neville stood, pushing back his chair. "Your nephew's Saturday night cockfights and unpaid debts are common knowledge. I don't care how you explain the stolen money, Willard. Blalock can say he's mistaken, or you can have the money suddenly turn up, but I expect a written statement to Sheriff Dix clearing John Henry's name within the hour."

"NEVILLE, YOU WERE WONDERFUL," Anne Aletha said as he turned the mare and buggy toward home. "How did you know for sure that Blalock took the money?"

"I didn't until Willard told us he'd sent him away for a few days. Willard is aware of his nephew's gambling debts, and he wouldn't have done that if he thought Blalock was innocent. I think he just hoped the whole incident would blow over and be forgotten. From all accounts, Blalock is a regular with gamecock fighting."

She shuddered at the cruelty of strapping razor-sharp steel spurs onto the poor birds and then tossing the roosters into a pit to fight to their death. "But how did Jenkins get involved?"

"With Sheriff Dix away, he probably saw an opportunity to further the Klan's cause—a way to present himself as protecting the townspeople. Sheriff Dix made a grave mistake this summer when he deputized Jenkins after Hamp Smith's murder. You saw the way the Klan moved into Ray's Mill, first swaying Preacher Elrod to support their cause and then getting men like Jenkins to recruit."

"Well, it seems to me that advertising themselves as seeking good Christian men of a high class order and then taking the likes of Elmore Jenkins would lead any decent man to question the Klan's rhetoric. How can upstanding men in this community be so deceived?" She scoffed at the absurdity.

"Unfortunately, you'd be surprised, Anne Aletha. I do think it's a good idea for John Henry to stay out of sight for a while, even when his name is cleared."

They rode in silence.

"Any word from Frank?"

"Nothing since the July offensive began. I know he's on the Western Front. The papers say the Allies have gained more than 200 villages."

"Yes, the Allies now have thirty-one divisions and more than a million men over there."

"President Wilson says he's determined to bring the war to a conclusion by concentrating all of our forces there."

When they reached Miss Effie's, Neville slowed Bella to turn onto the millpond road just as something startled the old mare, sending the buggy sharply around the corner. Anne Aletha slid sideways, almost into his lap.

"Whoa there girl." Neville reined in the mare as he put his arm around Anne Aletha. He smiled as she righted herself. "I bet you think that's an old trick to get lovely young ladies in my lap." There was a teasing note in his voice. "I assure you it's not. She spooks easily in her old age." He leaned over to retrieve the leather satchel that lay overturned at their feet. "I brought you a couple of books I thought you'd enjoy. Two of your uncle's favorites. I look forward to your thoughts."

She touched the soft calfskin, inspecting both of the lovely antique volumes. She opened them, careful of the old spines. "Thank you. I haven't read them, but Uncle Carter extolled the virtues of both. He often spoke of Lucretius's poems about nature and the universe, and how we humans ought to live in it. He said that Lucretius thought nature was beautiful, deadly, fascinating, and purposeless. And that once man could see how it works, he could free himself from the superstitious fears of the gods."

"Yes, Lucretius tried to rid his Greek contemporaries of the myths that he felt enslaved their lives. And you'll find Marcus Aurelius is a good contrast because he believed the events of the world were determined by the gods. As a Stoic, he thought we should try to control only the things we can, like opinions, emotions, and desires. And then live with what is outside our control."

She nodded, admiring his prodigious mind, wondering again how twins could be so opposite and her feelings so divided, wishing she could control her own desires.

As he slowed the mare and the farmhouse came into view, she turned toward him and placed her hand on his arm. "Thank you for defending John Henry, Neville. I don't know what I would have done without you."

For several long seconds, Neville looked at her. "Send John Henry away for a while and take heed, Anne Aletha. You're playing with fire."

14

AT DAWN, she slid the chamber pot beneath the bed, debating whether to crawl back between the sheets. The katydid outside her window had just now hushed. How could an insect only a couple of inches long make so much noise? She'd read that the males were the noisy ones. They'd sing from dusk till dawn, rubbing their back wings together until they found a mate. Like the one outside her window that must have just found one. Now with daylight, the steady hum of cicadas would soon fill the air while the nocturnal katydids slept. Most nights she loved their sounds and missed them in the stillness of winter. But last night, they kept her awake. That and her worry for John Henry. She'd convinced him that he and Peety should stay with Alex and Nellie a few more nights—although Peety now preferred the schoolhouse. His tender nose had run afoul too often of Cicero's swats.

Putting on her bedroom slippers, she took the water pitcher off the washstand and carried it down the dark hall to the well on the back porch. A sleepy dew-covered Cicero greeted her, lying stretched out on top of the water shelf. She leaned over and kissed his damp fur as he stretched and purred. A chipmunk tail from the previous day lay on the top step. She shook her head and smiled, adding this most recent conquest to his other trophies on the windowsill.

After drawing up a bucketful of fresh spring water and filling her pitcher, she returned to the bedroom to brush her teeth and bathe. It was still early. She'd have time to take the children's slates to the schoolhouse, along with Peety's leftovers, before Nellie came to make breakfast. If she had a slate for every child, she'd be able to leave one grade doing their sums and another doing their penmanship assignments while she gave a lesson to the next grade.

She gathered the box of school slates from the back porch and crossed the foggy yard, stopping to feel the sheets she'd boiled yesterday but neglected to take off the line, now damp with the dew. Hugging the box to her chest, she hurried to the schoolhouse.

Navigating her way in the fog, she ducked beneath the low limb of the pecan tree, ever vigilant of the late summer spiders that wove their huge webs between the low-hanging limbs, and shivering at the thought of being ensnared in one. That's odd, she thought, as she approached the schoolhouse. Usually, Peety ran to meet her. Especially if she had a dishpan full of table scraps.

"Peety?" she called. No answer. Her pulse quickened as she put down her armful and ran up the steps yanking off the crude drawing nailed to the door. A picture of a black ape with a pea-size brain stared back at her. The words NIGGER TEACHER were scrawled across the bottom. She crumpled it in her fist as needles of fear pricked her skin. "Peety? "

A whimper came from beneath the porch. She ran back down the steps squatting to look under the schoolhouse. Peety lay in his dug out sand hole.

"Peety? Come here, sweetie," she coaxed, reaching for him. He didn't budge. She got down on her hands and knees, poking her head and shoulders as far under the house as they would go, hoping she wouldn't have to crawl under to get him.

"Baby, did they scare you?"

A wet snout nuzzled her hand. "Come on, boy," she cooed, backing out bottom first, afraid he was hurt. He crawled out with his tail wagging.

"Oh Peety," she cried, pulling him gently into her lap. He was unharmed. She buried her head in his sandy fur. "It's all right, sweetie." Her cheeks flushed with anger. "I know it was that damn Elmore Jenkins. I swear next time we're going to fill his sorry tail full of buckshot."

Peety stood and shook himself, then settled next to her on the ground. For a long time they remained, looking out at the dirt swept schoolyard.

THIS CHICKEN RULES THE ROOST, thought Anne Aletha, as Nellie's best-laying Rhode Island Red stared back at her in defiance. Though the hen made soft clucking noises that sounded friendly, she hesitated. Egg gathering was her least favorite chore. Chickens seemed to sense her fear of being pecked, and they never relinquished them easily. Even as a child it seemed that she was the one most often sent to retrieve a last-minute needed egg. Especially if her father requested a sugar-dusted teacake to go with his buttermilk at suppertime, which he did nearly every night.

She held her breath, then gently slid her hand beneath the warm tail feathers. "Ouch!" she cried, jerking her hand away to inspect her thumb. The damn bird had drawn blood. Defeated, she wiped her wound, picked up the empty egg basket and stomped out of the barn.

"Anybody home?" called a soft spoken voice from the side yard.

"Maidee! Wait there. You'll soil your shoes." Anne Aletha hurried toward her friend, stepping around a large pile of Sulky's manure Alex had shoveled for the garden.

Maidee grinned, waving a letter. "It's from Frank!"

"Oh, I'm so relieved." She took the letter and held it briefly to her heart before tucking it into her apron pocket. "Thank you for bringing it, Maidee. Can you visit for a few minutes?"

Maidee shook her head. "Mother's in one of her snits. But there's something else I wanted to tell you." Her tone grew serious. "My cousin Henry admires your intentions, but he wants you to know there's talk of reprisal. He heard Jenkins tell some of the men at the turpentine still yesterday that they had to 'keep the jungle apes in line.'"

Anne Aletha's shoulders sagged.

"I thought you should warn John Henry."

"Yes, I'll have Alex send word to him. Neville says that in the past my Uncle Carter's standing in the community helped keep the anti-Negro sentiment at bay. But now, I fear no one will take a stand."

Maidee nodded and said almost in whisper, "You must be careful, dear friend."

She watched Maidee leave, thinking of John Henry hiding in the lean-to in the swamp and suddenly visualized the image of a Klansman's noose hanging from Cat Creek Bridge. Her fingers tingled with fear as she opened Frank's letter.

July 23, 1918
Somewhere in France

Dear Sis,

Please don't think me brave. You asked me how I live with the constant fear of death but every soldier here is just trying to stay alive and carry out orders. It seems we all enlisted to save the world from the terrible Huns, but now it's really just about saving yourself and your buddies. They become your family.

I guess when your time comes, it's gonna get you. I'm reminded of this every day. Three nights ago, our truck got stuck in mud. (All it's done is rain since we got here.) We decided to stay there all night. The truck was so overloaded, it was hardly possible to find standing room and we were all dead tired. I saw a haystack in the field and crawled into it. Best night's sleep I've had in months. But two of the men weren't so lucky. They bedded down under the truck to stay dry. Evidently the spot had been recently gassed. It seeps into

the ground and leaves a residue. One man died after much
suffering and the other is clinging to life.

Mud, stench, death and fear. That's what war is Sis. But
I'm coming home.

Your loving brother,
Frank

SOMETIME DURING the middle of the night, the
bedroom curtains rippled with a soft easterly breeze.
Whether it was the barely perceptible odor of woodsmoke
or the sound of something amiss while she slept, Anne
Aletha awoke suddenly and flew out of bed. She knew
something was wrong. Scrambling in the dark, she felt
around in the bottom of the chifforobe for her oxfords,
cramming her bare feet into the sturdy leather lace-ups as
fast as she could. Her nightdress didn't matter. When she
looked out the window, the night sky looked light.

From across the pasture, she saw the cedar-shingled
roof of the schoolhouse in flames. Holding up her
nightgown and trying not to trip as she ran, she watched
the burning cinders light up the sky. Even a bucket brigade
couldn't save it now.

Breathless, with her legs trembling, she stood in the
yard cursing the cowards that did it. Torches made from
tree branches and burlap that had been doused with
kerosene littered the yard. She raced up the steps as smoke
billowed from the roof, hoping to at least save the books.

Quickly, she ran to the bookcase in the back of the
smoke-filled room making an apron of her nightdress and
grabbing the primers, the spellers, the geography books,
Robinson Crusoe, Pilgrims Progress. Holding her breath,
she dashed back through the smoky room and out to the
porch, hurling the books as far as she could throw them.
Then she heard something. A whimpering?

"Peety! Peety!" she screamed. Was he inside the
schoolhouse or under it? She ran down the steps to search

beneath the porch. Empty. Scrambling back up the steps, she went inside. Soon the walls and roof beams would be engulfed in flames. Coughing, she buried her nose in the sleeve of her nightdress and groped her way to the wood stove in the middle of the room. No Peety.

Flakes of ash and burning cinders rained down on her head and shoulders. She shook her head trying to brush the stinging embers from her scalp, smelling the scorch of singed hair. Unable to breathe, she turned to flee. Where was the door? The room spun. Panicked, she stumbled and fell, her head slamming against the log bench before strong arms and darkness enveloped her.

ANNE ALETHA FELT Nellie gently dabbing salve on the blisters running up and down her arm and shoulder. Nellie's hand felt cool and soothing to her scorched skin, like submerging herself in the black waters of the millpond on a hot day. She tried to smile at Nellie, but it hurt, like there wasn't enough skin to cover her face. Then she tried to swallow, and that hurt too. Her words sounded raspy and hoarse. "Peety?"

"Shh, Miss Aletha, don't try to talk," said Nellie. "Just lay real still. Doc Clements says I's got to put this ointment on you. You done got blisters all up and down your arm and shoulder."

She closed her eyes feeling the pulse of each heartbeat in her throbbing head. Had she dreamed a glancing blow to her head and someone lifting her? Now, she was in her own bed.

"He say you's mighty lucky. Got yourself a concussion. But the burns ain't gone deep. They's just gonna scab and peel." Nellie was applying long strips of a bed sheet over the burns.

"But Lordy, you done scared the daylights out of us, and praise the good Lord for sparing you. If Mr. Patten ain't done found you when he did, you wouldn't be in this here bed."

She frowned. "Patten?"

Nellie shook a medicine bottle of brown liquid against the palm of the hand. "This don't taste good, but Doc says I got to give you two swallows every couple of hours. Now open wide."

She made a face, grimacing as the foul tasting tincture of laudanum entered her mouth. "Ugh," she whispered, shaking her head. "Peety?"

"Shush now. You ain't suppose to talk. Everybody fine. We ain't seen hide nor hair of that mutt but he be hightailing it home lickety split as soon as he get hungry."

She heard Nellie's evasive answer but closed her eyes, unable to stay awake a moment longer.

Somewhere in her dreams, the lumber mill's noonday whistle sounded. She opened her eyes as sunlight flooded the bed. Could it be midday? She turned over wincing as she forgot her bandaged arm and shoulder. She tried to untangle her muslin nightdress that had twisted into an annoying wad around her waist, but she couldn't do that either. Voices floated from the kitchen and she could hear snatches of conversation.

"That good, Miss Jincy," said Nellie. "Just stir the sugar real slow till it turn a caramel color. We done used up our sugar rations for the month but Miss Aletha don't like nothing better than a caramel cake."

"When is she gonna wake up, Nellie? And what if she asks about Peety? Are we going to tell her?"

"Miss Maidee'll be along soon and she'll know what to say."

When she awakened again, Maidee stood at the side of the bed. Anne Aletha reached for her hand thinking how pretty she looked in her print dress of delicate rosebuds.

Maidee squeezed her hand. "Hello, Anne Aletha. Don't talk now. We don't want to tire you out. Somebody else is here to see you."

Jincy stepped out from behind Maidee, grinning. She went around to the other side of the bed and sat down shyly at her feet.

"So glad to see you," Anne Aletha said in a hoarse whisper, feeling the lump in the back of her throat and the sting of unwanted tears.

"Shh …" said Maidee, patting her hand and reaching for the handkerchief in her pocket. "It's all right, Anne Aletha. It's over now and they won't be back again. Patten and Neville have millworkers guarding the house. And cousin Henry says to tell you there will be consequences for Jenkins."

She nodded, wiping her tears with Maidee's handkerchief. All she could think about was the school, with everything lost, and of Peety.

Jincy shyly patted her toes. "Miss O'Quinn, guess what showed up on our doorstep? A puppy! Queenie says I can keep him as long as he doesn't bother mama cat and her kittens. And guess what? Mama cat thinks he's one of her kittens. She's catching field mice and flying squirrels and bringing them for the puppy to eat!"

It hurt to talk but she tried. "Oh … that's wonderful, sweetie. Will you bring him to see me?"

Nellie bustled into the room carrying a tray of eggs and grits. "Miss Aletha, I told them that you ain't had nothing on your stomach since midday dinner yesterday. See if you can eat a little something and then Miss Jincy's baked you a surprise."

Maidee and Jincy helped her to sit up, fluffing her pillows. "Thank you," she whispered. "Did Peety come back?"

Nellie and Jincy both glanced at Maidee.

"Peety hasn't turned up yet, Anne Aletha. But he will. Now try to eat a few spoonfuls of eggs and grits and maybe a little later you can have a piece of that caramel cake Jincy helped bake."

Lifting her spoon, she tried to smile, appreciating their attempts to cheer her. But she felt too burdened and sad and hoped they would soon leave.

BY THE END of the week, Uncle Doctor lifted his bed rest restrictions, Nellie hovered less, and Anne Aletha's skin itched in all the impossible-to-scratch places. Since she'd done nothing but sleep for a week, she found herself trying to sort the days from the nights, with sleep eluding her. The parlor clock chimed one in the morning and she snuggled down further into her aunt's old patchwork quilt in the porch swing with only the lamp light coming from her bedroom. Clouds obscured the moon and she wondered if one of Patten's millworkers still watched the house. Sheriff Dix had made perfunctory inquiries, but it was clear he thought it only the loss of a cotton shanty and the consequence of her outspoken, misdirected opinions. The burned remnants of a Klan hood and the crumpled crude drawing nailed to the schoolhouse door seemed of little interest.

She set the swing in motion, pushing off the plank floor with her bare feet. What if she had to return home? Her stomach knotted at the thought. She'd been so sure she could succeed, though everyone said the land and the house should have gone to her older brother. But why had her uncle willed it to her if he didn't think she was the one best suited?

She let the swing come to a rest, sinking into her melancholy thoughts. She must have dozed for footsteps on the porch startled her awake.

"You're up late again tonight, Anne Aletha," he said, towering above her. "Can't sleep?"

Suddenly, she realized Patten had been the one watching the house and not one of his millworkers. She sat up straight in the swing pulling the quilt closer to her body.

"I haven't had the chance to thank you since the fire. You saved my life."

"You protected Jincy in the storm. We're even now."

"But how did you know they planned to torch the schoolhouse?"

Surprising her, he sat down on the swing, but did not answer the question. The swing's annoying metal chain groaned in protest and she wondered if it would hold them both.

He withdrew a silver whiskey flask from his back pocket and offered her some.

She shook her head. "No thank you. Mother always took a dim view of whiskey drinking and my father had to hide his whiskey barrels in the smokehouse. Whenever she discovered one, she'd pull the plug with both indignation and delight."

"Seems a shame, wasting good corn whiskey." He took a long swallow.

For a while they sat in the stillness, neither making an effort to talk. He looked at her quizzically, then reached over and touched the back of her neck. "You cut your hair."

His touch startled her. "Yes, Nellie did. She cut off all the singed parts. Now it's shorter than a bob."

A note of regret crept into his voice. "I'm sorry, Anne Aletha. I'm sorry I couldn't stop them."

She heard her own bitterness. "Oh, I don't know. Maybe it doesn't make much difference anyway. The town finds me unacceptable. Without pupils to teach ..." She let the sentence go unfinished. "But what about you? What about the mill?"

"If the war ends before next spring and we can't get another loan, we'll have to sell." He stood returning the whiskey flask to his pocket.

She felt a stab of disappointment at his leaving.

"It's cooling off," he said, his voice little more than a whisper. He held out his hand. "Let's go inside, Anne Aletha."

She looked up but made no reply. Had melancholy weakened her resolve? Or, had she known from the first day she saw him on horseback that this moment would come? She stood.

He took the quilt from her, draping it across her shoulders, but made no other move. In the silence, a moth flung itself noisily against the screen of the bedroom window. Finally, she turned and led him from the porch into the bedroom, covering the rumpled bed with the quilt.

He leaned over the kerosene lamp on her nightstand and blew out the flame before taking her into his arms. Her heart raced so fast inside her chest she wondered if he could feel it beating. He lifted her chin and kissed her, a long, unhurried kiss.

"I want to finish what we began, Anne Aletha," he whispered.

She stood still as he unfastened the buttons of his shirt, removing it. The muscles of his bare chest reflected between the fleeting clouds of the half moon. He cupped her face in his hands. "Is your shoulder painful?"

"No, it just itches," she answered with a nervous laugh.

"Will I hurt you if I lift the nightdress over your head?"

She shook her head, helping him lift it over her shoulders. He removed his trousers and pulled her gently down across the bed. When he leaned over and kissed her, the shock of his naked flesh against her breasts startled her.

He raised himself and looked down at her, as if asking permission one last time. But she heard no more admonishments in her head as he lowered his lips to hers, and she returned his kiss, leaving her girlhood behind.

THE NEXT MORNING, Anne Aletha flew out of bed at the sound of pots and pans banging in the kitchen. Nellie was already making breakfast. Wincing, she quickly peeled the nightgown over her shoulder to have a quick sponge bath. Did she still smell of Patten, she wondered. Just as she changed into a fresh gown and smoothed over the patchwork quilt that now held a multitude of sins, Nellie called.

"Somebody waitin' on the porch for you, Miss Aletha."

She groaned. Surely it wasn't John Henry. He'd promised to stay at the lean-to in the swamp a little while longer. Sliding her feet into slippers, she padded into the kitchen.

Nellie grinned. "See what I told you? He come back. Just sittin' at the backdoor waitin' on breakfast. John Henry gonna be mighty happy."

Peety sprawled sideways on the top step, tail thumping. She dashed out the screen door and knelt down, burying her face into his singed, dirty fur, kissing each lopsided ear. "Oh, Peety, where have you been? We've been worried sick."

"He just scared, that all. Had hisself a good hiding place till hunger drove him home."

"Can Alex get word to John Henry?"

"Yes'um, sure can and I gonna cook that mutt a good breakfast. Don't look like he eat nothing for a while." She turned and studied Anne Aletha. "Ain't you slept?"

Blushing, she shook her head and lied. "I guess I've still got my days and nights mixed up. And I itch something terrible." Now she was certain Nellie and Alex hadn't heard Patten last night.

"Go on back to bed and I'll mix up a little salve."

She hugged Peety once more before retreating back to the bedroom. "I'll wash him this afternoon."

She plumped the feather pillows and got back into bed thinking about her mother's dozen pregnancies. About the brood of children that marriage produced and the few ways to prevent it. She cringed at the thought of jeopardizing her independence. Something else nagged at her too. It was doubt. How had Patten known the Klan intended to set the fire and why had he been so evasive? Perhaps he found the Klan's anti-union rhetoric attractive. Most Southerners, especially those who owned mills and factories, had an inbred reluctance to unions. Her father and brothers certainly did. But how could he condone the bigotry and violence of the Klan? And the reprehensible acts that had been committed? She remembered the familiar blue eyes beneath the hooded mask at New Ramah and wondered: could they have been his? Recoiling at the thought, she threw off the bed sheets. It was too hot to sleep.

At the wash basin, she spit out toothpowder and rinsed her mouth, then stood naked in front of the chifforobe mirror. She looked the same and felt the same, but she was a woman now.

15

IT WAS THE FIRST OF OCTOBER and goldenrod bloomed in the ditches along the roadside, swaying like yellow feather dusters as Sulky lumbered down the lane toward the colored quarter. Soon, the hickories, sweet gum, and sycamores would blaze yellow against the sky and the burning piles of fallen leaves would scent the air with autumn. Perhaps another couple of months before the cold, she thought, happy to put off winter.

Nellie tightened Sulky's reins as they crossed over the railroad track. "Queenie say folks is scairt it's the Spanish sickness and won't nobody go near Willa Mae's cabin. They say she done took sick two days ago and that there ain't a speck of food in the house."

Anne Aletha, alarmed by the growing new threat of the Spanish Influenza, tucked the tea towel further down between the clattering quart jars of chicken and rice as they passed over the track. Just three weeks ago, Boston's Fort Devens reported the first outbreak of the mysterious disease, and now it was spreading rapidly to civilian populations throughout the country. "Neville says our crowded army barracks are just powder kegs waiting to explode with influenza. Augusta's Camp Hancock reported over seven hundred new cases yesterday." She let out a sigh, settling the food basket between their feet, wondering if Frank wasn't safer in the trenches than in the barracks. She hadn't heard from him in over a month.

"Them poor boys ain't got no chance," said Nellie. "And Miss Jincy and Mr. Neville up there in Atlanta in all them crowds."

She hoped Neville succeeded in his last-ditch effort of securing a bank loan. He had admitted difficulty in meeting last month's payroll. And she had been glad he'd taken Jincy with him to visit a cousin. Especially if the rumors of Patten's heavy drinking were true. Though still stirred by the thought of him, she'd avoided him since his visit to her bed, and her doubts had continued to fester. Like Saint Augustine's *Confessions* in which he wrote of his struggle with the bodily desires that seethed within him, she too struggled with a desire that overruled her reason.

Yesterday's shower had muddied the road and Anne Aletha glanced up at the clouds beginning to pile on top of one another, noting that the wind had turned to the east. "We might get a little more rain today."

"Yes'um, and the flies is biting real bad. Always bite before the rain."

Soon they entered the colored quarter where a large flock of guinea hens roamed freely among the cabins, squawking loudly and announcing their arrival. Most folks welcomed the black and white speckled birds with their buzzard-like heads for their early warning of visitors. Her mother especially appreciated the noisy fowl when they foraged in the pecan orchard near the road, always warning her of the first sign of company and allowing her time to run change her apron and powder her nose.

A cluster of small gray cabins stretched out along both sides of the lane. Queenie's, the only whitewashed cabin in the quarter, stood third on the right. Her dirt-swept yard had been the recipient of a multitude of pass-alongs over the years and most had taken haphazard root. But it was Queenie's sugar cane patch out back that she was most proud of.

"Queenie got herself a right good stand of cane this year," said Nellie. "When she send out the word, folks come from all around with their empty fruit jars. Best cane syrup this side of the county. You wait and see."

"It won't be long till cane grinding," Anne Aletha said, thinking of home. Her father always waited till the first cool spell so the yellow jackets could be kept at bay. The work would begin at daybreak and go late into the night. She and her siblings would sit under the large oak near the cane patch watching the mule, harnessed to a long cypress log, plod around and around in a wide circle as her father and older brothers fed the juicy sugarcane stalks into the cane grinder and the green juice gushed into a barrel. Then the raw juice was cooked for many hours in a huge cast iron pot and stirred constantly until the batch turned into a sweet, dark amber syrup.

"My father always says there's nothing better than that first cup of fresh cane juice after a long night's chilly work."

"Yes'um, I remember us youngins gettin' to stay up till the wee hours. Got to dip our cane stalk down into the stir-off pan and get a little sweetening. To us children, it was as good as Christmas."

Further down the lane, Nellie reined in Sulky, calling out to an elderly white-haired man half dozing on his porch, beside him an assortment of cane fishing poles and bait cans. "Catfish! You feelin' better? Glad you up and about."

The old man grinned, righting himself and spitting juice into the snuff can beside him. "Yes'um, Miz Nellie," he said, wiping his mouth on his shirt sleeve. "Tell John Henry I ready to do a little fishing. They's biting good."

"I'll send him around," called Nellie, waving goodbye. "Catfish a good man and done took in John Henry when his ma die and his pa ran off. Learned him to hunt and fish, and look after hisself. Built that old lean-to on the pond so they could gig frogs. John Henry say Catfish can smell where them fish is hiding. Know just which cypress stumps they's under. He probably stay with Catfish come winter."

Though John Henry had remained out of sight after Jenkins and the fire, he now seemed content spending his days helping Alex and Miss Effie with chores and taking the occasional odd paying job. Nellie continued to feed

him, and he and Anne Aletha both looked forward to their
late-afternoon lessons on the back porch. He thrived in his
newfound world of knowledge.

Nellie whoa'd the mule in front of a tarpaper shack
at the end of the road and scowled. "Look over yonder,"
she said, shaking her head. "Willa Mae sick in the bed and
Roscoe up there drunk on the porch. Shame on hisself.
Roscoe! "

The man with graying whiskers appeared old enough
to be Willa Mae's father. He gave no response, tilted back
asleep in a broken-down, cow-hide chair against the wall.
Anne Aletha wondered that the legs would hold him. The
door to the cabin stood open. "Do you think the children
are inside?" she whispered.

"Yes'um. Just set them jars on the porch for when he
wake up."

"I better look in on her. You stay in the wagon. I won't
be long."

Gourds hung from a vine that almost covered the
sagging porch, and she ducked beneath them to climb the
steps, skirting the splintered middle step. Roscoe snored
slack jawed, a brown jug and corncob stopper beside his
chair. She set the food basket next to the whiskey.

In the middle of the doorway, a jumble of Sunday shoes
were turned upside down, an old Negro superstition meant
to ward off evil spirits. She stepped over the pile of shoes
and entered the darkened room, smelling the familiar odor
of sickness. A dingy bed sheet partitioned the sleeping area
where Willa Mae lay on an old rope bedstead. On the floor
next to her, the baby lay sleeping in the middle of a corn-
shuck mattress while the little girl with pigtails played with
a sawdust baby doll and sucked her thumb.

"Is your mommy sick?" she whispered, walking
over to the bed where Willa Mae labored to breathe, her
head kerchiefed and a small red-cloth bag filled with
folk remedies of roots and herbs hanging from her neck.
Another superstition to make sure her illness would pass
away in the night.

"Willa Mae?"

The young woman groaned, then shivered, but did not open her eyes.

Anne Aletha felt her fevered forehead, pulling up the threadbare quilt to cover her thin shoulders. Something that looked like blood had spattered her camisole and quilt.

Roscoe shuffled in beside her, stoop shouldered and weary. "Got the shivering fits day 'fore yesterday. Been coughing two days now. Plumb wore herself out."

"We brought aspirin for the fever and some chicken and rice to keep up her strength. But I think we should send for Doctor Clements. Nellie and I'll leave word in town."

He nodded, the whites of his eyes bloodshot and yellow. "Yes'um. I be obliged."

An uneasiness settled over Anne Aletha and she hurried to leave the sickroom, trying to hold her breath until she reached the water shelf on the front porch. Almost tripping over the shoes in the doorway, she exhaled with a loud rush of air. The influenza had come to Ray's Mill. She was sure of it.

"Can someone take the children till Willa Mae is better?" she asked Roscoe, as she poured water from the well bucket into a rusted tin pan and scrubbed her hands with a thin sliver of lye soap. "We don't want them getting sick." Shunning the grimy rag that hung on a nail, she swiped her hands down the front of her skirt and reached into her pocket for the aspirin tablets.

"Yes'um," said Roscoe, wrapping the tablets in a soiled handkerchief and placing them in the front pocket of his resin stained overalls. He turned and nodded to Nellie in the wagon.

Nellie nodded back, withholding her scorn.

"When she wakes, give her two aspirin tablets for the fever and see if she'll take a little broth," she instructed. "We'll leave word at the drugstore for Doctor Clements."

Nellie guided Sulky back down the lane, giving her a sideways questioning glance.

Anne Aletha shook her head, hesitant to alarm her. "I don't know. It could be influenza. She has all the symptoms."

Sulky jostled them back across the train track as Nellie turned to her in alarm. "Lord a mercy. That poor child ain't yet twenty. And—oh sweet Jesus, you might is caught it too."

Anne Aletha and Nellie arrived in town to find a small crowd gathered around Uncle Doctor's Model T in front of the corner drugstore. "He's early," said Anne Aletha, knowing that he didn't see patients until Wednesday afternoon. Was it the novelty of his new motor car or something else? A group of Negroes stood apart, huddled nearby.

"Look like something going on," said Nellie, pulling the wagon alongside the feed mill store.

The old men on the bench glanced in their direction but were soon diverted when Mr. Wilcox came out of the barber shop and placed a closed sign on his door at ten o'clock in the morning, then strode toward the drugstore. Shortly afterward, three ladies, without parcels, left the dry goods store, hurrying toward the drugstore. Across the street, the widow Dew came out from the telegraph office and shuffled past their wagon toward the drugstore, her plump, short arms swinging ape like from her side, propelling her body forward.

Anne Aletha spoke as she passed. "Morning, Mrs. Dew."

The widow Dew glanced up but did not return the greeting. Her mother's warning of ostracism had proven correct. What people thought about you did matter, especially if your wages depended upon them.

Moments later, Uncle Doctor emerged from the drugstore and waited to address the crowd. He placed his leather satchel at his feet and removed his hat. The expectant crowd hushed. Only the hammering of the blacksmith's anvil could be heard the next street over.

"Doc," the widow Dew called, tugging at the dress hiked up over her voluminous abdomen. "What's this we hear about them quarantining Barwick, Georgia?"

"Yeah, Doc," yelled Wade Madry from Uncle Doctor's Model T. He and another man were now comfortably seated on its running board. "We heard they closed Barwick's drugstore."

Uncle Doctor nodded, grim faced. "That's right folks. Barwick's shut down. They reported thirteen influenza cases yesterday. Had to send out appeals for help when both their doctor and druggist took ill. Quitman's the nearest town and they sent their druggist over to help out. But the whole town of Barwick's under quarantine."

Anne Aletha stood up and waved from the wagon, calling over the murmuring crowd. "Uncle Doctor, Nellie and I came to leave word for you. We just took food to Willa Mae and she's very ill … with all the symptoms of influenza."

Uncle Doctor frowned and the Negroes gathered in closer to hear. "I'll see her first thing. Folks, it may have reached us. People can go from well to sick in just a few hours."

A plume of peacock feathers bobbed among the heads of the gathering crowd. "Excuse me, *please* let me pass. I must speak to Doctor Clements." There was polite mumbling as Florence Mobley pushed her way through, waving a telegram.

"Gentlemen, let the lady pass," said Uncle Doctor, beckoning her toward him. The crowd parted.

She handed him the telegram, her voice quivery with excitement. "Our Red Cross chapter just received word this morning from Atlanta. Augusta's Camp Hancock is asking for 100,000 face masks as soon as humanly possible. Our members need all the help we can get." She paused catching her breath before turning to address the crowd. "We must try to keep the influenza from spreading, especially from the troops into our towns." She held up what looked like small strips of gauze or cheesecloth.

"These masks are very simple to make. Our chapter has all the materials on hand, so it's merely a question of securing sufficient labor. Supplies may be picked up at my millinery shop. Any help will be welcome, gentlemen included." She searched the crowd. "I believe Mr. Attaway has fashioned one for himself."

Ralph Attaway stepped out from the crowd, strutting about in demonstration of the makeshift mask before pausing to yank it down. "Doc, they say folks are turning black and blue with it. That you can't tell the colored from the white!"

Uncle Doctor interrupted. "Thank you Mrs. Mobley, Mr. Attaway. I know everyone is willing to help. Because of the contagion, they're taking precautions up North and Washington has issued orders, with President Wilson's approval, to stagger work hours to prevent crowding on the street cars. I think the government will leave it up to the discretion of individual communities to close their churches, schools, and moving picture houses, those that have them. We're going to have to depend on our own resources because as you know we have an extreme shortage of nurses and doctors due to the war effort. Anybody with two hands can help."

"What about our Liberty Bond drive this Saturday?" the widow Dew asked.

"Cancel it. If the influenza has begun, we should take heed immediately."

LONG PAST MIDDAY DINNER, Anne Aletha heard the thud of Alex's work boots on the back porch as he sat on the three-legged milk stool and removed them. Relieved, she called to Nellie. "He's back." Since the fire a month ago, they now worried whenever Alex was delayed, afraid he'd met with some meanness or a taunt by white men just waiting for the misstep of a colored man.

The screen door slammed behind him as Alex carried in a large basket of soiled laundry. Careful not to track in any unnecessary dirt that Nellie would have to mop, he walked barefooted into the steamy kitchen where flatirons heated on the wood stove.

"We was gettin' worried," said Nellie. She wiped her face with her apron and added more sticks of kindling to the wood stove pointing to the corner where he was to set down the laundry basket.

"Had to wait on Miz Terry's house girl to fetch all them curtains off the windows. She want 'em day after tomorrow, but say no hurry on the tablecloths."

Nellie frowned before returning to her ironing. Carrying food to Willa Mae that morning and yesterday's rain had set them back a day. "That may be the last washin' on them dotted Swiss curtains. I done mended them too often. Well, never mind. We's laid a plate for you. You might as well eat here. Go on and wash up. I know you hungry."

Alex took off his dusty felt hat ringed with sweat and hung it on a peg by the door, then poured warm stove water into the blue enamel dishpan to wash up.

Cicero meowed at the screen door and Anne Aletha stopped sprinkling the boiled shirts to let him in. He had cobwebs in his whiskers and most likely had spent the morning napping in the rafters of the smokehouse. "Did you hear anything else in town about Willa Mae?"

Alex shook his head. "No, ma'am. Doc Clements still ain't back from the quarter yet."

Cicero yawned, positioning himself beneath the table in readiness for leftovers. Alex sat down as Nellie placed a warm plate of black-eyed peas, fatback, and a hoecake in front of him. She resumed her ironing.

"Y'all seen Miz Effie this morning?" he asked, sopping up the black-eyed pea juice with his hoecake. "Passed her nanny goat just now. Bleating like she need milking."

Anne Aletha and Nellie both frowned.

"Ain't no washin' on the line neither," he added.

Nellie stopped ironing. "Less she sick, that wash be on the line."

"She might have taken ill, Alex," Anne Aletha said. "We better go check on her after you finish eating."

"Yes'um. I be done in a minute. I ain't unhitched Sulky yet. We take a little feed corn just in case."

Anne Aletha left him alone to eat. Though Nellie and Alex were like family now, no amount of coaxing could persuade them to share their meals with her. Nellie prepared three meals every day, setting a single place at the kitchen table for Anne Aletha before carrying their own food back to their cabin. Would the racial boundaries and taboos of the South ever be overcome?

As a precaution to the contagion, she went in search of her uncle's stack of handkerchiefs. Opening the top left drawer of his walnut dresser, she selected a large white linen monogramed with his initials. This would cover both nose and mouth.

Tethering Sulky to the sweet gum tree behind Miss Effie's property, Alex swung the hemp sack of cracked corn over his shoulder. Except for the crunch of prickly sweet gum balls beneath their feet, silence pervaded. "Where is they all?" he asked.

"Something's wrong, Alex. It's too quiet." Dead leaves rustled as they climbed over the split rail fence and walked toward the outbuildings at the back of the house.

"Miz Effie?" Alex hollered.

The privy behind the barn stood partially open and he waited a discreet distance while Anne Aletha peered inside. A green lizard warmed itself in a ray of sunshine on the wall as blowflies buzzed noisily in the lime beneath the two-hole outhouse. She shook her head and continued.

Outside the barn, Alex kicked at the remnants of cold ashes under the iron wash pot. They ducked below the low empty clothesline, stepping around the rinsing tub and wash board.

Her concern increased when she saw the water trough. "Look Alex, the trough is empty." She knew Miss Effie would never leave the goats without water, a crucial requirement, especially in summer. The elderly lady treated the playful, affectionate goats like children and was often seen taking them on walks to nibble their favorite blackberry bushes, honeysuckle and poison ivy vines.

They stepped inside the barn and it too was empty. Since goats didn't like to get wet, they slept on wooden shelves built off the ground. The milking table stood next to the shelves with a feeding bucket on the wall and this was what Buttons, the nanny goat, ate from while Miss Effie milked her.

"It ain't been raked out in a day or two," said Alex

They walked next door to the chicken coop. Inside, a sitting hen eyed them motionless in the straw, an empty water pan turned upside down. The bantam rooster that usually teetered on the hen house roof was nowhere in sight.

They paused in front of the old smokehouse that Miss Effie used for storage. The door creaked open and they stepped down onto the dirt floor. The cool, dark interior smelled pungent with old hickory ash and once cured hams. A thick layer of grime coated old fruit jars, rusted farm equipment, and a discarded spinning wheel.

They squinted in the sunlight as they stepped back outside.

Suddenly, Alex stopped and pointed toward the house. "Look-a-there, Miss Aletha. There they all is."

Buttons snorted on the porch, bleating in panic while the baby goats huddled against her side.

Anne Aletha took the feed bag and knelt down, holding kernels of corn in the palm of her hand. "Come on, Buttons," she coaxed.

The goats galloped down the steps with tails wagging, their delicate legs and small hoofs splayed in all directions. She gathered them against her, soothing and petting, feeling their warm little bodies and rapid heartbeats. With only eight tiny white front teeth on their lower jaws and none on their upper, they gently gobbled the corn from her hand.

Soon, the chickens and rooster emerged in a squawking ruckus from beneath the house and took flight toward the corn as Alex scattered more feed.

Buttons bleated again, pawing the ground then squatted to urinate, her udders painfully engorged. Though the baby goats now nursed only on occasion, she still gave Miss Effie almost a half-gallon of milk a day. "Alex, you better take her to the barn and milk her. I'll go inside."

"Ain't sure what you gonna find."

She hurried across the yard, past the giant fig tree by the back porch and up the steps, her heartbeat as rapid as the goats'. She thought of Miss Effie's offer to protect John Henry and her many kindnesses to Nellie and Alex after her Uncle Carter died. Please let her be all right, she whispered.

Nothing seemed amiss on the porch. The rag rug by the backdoor, Miss Effie's little ladder-back chair sitting next to her spittoon, her sewing basket of cloth scraps nearby. She peered through the torn screen door.

"Miss Effie?" The sagging hinges squeaked loudly when she opened it. Inside, a huge cockroach scurried over the canning jars on the worktable, taking refuge beneath the end of season tomatoes. She shuddered. "Miss Effie? It's me, Anne Aletha."

A faint voice replied. "Here …"

She rushed back to the small sewing room off the porch. Miss Effie lay in bloomers and camisole on a daybed of ticking strewn with brown-tissue dress patterns, buttons, and colored threads. At the end of the bed, a rusted dressmaker form stood silhouetted in the light of the window and looked just like a person.

She reached down and touched the woman's frail, clammy arm. "Oh, Miss Effie. You're ill."

Miss Effie stared at the ceiling, large dark splotches spotting her cheeks and throat. Black drool crusted the sides of her mouth and Anne Aletha didn't know if it was blood or the pinch of snuff she usually kept tucked inside her bottom lip.

"I'm so sorry we didn't come sooner. Alex just heard Buttons bleating a little while ago."

"Thirsty," she slurred, laboring to breathe. Her false teeth and spectacles lay on top of the foot-treadle sewing machine.

"Alex is milking Buttons. I'll go draw up some cool water and send him for Uncle Doctor. You rest now and I'll be right back."

Miss Effie closed her eyes, and Anne Aletha quickly opened the door to the porch in the hot stuffy room. Tying her uncle's handkerchief around her neck and raising it to cover her nose and mouth, she dragged the butter churn over to prop open the door. Miss Effie had been unable to make it to the privy.

Fear coursed through her as she raced to the barn, scattering the cackling chickens and the pecking rooster. "Alex," she shouted, yanking down her mask.

Buttons, perched on the milking table, looked around in alarm. Anne Aletha lowered her voice, trying to still her shaking knees. "Oh Alex, Miss Effie's real sick. Can you go find Uncle Doctor?"

He frowned, his sure, gentle hands squirting frothy white milk into the pail. Buttons resumed eating from the feedbag on the wall. "If he still be here. Might already be gone back to Adel."

"She's sick, just like Willa Mae."

"I take Sulky and find him. Be careful, Miss Aletha. It's real catchin'."

"I will. She's thirsty and I'm going to draw up water. I'll water the animals too."

Anne Aletha swallowed hard, raising her mask before reentering the room. Her mouth kept filling with saliva. The room's heat and stench had dissipated, but Miss Effie struggled for breath. She set down the water bucket. "Uncle Doctor's on his way," she soothed, praying that Alex could find him.

She reached down to cup Miss Effie's sparrow-like head. The sparse oily hair was matted with sweat. She felt revulsion at the thought of touching her, then shame at her reluctance. What if Frank were sick with fever and thirsty somewhere?

"Just a little sip," she coaxed, dipping the gourd into the cool water. Miss Effie panted for breath, spilling most of the water over her parched blue lips and down her chin and chest. She was unable to drink.

Anne Aletha lowered her head gently back down on the pillow and wet a soft muslin cloth for her forehead." There," she whispered. "This will cool you and help bring down the fever."

Miss Effie's cloudy brown eyes searched Anne Aletha's masked face.

She squeezed her hand. "You rest till Uncle Doctor arrives. I'll go water—" Footsteps on the porch startled her. She turned. "Alex? Don't come in. Did you find him already?"

Buttons stood in the doorway.

"Buttons," said Anne Aletha.

Miss Effie turned, reaching out a thin, knobby hand to the goat as her delicate hoofs pattered across the floorboards to the daybed.

Anne Aletha eased out of the room with the water bucket, leaving Miss Effie and Buttons, her throat constricted with tears.

FEAR CHURNED HER STOMACH as she carried water to the barnyard animals. How did Frank and his fellow soldiers live daily with the threat of death? She felt the baby goat nibbling her skirt pocket and turned to see the billy trailing behind them. They waited for her outside the chicken coop as she filled water pans and then they frolicked ahead to the barn, playful as clowns, jumping on tree stumps, playing king of the hill all along the way. Soon, when the male goat matured, he would have to be separated from his mother so that her milk wouldn't be tainted with his odor. Maybe that was why Miss Effie did not name the billys. Stooping down, she petted their long snouts and thin little beards, giving extra attention to the billy. Inside the barn, she filled their water trough, letting them drink until the girl, imitating her mother, jumped up on the milking table and nuzzled the empty bucket. After she located their feed, she left them to eat while she raked up the fouled straw and replaced it with fresh.

Far off in the distance, she heard the putt, putt of Uncle Doctor's Model T. Relief surged through her and she threw down the rake, racing from the barn to the front of the house, scattering the chickens again and trampling a row of collard seedlings. Her chest heaved. "Oh, Uncle Doctor, I'm so relieved you're here."

He stepped from the motor car, rumpled and solemn. "It's begun, Anne Aletha."

Her voice quavered. "Willa Mae?"

He nodded. "I'm afraid so. And I'm on my way to see Luella Sirmans next."

She sank down on the porch steps. Her fingertips tingled. "Will Willa Mae die? What about her children?"

He shook his head. "I don't know. There's an appalling loss of life in the army camps. Fort Devens is averaging over a hundred deaths a day. The men are drowning in their own fluids, much like Roena."

"What can we do?"

"Patients will need hydration, nourishment, and bed rest to survive. The germs are most likely airborne and highly contagious. You mustn't expose yourself, Anne Aletha. The newspapers are leading the public to believe that fear is worse than the disease, but that's nonsense. Wear a mask and wash your hands. The disease is deadly."

"Miss Effie can't breathe and she has dark splotches on her cheeks."

He frowned. "I'll take a look and give her something to ease her breathing. You go home, child. Wash yourself, your hair, and your garments."

"Are you going back to Adel?"

"In the morning. The infirmary will be full. I'll be at Roena's tonight."

"Shouldn't I sit with Miss Effie?"

He shook his head. "She'll sleep the night. Come back in the morning. Y'all prepare food for those who are ill and you and Alex check on the Sirmans tomorrow for me. He'll need to help with the livestock. Patten telegraphed Neville to remain with Jincy in Atlanta."

16

THE NEXT MORNING a dense fog loomed over the barnyard like the heaviness of their dread. Sulky lifted a hoof and stomped the dew-damp ground as Alex fumbled with his bridle. Slipping it over the old mule's head and long ears, he placed the bit between the mule's lips. "He know something wrong," said Alex, his erect shoulders slumped and his usual whistling silenced.

"Bet that old hooty owl done spooked him too," said Nellie. "Screeched most the night. They say that mean tragedy's a-comin'. We suppose to throw salt in the fire and tie a knot in the bed sheets."

Fear knotted Anne Aletha's stomach too. The night's disturbing dreams had drained her. Miss Effie kept calling and she was unable to reach her because the millpond had flooded the road. When she tried to find the rowboats on the embankment, they were nowhere to be found and she spent the whole night searching. She awoke exhausted.

Nellie handed Alex a pail of warm, buttered sweet potatoes and the milk bucket.

"Maybe Miss Effie be feeling better this morning. She won't mind if you carry the Sirmans boys some milk."

Alex loaded the bucket and pail into the wagon. Sulky's ears pricked forward.

"Listen…" said Anne Aletha. In the distance, a church bell tolled three times.

"Oh lawdy. Somebody dead," said Nellie.

"Sure nuf. Ringing this time of mornin', somebody done died," said Alex.

"Reckon they for Willa Mae?" asked Nellie.

"Sound like Beaverdam," said Alex. "Too far away for New Ramah. Ain't the colored church 'cause we don't got no bells."

Nellie handed Alex a large red bandana. "Cover your face and don't touch nothing but the animals. You got your mask and gloves, Miss Aletha? Just set the taters on the porches."

Anne Aletha checked her pockets for her aunt's white cotton gloves and climbed into the wagon. "Don't try to wash those curtains, Nellie. We'll do it later. I don't think folks are going to be concerned with laundry right now."

Alex clucked to the reluctant mule and the buggy lurched forward into the ruts of the side yard and out onto the lane. They rode the short distance in silence.

At the end of the road, Alex frowned in puzzlement, bringing Sulky to a halt along the side of Miss Effie's house. "Look like Mr. Patten and Mr. Clyde is delivering something yonder to Miss Effie."

She tensed. Patten climbed down from the wagon looking thinner and she knew that the rumors of his drinking were true. Though she felt no remorse, their night together had been a night of lust, not love, and she did not intend to repeat it.

Clyde went to the back of the wagon and jumped up in the wagon bed, spry for a man his age and with his bowed legs. He hoisted down a pine coffin.

She let out a sob, grabbing Alex's arm. "No!" she screamed, scrambling down from the wagon.

Patten turned in her direction and scowled, his jaw clenched. "Don't come any closer, Anne Aletha," his tone brusque and dismissive. "There's nothing to be done here."

She stumbled across the yard. "Oh no, is Miss Effie dead? Oh, please tell me she didn't die alone." Her face crumpled as she wept into her hands.

"Miss O'Quinn," said Clyde, his voice tender. "Doc Clements wants her in the ground right away. Our men at the mill are building coffins."

She wiped her wet cheeks and counted coffins. "Three?"

"He says more will be likely to get it," said Clyde. "They're dropping like flies in hard hit places like Philadelphia. Forty-five hundred people have died there so far and they're stacking the bodies like firewood 'cause the morgues are overwhelmed. The gravediggers won't work and they're telling people to put the corpses on the front porch. Families are having to dig their own graves."

Patten interrupted. "Go home, Anne Aletha." Both men turned to their task, putting on work gloves and mask before carrying Miss Effie's coffin through the front door.

She called after them. "We came to milk Buttons and carry food to the Sirmans…"

The screen door slammed behind them.

ANNE ALETHA SHIFTED the boney protuberance of her bottom on the hard wagon seat, careful not to jiggle the full pail of Button's milk between her legs.

Alex glanced sideways at her, giving the mule's reins more slack. "Doc Clements know best, Miss Aletha. He said go home and leave Miz Effie 'cause wasn't nothin' you could do but get sick yourself."

She nodded, not bothering to wipe her tears. Why hadn't she at least sat on the porch within earshot so Miss Effie would know she wasn't alone? Neighbors always helped neighbors. Barn raising, hog killing, cane grinding … that's what you did for one another. If a man fell ill, you gathered his crop; if a woman took sick, you brought food for her family. She only hoped the laudanum from Uncle Doctor had eased Miss Effie's struggle.

They remained silent with only the creak of the wagon wheels. A woodpecker drilled in a dead tree nearby and she looked up through the trees to see that the sun was now high in the sky. "Miss Effie said that goats can die of loneliness—" Her voice choked.

"Then we bring them home till they sorts out her kinfolk."

She turned, squeezing his arm. "Oh Alex, yes. Let's get them this afternoon. We'll bring Buttons' milking table, and John Henry and I can take them to the woods to forage." That morning, the goats had eagerly come to her side and seemed to want attention, especially the little billy she called No Name.

"Yes'um, that be a good thing. We best bring the chickens too."

She swiped again at her tears. Sweet, gentle Alex, with a heart as tender as Frank's. Miss Effie would rest easier.

Sulky dropped a pile of manure, picking up his pace as the road bent to the right. Soon, the Sirmans' house came into view. Set in a grove of trees, it had gingerbread trim around the eaves and strange-looking lightning rods that reached up from the gabled roof. They reminded her of toy soldiers standing sentinel and she wondered if the rods really deterred lightning strikes.

Alex guided the wagon beneath the shade of the shiny barked sycamore tree, half of its yellow leaves already fallen. "Some kinda sign on the door."

Her heart sank as she looked back. A black shawl draped the door with a sign scrawled in block letters. INFLUENZA.

Beneath the porch, a mottled-looking mutt peeked out and barked. The front door opened immediately. Mr. Sirmans, a tall man with deep-set eyes and heavy eyebrows, stepped out on the porch.

"Doctor Clements asked us to bring food and see if Alex could help with the livestock," she said. He nodded, removing a handkerchief from his back pocket to wipe his eyes.

"My missus passed in the night."

Alex groaned. "Oh Lord have mercy."

Anne Aletha's hand clutched her throat. "Oh no, we're so sorry."

A heartrending cry came from within the house. "Mama …"

"Miss, can you take a look at my youngest? He's the worst off with the fever. He don't know his ma is dead yet."

She looked at Alex and saw the fear in his eyes. "I'll be careful," she whispered.

How could she refuse? Her heart beat faster as she removed her hat and tucked as much flyaway hair as possible behind her ears before tying her mask. Would two handkerchiefs be better than one? She slipped her aunt's cotton gloves over trembling fingers. Her uncle said that sometimes courage was having no choice.

She entered the deep gloom of the front parlor where only a dim glow shone from a kerosene lamp. On the mantel, the hands of the clock were stopped just past midnight and the mirror behind it was covered in black. Such nonsense, she thought, that people believed a soul could escape through a glass mirror.

Three pallets were spread out on the floor near the hearth.

"The light hurts their eyes," said Mr. Sirmans.

Timothy, the youngest whimpered, kicking off his covers. "Mama …"

She knelt down and removed her gloves, gently touching his flushed forehead, remembering this littlest boy at the pond swatting mosquitoes, chased down the lane by his big brother brandishing a giant snapping turtle. Never again would he fling himself into the protective arms of his mother.

"Mama …"

She caressed his cheek, choking down a sob, trying to remember what Uncle Doctor said to do. "Bring whatever ice and rubbing alcohol that you have, Mr. Sirmans, along with some aspirin tablets. We must bring down the fever."

The oldest boy coughed and she moved toward him. Blood crusted his nostrils and he smelled of vomit, but his forehead felt cool to her touch. Had his fever broken? He watched her with sad eyes. This boy knew his mother was dead.

The middle child slept, a strangled wheeze but he was not fevered. Please let them live, she pleaded.

LATE THAT AFTERNOON, she sank exhausted into her unmade bed, not bothering to remove the scoured dress still warm from Nellie's iron, nor comb her wet tangled hair. Nellie's boiling wash pot in the backyard had awaited every stitch of their clothing, including Alex's old felt hat, and though they grumbled, they complied, grateful for her diligence against this lurking unknown disease. She wondered if this new pestilence would be like the plague of the Middle Ages that had wiped out a third of Europe's population. No one knew.

She closed her eyes and sighed, feeling the tautness in her shoulders slowly relax. She must write home tonight. Had the influenza reached Odum yet? She longed for the safety of the world she'd once known. Before the war, the lynchings and this deadly epidemic.

She thought of the riverbank and its earthy smell. The cool quiet of the majestic forest of cypress trees along the river. It was her favorite time of day when the light ebbed and the golden leaves floated lazily down the Altamaha, bobbing and swirling. Usually the belted kingfisher kept her company with his rattling cry, fishing from his favorite cypress branch. But she must watch the sun's descent and not get caught past dusk in the boggy forest. The ferocious wild hogs her brothers tagged and released in the spring were now fattening on forest acorns. And soon the huge beasts would be recaptured for slaughter, her brothers taking great care not to be gored by their tusks.

In the distance, she heard a pounding, and placed her ear to the ground. Could it be wild hogs? She'd neglected to look for the heart-shaped footprints of their hoofs. The pounding grew louder. Should she run? But she mustn't trip on the cypress knees in the dark, for the roots of the cypress tree rose up like tombstones all around the forest floor.

She lurched and opened her eyes. Someone was knocking at the door. Groggy, she stumbled out of bed, rushing barefooted to the front door. "Neville …"

He leaned heavily on his cane, a newspaper beneath his arm. "My God, Anne Aletha, are you ill?"

He reached for her and she crumpled against his wrinkled shirt, smelling the stale, sour smell of his travel. He must have come straight from the depot. "No, no. I'm fine. But Miss Effie's dead and Luella Sirmans and maybe Willa Mae," she said, sobbing against his chest.

"Oh, my dearest Anne Aletha," he said, caressing the still damp curls at the back of her head. "Let's go sit down."

Limping into the parlor, his lameness exaggerated by fatigue, he lit the lamp on her uncle's desk and beckoned her beside him on the settee. "You're very pale. I'm worried about you."

"I'm fine, but I'm so afraid, Neville. Who will be next? It's wiping out entire families from dawn to dusk!"

He covered her hands with his own. In the lamp light, she saw the weariness in his slackened jaw and the concern in his kind blue eyes.

"The epidemic is spreading rapidly. The surgeon general has called for a nationwide ban on all gatherings. I left Jincy in Atlanta with her cousin till the contagion passes."

"I'm glad. We've been so worried for you."

"Any word from Frank? It's hitting the troops overseas particularly hard. I brought newspapers for you."

"No, but General Pershing reports that there have been further advances by American forces along the Meuse River and Argonne Forest. I think Frank is there. And the papers said that our aviators have shot down more than one hundred hostile planes and twenty-one balloons since September twenty-sixth."

"Yes. Fortunately, we were able to get our troops overseas and ready to fight much earlier than our enemies expected." He stood. "I want you to rest. I'll stop by tomorrow with more news on the influenza."

Anne Aletha walked him to the door. "Thank you, Neville. Before you go, did you meet with any success at the banks in Atlanta?"

He responded with a weary shake of his head. "No, but it seems the least of our worries at the moment."

17

"AIN'T NOBODY gonna lay right for a day or two," said Nellie, fanning herself at the work table beneath the shade trees. "They gotta work out their pecking order."

Anne Aletha plucked three warm, damp, rust-colored eggs from her apron pocket and placed them in the basket on the table. Peety drowsed beside them with one eye open on the skittish new chickens.

Since daybreak, Alex and John Henry had worked on a makeshift chicken coop and now Miss Effie's flock was safely penned inside. Especially since no one knew what Peety would do with the new flock. The other hens milled about in the barnyard, cackling and pecking, one chasing a grasshopper while Nellie's best-laying hen had a dust bath.

Miss Effie's bantam rooster crowed again in the chicken coop and startled them all.

"If he keep that up every hour, we gonna stew him," said Nellie, looking weary.

"Are you sure you're feeling well, Nellie?"

"Yes'um. Just wondering who gonna get it next."

She nodded. They were all drained and agreed not to even bother doing laundry. With death lurking all around them, Mrs. Terry's curtains didn't seem to matter.

The hammering in the barn stopped and soon Alex and John Henry came out to join them. Stretching, Alex placed his hands on the small of his back and the pungent liniment for his lumbago wafted toward them. "Ain't heard no church bells this morning."

"Yes, and I pray the Sirmans boys are better. Y'all come rest a while and I'll read the newspapers Neville brought last night."

Alex sat on an old rain barrel while John Henry paused to kick at a clump of dirt, hoping to unearth a plump worm for his afternoon fishing. It would be pocketed, squirming, into his overalls and later added to his bait can of earthworms.

Buttons and the baby goats lay napping, curved against each other, sheltered against the shady side of the barn while Alex and John Henry worked to complete their wooden sleeping platform. Buttons raised her head at the sight of John Henry. She'd immediately attached herself to him, following him everywhere, butting his hand for head rubbings. Like Peety with school erasers, Buttons snatched anything out of back pockets, including John Henry's penmanship papers, devouring them before he could retrieve them. So far, Peety and Cicero had watched the goats with interest, but kept their distance.

"Can I study on the newspaper when you're done, Miss Aletha?" asked John Henry.

"Yes and circle all the words you don't know. Then we'll go over the new ones."

She opened the Wednesday edition of the *Atlanta Constitution* and scanned the front page to read the headlines:

> The Spanish Influenza continues to spread in all the army camps. More than 14,000 new cases were reported during the twenty-four hours ending at noon today. The total number of cases is 88,000 in all the American camps.

Alex whistled, shaking his head.

She realized Frank was in even greater danger. After Neville left last night, she'd checked the Honor Roll section of the newspaper reading about the difficulties of reporting casualties and getting that information back from the field hospitals. She'd learned that in large warfare, units under heavy fire that were losing men on the way couldn't pause to check casualties. That must come later from the dressing stations, hospital or burying parties.

She continued to read the headlines:

> The Atlanta City Council passed an ordinance Monday afternoon that for the next two months churches, schools, movie theaters, pool and billiard rooms, and dance halls will remain closed as a precautionary measure against further spread.

"Two months?" said Nellie. "Lord a mercy."

"Yes," Anne Aletha agreed, wondering about Miss Perkins and the start of school. She read the next headline. "Americans Press Enemy. American forces are Northwest of Verdun. General Pershing's infantry today again went into action on the left wing of Argonne Forest. In addition, 350 U.S. aeroplanes went on a bombing raid and did big damage dropping 32 tons of explosives on German cantonments."

"We's got 'em running now," said Alex. "Mr. Frank be coming home soon."

"Neville says the fact that we were able to get all of our troops over so quickly—"

Peety growled and jumped to his feet barking.

Ralph Attaway burst from around the corner of the house, hatless and flushed, stomping toward them. "I figured you were around back."

John Henry grabbed Peety, shushing him while Nellie hoisted herself out of the chair.

"Mr. Attaway," said Anne Aletha. "We didn't hear you. Is something wrong?" His flu mask hung from around his neck in addition to a string of garlic and camphor balls. "Miss Maidee needs you right away."

Anne Aletha's breath caught. "Oh, no! Is she sick?"

He shook his head, waving away the pesky gnats that hovered around his eyes. "Miz Mobley's dropped off three children orphaned by the influenza. Their parents were tenant farmers over in Hahira. An infant and a little boy and girl." He gestured their height. "Miss Maidee wants to know if you can keep the brother and sister a couple of days till kinfolk are found."

She hesitated. Would the children infect them all? But the thought of orphan children wrenched her heart. She looked at Nellie.

"I'll go make up a cot," said Nellie.

"I brought the carriage to carry you over, Miss O'Quinn. Miss Maidee and her mother got the infant in a dresser drawer and it ain't stopped squalling yet."

Anne Aletha removed her apron, feeling shame at her hesitancy but aware of the withering fear in risking the lives of those you love.

Ralph Attaway slid aside the stack of Liberty Bonds on the carriage seat to make room for her. How many people would answer the door to listen to his appeal or pay on their installments with the deadly threat of influenza, she wondered. But she had to admire him. He took his patriotic duty seriously. With a twinge of pity, she found herself softening toward him. Had she been too quick to judge?

"Do the children know their parents are dead?" she asked, worried that she might need to console them with stories of heaven.

"Miz Mobley didn't know. Just said there was blood everywhere in the bedroom. The parents had coughed it up on the pillows, sheets and even the walls."

She grimaced. "Oh, those poor children."

TWO SMALL SOLEMN-FACED children clung to each other on Maidee's porch swing. Holding hands, the little boy sucked his thumb and his sister clutched her doll.

"Oh dear," she whispered, feeling her eyes prick with tears. She lowered her mask so as not to frighten them.

Ralph Attaway tethered the mare and held out his hand to assist her down from the carriage. "Miss Maidee's out back in the kitchen. Go on in the parlor and I'll tell her you're here."

She climbed the porch steps, smiling. "Hello there, my name is Anne Aletha. What is yours?"

The children stared back at her, their cheeks encrusted with dirt and tears.

She sat down next to them on the swing, but they slid further away, pressing themselves to the edge. They appeared close in age, barefooted and thin, with chigger bites covering their legs.

"Do you like teacakes and lemonade?" she asked.

They did not respond.

She continued. "I'm going to take you to my house for a few days. This afternoon we can go wading in the pond. Would you like that?" And wash off some of that dirt, she thought.

Were they mute? she wondered. "Stay here and I'll be right back." She reached over to touch and reassure them, but they drew back, like a cat that didn't want to be stroked.

Inside Maidee's hallway, she paused for a few moments to stare in amazement at all the clutter. Nothing had been thrown out in years, if ever, and everything teetered, threatening to topple. Piles of old newspapers and stacks of magazines crammed the maze-like interior so that she could barely squeeze through the hallway to enter the parlor. And in the parlor, there was no place to sit. Hat boxes spilled over with receipts, and stacks of ledger books perched precariously on both the settee and slipper chairs. Bric-a-brac, figurines and photographs filled the curio cabinets. Even the walls were crowded with a host of grim-faced ancestors in dark oval frames peering down at her. She smiled, feeling a little less eccentric. So, this was why Maidee and her mother did not receive callers.

An infant wailed and Maidee called from the hallway. "I'm coming, Anne Aletha."

Moments later, Maidee entered the parlor, breathless and in disarray. "Oh! Goodness gracious, please excuse the mess. Thank you for coming."

Anne Aletha smiled at her friend, uncorseted in a shapeless housedress with loosened hair halfway down her back and a shawl thrown across her shoulders. She was flushed and lovely.

Maidee blotted sweat from her upper lip and embraced her. "What a dear you are to come."

Anne Aletha hugged her in return.

"I'm heating milk for the baby. The poor little thing is ravenous. We've fashioned him a crib out of a dresser drawer, but it's been years since I've changed a diaper. And I'm afraid Mother might drop him!"

"Oh, those poor children. Do they understand that their parents are dead?"

"I don't know. Mrs. Mobley says the parents were sick for days. The Red Cross is sending out desperate appeals for help. They're begging neighbors to take in the children when the parents are dead or dying. It seems to be killing our most productive and vital."

The man in the moon
Looked out of the moon
And this is what he said,
'Tis time that, now I'm getting up
All babies went to bed..."

ANNE ALETHA PAUSED, listening for sounds from the cot at the end of the bed. Softly, she closed the book of nursery rhymes and crept out of bed. Finally, they were asleep, head to toe on the cot, a thumb in each mouth. Though the children had not yet spoken, they'd spent the afternoon with John Henry exploring. Piling them into the wheelbarrow, he ferried them first to see the giant wolf spider suspended in a web in the mulberry tree waiting for prey. Then they visited the huge gray paper hornet's nest in the hickory tree near the creek, watching the wasps enter the tiny opening. Next, they climbed into the corn crib to see John Henry's summer sleeping pallet, inspect his orange crate full of school books and crawl beneath the corn crib to see Peety's scavenged booty. In the barn loft, they retrieved the shed skin of a rat snake and helped John Henry dig earthworms behind the privy for tomorrow's fishing expedition to the millpond. Like Miss Effie's goats, by dusk, the children were clinging to John Henry like fig ivy.

At supper, they fell on their food, bolting down beans and rice and two of Nellie's fried hoecakes. Only at bedtime did they balk at any mention of bathing.

"There be time for washin' in the mornin', Miss Aletha," Nellie whispered.

She leaned over and pulled the summer quilt top over their thin little necks ringed with dirt. She longed to feel their foreheads for fever, but feared waking them and wondered if they would all sicken with influenza. Uncle Doctor said the contagion could take two to three days to contract, so they would just have to wait and see.

She thought about her cowardice that morning and crawled back into bed feeling fresh shame that she'd hesitated to take the children. Nellie had not. And she was grateful they had done the right thing. Even Ralph Attaway was still going door to door selling Liberty Bonds, and Patten and Clyde were endangering themselves every day delivering coffins to inter the dead. Risking oneself was the best of human nature.

She snuffed out the lamp, doubtful that sleep would come. The branches of the tea olives stirred in the breeze and the fragrance of their second blooming wafted into the room, smelling of home. She hoped the influenza had not yet reached Odum and that her family would remain safe in the country.

Sometime in the night the bottom of a calloused foot scraped against her leg and she awoke. The children lay beside her in the bed. As she snuggled their rank little bodies closer, her heart surged with joy. If only she could keep them safe and take away their sorrow.

"HE DID IT," wailed the little girl, stomping the floor and trailing Anne Aletha down the hallway the next morning. She clutched a tattered rag doll to her chest and her tiny belly protruded over dirty underpants that she refused to remove.

"Did not," her brother cried, carrying the shed skin of the rat snake.

"Did so!"

Anne Aletha paused at the hall table, holding the urine-soaked sheets at arm's length. "Shhh," she said. "It doesn't matter who wet the bed. Let's leave the snakeskin here till after breakfast." She hoped Nellie wouldn't catch sight of it. She'd shriek.

In the kitchen, Nellie perched on the milking stool in front of the wood stove, waiting with the large galvanized washtub full of warm bathwater. When they entered, she pounced with expert speed, snatching up each squirming child, cajoling and stripping them of soiled underpants before submerging their little bottoms into the warm soapy water.

"Ain't never seen me a youngin' yet that likes to take a bath. Ya'll is no better than a cat. Why, one time, we had to wash poor ole Cicero 'cause a polecat done sprayed him. Stunk him up so bad he couldn't stand his ownself."

Anne Aletha chuckled as Nellie soaped and scrubbed, ignoring their squeals of protests.

"Close them eyes for the rinsin'," Nellie said to the little girl. "And Miss Aletha gonna dry you. Then after breakfast, I gonna make that baby doll a brand-new dress. How would you like that? Can't have her going around half naked."

Anne Aletha readied a drying towel and clean underwear from their knapsack as Nellie's ample arms lifted the little girl to her.

"And when John Henry's done finished his chores," she said, rinsing the little boy. "I bet him and you gonna have time for a game of marbles."

LATER THAT MORNING on the porch, Nellie tied a final knot in the hem of the yellow gingham doll dress. Biting off the end of the thread, she grinned and shook out the miniature garment. "You wants to dress her?"

The little girl nodded with a shy smile, reaching for the doll dress.

Anne Aletha and Nellie exchanged glances. Though still watchful and quiet, the children seemed less solemn today. But she felt sure they had witnessed their parents deaths.

Keeping each other always in sight, the little girl glanced over at her brother and John Henry playing marbles in the dirt before settling herself on the porch swing. Then she dressed her baby doll.

Rummaging through her basket of cloth scraps, Nellie extracted a small piece of lawn cotton. "Look-a-here, child. 'Fore Miss Maidee come for you tomorrow, we's gonna make your dolly a frilly apron—" She stopped mid-sentence.

Peety snarled and the boys stopped playing marbles. Bicycle tires crunched on the rutted lane and soon the Western Union boy swung into the yard.

Anne Aletha stiffened, lifting the newspaper and pan of snap beans off her lap, aware of the smallest detail: the scolding of the house wren in the hawthorns, the fluttering of the falling sycamore leaves to the ground, the clink of the boy's marbles just moments before.

"Lord have mercy," murmured Nellie.

The young man rested his bicycle against the catalpa stump, calling up to the porch. "Telegram for Miss O'Quinn." Respectful, he remembered to remove his cap as he approached.

She could hardly breathe and her heart thudded as she grasped the banister rail of the steps, not trusting her knees. The youth's face had a look of sympathy. He wasn't much younger than Frank, with fuzz on his chin that he hadn't yet begun to shave.

Moments passed in the unnatural stillness. She felt Nellie at her side and a comforting arm encircled her shoulder. She reached for the envelope. Her clumsy fingers opened it and the tissue-thin sheet of yellow paper crinkled as she unfolded it.

She read aloud the capitalized words with no punctuation.

FRANK WOUNDED STOP PRAY AND BE STRONG STOP DO NOT COME HOME STOP FLU RAMPANT IN NEARBY JESUP STOP LETTER IN POST STOP

LOVE MOTHER

The youth replaced his cap and turned to leave.
Her voice quavered. "Let me get my change purse."
He shook his head. "No, ma'm, but thank you."
Nellie took charge. "John Henry, Miss Aletha and I is going to the parlor. There's biscuits and taters on the stove. Y'all take them and go along fishing now."

Nellie closed the parlor door softly behind her as she left and Anne Aletha sank down into her uncle's sagging armchair.

"Oh Frank," she cried, no longer able to suppress her sobs. Was there no sense to be made of life?

She ached to be at his bedside. Was he in a field hospital near the trenches, alone and in pain? She tried not to think of his wounds: blistered and scorched lungs from the deadly mustard gas or blown-apart limbs from shrapnel and mined fields?

A wave of homesickness swept over her. Suddenly, she longed to be home with her family. To embrace each and every one. She knew that unless the influenza prevented him, Preacher Burke would ride out to visit the family after supper this evening. They would join hands as they did at family mealtimes when the food was blessed and he would read scripture passages in his quiet conversational voice, offering them comfort. She envied them their solace but knew that her battle between faith and reason was lost long ago.

"Providence or chance?" she asked aloud, thinking of her uncle and their many discussions of the mysteries of life and the randomness of death. She remembered the solemn Christmas after their little Claire had died of typhus and her Uncle's sad but stoic acceptance.

"Chance," she answered aloud, leaning her head back against the freshly starched antimacassar. Closing her eyes, she could see Frank's mischievous grin. She always knew by the cock of his head if he was up to some devilment. And though he delighted in playful fun and pranks, he was never mean-spirited. Always loyal to a fault, everyone agreed.

She recalled a childhood Sunday afternoon when their nearest neighbors visited and her two middle brothers laid in wait outside the privy for the little Parnell boy to go inside. Just as he settled himself on one of the cutout holes, the boys snuck up and shook the outhouse. To their dismay, the tiny child slid through the adult hole bottom first into the lime and excrement. His screams brought everyone running. But it was Frank who received the undeserved blame and punishment. Never one to snitch on his older brothers, he was made to retrieve and wash the child, and to cut his own hickory switch for the whipping that followed behind the smokehouse once their company departed.

A little while later in the quiet house, Cicero pawed at the closed door to be let in. "There you are," said Anne Aletha, knowing he'd only ventured out from his hiding place in the absence of children. They returned to the chair where the old tom wove between her legs before settling himself on her lap, kneading and purring. "Please let

Frank live," she whispered. He could come here to live, she thought, but the bleak prospects of paying spring's property taxes and her father's one-year stipulation darkened her future. Since her arrival in May, she'd failed to enlist a single student. If school started in November, Miss Perkins would surely be asked to return.

A large black fly buzzed against the window screen, catching Cicero's attention, and he jumped down to investigate. The setting afternoon sun seeped through the magnolia leaves, reminding her of the shortening days of fall and the melancholy of its dying season. She sighed. The children would soon be back and Maidee would come for them tomorrow. This was their last night.

She stood up and walked over to the Victrola. Unlike the orphans' parents, Frank was wounded, not dead, she reminded herself. She selected a boisterous Sousa march, knowing the children had probably never seen a gramophone.

18

THE NEXT MORNING, Alex shuffled across the yard carrying a small bundle of kindling. Each day he moved more slowly and Anne Aletha knew he was too old to be chopping wood and building chicken coops. But neither he nor Nellie would slow down.

She leaned over the well and dropped the bucket down bringing up the cool fresh water. The heat had not yet broken and she unbuttoned the sleeves of her blouse, rolling them back up to her elbows. Her puffy eyes itched but she tried not to rub them, knowing more tears would soon follow with the orphans' departure.

Alex climbed the porch steps. "We's gotta trust in the Lord, Miss Aletha. Mr. Frank gonna come home. I know he is."

She smiled and nodded. "Mother's letter will probably come tomorrow and we'll know more."

He tossed the kindling into the wooden box with a loud crash, and then removed his straw hat, mopping his face and neck with a rag.

"I sure wish the children could stay longer."

"Yes'um. They just settling in."

Nellie and the little girl gathered eggs in the backyard. Beside them, Peety eyed the hen with an injured wing. She knew Nellie would soon stew it.

"Chickens is laying good this morning. Reckon anybody's gonna find Miz Effie's kinfolk?"

"I don't know. Mr. Neville said there's a cousin up North somewhere. Perhaps Maidee will have some news. She'll be here in a little while, so I better go tidy the parlor." She paused. "You know, we haven't heard any church bells this morning."

"No ma'm. We sure ain't."

In the parlor, Cicero sprawled out on the blotting pad of her uncle's rolltop desk, yawning and stretching. This was his favorite place to nap and she knew they both felt her uncle's presence most in this room. It still smelled like him, his wooden pipe stand pungent with Prince Albert tobacco and his desk unchanged. The writing implements and round spectacles lined up neatly in their cubbyholes with his treasured volumes of Emerson, Aristotle and Thoreau shelved between the bookends.

She could hear his voice so clearly. "Only the seasons hold an orderly pattern, Anne Aletha. Dying never does." She took down a volume of Thoreau, reading one of its marked passages. *A measure of a man is how he handles adversity …*

An infant's wail interrupted her thoughts. Maidee had arrived with the orphans' baby sister.

"ANY FURTHER NEWS OF FRANK?" called Maidee, climbing down from the buggy.

Anne Aletha waved, hurrying to meet them, grateful for once that news traveled fast in a small town. "No, but I'm hoping for a letter from mother soon. He's alive, thank God."

Though neither wore face masks, Maidee embraced her, comforting her as no words could. She smelled of sour milk and baby talcum, and, though fatigue etched her eyes, she looked radiant. Maidee would have made a fine mother, and Anne Aletha often wondered about her friend's past suitors.

"I'll stop by Cora Lee's after I take the children to Mrs. Mobley's. She will have put up the mail."

From the basket, dainty little legs kicked in frantic fury. Maidee reached for the infant, cradling her. "She's a good baby as long you hold or rock her. Aren't you baby girl," she cooed. The child quieted.

Anne Aletha caressed the bottom of a soft tiny foot as eyes as blue as her siblings watched her. A pink satin ribbon held a wisp of golden hair. "I wish the children could stay longer. They've barely spoken, but I know they will."

"I do too," said Maidee, shifting the infant to her hip. "Will you bring the basket? And the newspaper. Let's sit on the porch for a few minutes."

She grabbed the basket and newspaper realizing that she would have no further need of casualty lists. Frank was a casualty now.

The porch swing squeaked as they settled beside each other, Maidee jiggling the contented infant in her arms.

"I hope their aunt is kind and patient," said Anne Aletha. "Do you think we can visit them?"

"I'm going to ask Mrs. Mobley to speak to the Red Cross worker in Hahira and tell her we'd like to visit. I think it would be good for the children."

"We haven't heard any church bells this morning. Has anyone else taken ill?"

"The dry goods store is closed till further notice," Maidee said. "Ralph told me Bernice was complaining of pain behind her eyes yesterday and spent the morning in the outhouse, but they don't think it's influenza. The squabbling sisters are recovering but are having to look after one another. And all the Sirmans boys are getting stronger each day."

"I'm so glad. Tell Ralph we'll have food for him to deliver tomorrow."

"I'll tell him. You know Willard's trying to keep the grocery open a few hours a day. Blalock took sick day before yesterday."

Anne Aletha felt remorse at having so little sympathy.

"I saved the newspaper for you," Maidee said, motioning to the headlines. "I knew you hadn't heard yet."

Anne Aletha frowned, glancing down at the folded newspaper in her lap.

SUFFRAGE AMENDMENT DEFEATED. WOMEN ARRESTED ON THE STEPS OF THE CAPITOL IN PROTEST AGAINST THE SENATE FOR THE FAIL- URE TO APPROVE THE FEDERAL AMENDMENT.

She frowned in disbelief. While there had been an indefinite postponement of the vote in June, both Republicans and Democrats had promised to support it. The damn politicians had reneged again on every promise. She grimaced, shaking her head. It had been an uphill struggle since Seneca Falls in 1848, and now, seventy years later, there was still no widespread support. Even among women, which baffled her more.

"I'm shocked too. Mother's right. She says even a Negro man can vote if he can pay the poll tax and pass the literacy test, but not us. However, I do have some good news. Cousin Henry let Jenkins go."

Anne Aletha turned to look at Maidee. "Really?" she asked, fearing it might make matters worse. "Do you think he'll leave town?"

"I don't know, but with only one arm, his work opportunities are limited."

As the noonday mill whistle blew, Maidee gathered the sleeping child. "I guess it's time to go, little pumpkin."

At dusk that evening, Sara delivered her mother's letter. Perched on the catalpa stump by the road, Anne Aletha squinted to decipher the words in the waning light. Relief swept over her when she read the first paragraph with news of Frank's expected recovery. But her shoulders slumped when she read the second.

October 4, Friday Evening

Dear Daughter,

I pray this letter finds you well and that the good Lord continues to spare us in this terrible time of war and pestilence. Preacher Burke brought the telegram out to the house himself this morning. We still await further details about Frank's wounds and convalescence. Though recovery is expected, I fear he's still not out of harm's way with the peril of this Spanish fever. So many have sickened and died. It has not yet reached Odum, but Jesup reported twenty cases and the Moreland family have all been stricken. Please do not expose yourself unnecessarily as it seems to be taking those in the prime of their lives.

I know that these words will be met with disappointment but your father is concerned that you have not yet been successful in securing a teaching position. Be aware that your brother Babe intends to ask for Clarise's hand in marriage at Christmas and perhaps thought should again be given to his better suitability in farming my brother's land. Now with the boll weevil infestation, they feel that tobacco has a new and profitable future. But we will speak of this at later date.

Continue to pray for your brother and please keep yourself well, dearest one.

Your affectionate mother

THE HOUSE AND YARD seemed so empty the next morning without the children. Anne Aletha tried to busy herself on the back porch as she waited for Nellie to deal the fatal blow in the backyard. And though Nellie was quick and efficient, with a way of stroking a chicken's head to calm it, she couldn't bring herself to watch.

Everything was ready in preparation: boiling water on the wood stove to scald the bird and loosen its feathers, newspapers and matches to singe the pin hairs off the carcass once they plucked it, and a bucket of well water to rinse off the whole smelly mess.

When the ax thudded against the tree stump, she winced. The poor bloody creature would be flopping about the ground headless till still. The barnyard went quiet. Even Miss Effie's noisy rooster ceased his constant crowing. He'd be next if he didn't hush up.

She cocked her head. In the distance, the putt, putt of a motorcar grew louder.

Nellie heard it too and called from the yard. "It coming down the lane, Miss Aletha."

Her pulse quickened with dread. Was Uncle Doctor bringing more bad news? Neville, Patten or Jincy sickened with influenza? She peeled off her apron and dashed to meet him, the screen door slamming behind her.

The Model T sputtered down the lane in a cloud of dust and a flock of crows erupted from the top of the loblolly pines. Uncle Doctor drove the damn machine way too fast. Sulky hated the noisy contraption too and he would soon bray from the barn.

Fortunately, John Henry and Peety were at the millpond so she didn't have to worry about Peety chasing the automobile wheels.

As the motorcar swept into the yard and the dust settled, her frown of concern changed to relief when both Uncle Doctor and Neville waved with smiles.

"We just stopped by to see if you need anything," Neville shouted.

Neither man wore a mask, though they dangled at their necks. Uncle Doctor, looking haggard, motioned her toward the car. Hundreds of doctors were dying of the influenza across the country and she feared for his safety.

"I don't want to shut off the motor and have to recrank this blasted thing," he yelled.

She grinned. Neville reached for her hand and squeezed it, his palm warm and soft. She stood on the running board and tucked her head inside the open window.

"Thank God you've been spared, child," said Uncle Doctor.

"And you too, I've been so worried for you all. I thought you were bringing bad news."

"We're still above ground," he said. "And the influenza may soon be on the wane. The state health chief says that there are as many cases of recovery as new cases. I'm seeing that over in Adel as well."

"Really? That's wonderful."

"And the school superintendent in Atlanta believes the schools may be closed no longer than two more weeks," said Neville.

"Then Jincy can return home," she said, jubilant while pushing the thought of Miss Perkins' return and her father's deadline quickly from her mind. Once the epidemic was over, would parents in Ray's Mill be meeting?

"And Frank too, when he recovers," said Neville. "The war will soon be over, Anne Aletha."

"Do you really think so?"

"If Wilson gets his way with the treaty and his fourteen points are accepted," said Uncle Doctor.

"We've won the war," said Neville, "but the other nations still want territory out of it."

"What if his League of Nations isn't accepted?" she asked.

Uncle Doctor adjusted the controls on the sputtering machine. "Then, child, someday I fear, not in my lifetime, but in yours, another war will surely come."

She stepped back from the motorcar feeling a sudden shiver.

"Are you sure you don't need anything?" asked Neville.

She shook her head. "Thank you. Maidee and Mr. Attaway are stopping by daily with mail and newspapers."

The motor car lunged forward. "Stay away from town a little longer, child, just to be safe," shouted Uncle Doctor. "And that was a mighty fine thing you did for the orphans."

As the automobile circled around the old oak tree, she waved goodbye, feeling pleasure with Neville's frank admiration. She had missed him and their comfortable companionship. Just like her Uncle Carter, he made her feel special.

19

AS THE LAST HUES of the sunset tinged the rosy sky, she lingered on the front porch waiting for all the light to fade. Cicero meowed on the back porch. If she was within hearing distance of his meows, he expected her to provide a short cut through the house, instead of the longer walk around the side. And, of course, she complied. They had just returned to the front porch when she heard loud shouts coming down the lane. Ralph Attaway barely brought the buggy to a standstill before leaping from the carriage with the October 12th edition of the *Valdosta Tribune*.

Had she actually hugged him? She couldn't remember. Only that she didn't even bother to change out of her house slippers before racing to Alex and Nellie's cabin. Her open-toe shoes slapped against her heels, filling with gritty dirt as she waved the newspaper. "Alex, Nellie! They've surrendered. The Kaiser's surrendered!"

No lamp light shone from their cabin in the dusk and she nearly trampled the onion seedlings Alex was waiting to plant in the full moon. "Damn," she mumbled, barely side-stepping them.

When she called again, a light came on and Alex opened the door, greeting her in his undershirt.

"Alex! The war's over," she shouted, scampering up the steps with the newspaper. "Germany's surrendered."

"Lord a mercy, Miss Aletha. Come on in. I get Nellie. She just resting."

As she stepped into the deep gloom of the cabin, he turned up the kerosene lamp on the kitchen table. Cobwebs hung from the rafters and the odor of ashes, sweat and liniment mingled in the tiny cottage. She and John Henry would need to give it a good scrubbing before winter.

Nellie appeared in the doorway in housecoat and slippers and Anne Aletha hugged her tight, tears choking her voice. "The war's finally over, Nellie."

"Sure nuf?" she said. "Hallelujah and thank you, Jesus!"

Anne Aletha pointed to Nellie's swollen ankles. "You all right?"

"I's fine. Just restin. Ain't even washed up the supper dishes. John Henry gone fishing and we's saved him a plate."

Alex removed the dirty plates and pulled up another chair. He sat down next to Nellie and moved the lamp closer to Anne Aletha's chair, nodding at the newspaper.

"What it say, Miss Aletha?"

She glanced at him noticing that the milky white cloud of his cataract was more apparent in the yellow lamplight. Then she read the headline:

GERMANS SURRENDER
Seated last night in the grand tier box at the Metropolitan Opera House in New York, President Wilson received from the Associated Press the unofficial text of the most momentous diplomatic note in the history of the world.

"Ain't that something," said Nellie, brushing cornbread crumbs off the oilcloth.

Anne Aletha continued.

Publication of the German reply to the President's inquiries as to accept all the terms he previously enunciated and to evacuate all occupied territory came as a complete surprise. The way in which the wireless dispatch of such tremendous purport sent out from the great German station at Nauen was made public shattered all diplomatic precedents.

"Praise the good Lord, Miss Aletha," said Alex. "Everything gonna be all right."

The text reached New York only a short time before Mr. Wilson and his party left the Waldorf Astoria to attend the concert for the benefit of the blinded Italian soldiers.

"Yes suh," Alex chuckled. "We done got 'em beat."

THIN CLOUDS SKIDDED across the November sky and Anne Aletha hugged herself against the cool breezy day as she hurried to meet Jincy. The Great War had ended in the early morning. And for the first time since the influenza struck six weeks ago, the sweet notes of Alex's whistling floated through the air. Everything seemed friskier. Cicero stalked the rustling leaves while the baby goats romped, kicking up their hind legs. Peety loped back and forth, dividing his time between helping Alex burn the brush pile and John Henry split the kindling.

No one had sickened in Ray's Mill in two weeks. While the epidemic continued and other cities still reported new influenza cases, Uncle Doctor thought that those susceptible in Ray's Mill had most likely already succumbed to the contagion. Millions had died all over the world and still no one knew the cause or the cure.

She pulled Toog's knitted blue cardigan tighter against her chest and repinned the tousled hair blowing loose from her clips. Patten would most likely bring Jincy and though she'd not seen him since Miss Effie died, her heart no longer quickened. Maybe now her mind told her what her body had not.

She checked her skirt pocket for Bella's treat, assuming he would bring the gentle mare. Moments later she heard Jincy's animated chatter and watched the mare plod toward her.

Jincy squealed, "Miss O'Quinn, guess what? Daddy's going to tie down the mill whistle at exactly eleven o'clock this morning and everybody's going to make a lot of noise to celebrate."

Patten reined in the mare, tilting his hat in greeting. "It's over, Anne Aletha. The Armistice was signed this morning and the guns were silenced at six a.m. Paris time."

Her voice choked with emotion. "The eleventh hour, of the eleventh day, of the eleventh month," she whispered. "I can't believe it's over."

"Yes," he replied as Jincy wiggled out of his arms, sliding down Bella's saddle.

"Careful now." He clutched her arm till her feet touched the ground.

Jincy threw herself into Anne Aletha's arms, her eyes sparkling, the spray of freckles still prominent across her nose and her pigtails braided with hair ribbons.

"Look how much you've grown since Atlanta. "You're almost as tall as I am."

Jincy beamed. "Everybody's celebrating, Miss O'Quinn. People are closing their shops and they're going to ring the church bells too."

"Well, we'll just have to make our own racket out here too. Run tell Alex and Nellie. We'll ring the old cow bells and beat the pie tins."

Jincy turned racing with excitement toward the house.

Anne Aletha looked up into Patten's bemused eyes. He watched her in silence with his knowing gaze, but she didn't blush. "Neville says you've put the mill up for sale. I'm very sorry."

He nodded. "It's probably already sold, but unfortunately to the lowest bidder."

She frowned. "Oh?"

"Hahira is the only mill willing to keep all the men on. But they're giving us less than we owe the creditors." He said it as a matter of fact, with no bitterness.

"What will you do?" She knew the millworkers were like family and admired both brothers for their loyalty.

"Take what we can get and figure out a way to pay the creditors the rest."

Bella whinnied and Anne Aletha remembered her sweet potato treat. "Oh, I almost forgot." She reached into her pocket as Bella nuzzled her hand.

"And what about the schoolmarm?"

She shrugged. "Miss Perkins will probably be asked to return. It seems everyone found me unsuitable." She fumbled over her next words. "And I won't be able to remain without paying pupils." Though she'd thought of nothing else for days, she spoke the words she'd been unable to utter.

He studied her, his face inscrutable. "I'm afraid Jincy's quite taken with you."

She nodded but couldn't speak.

Bella shook her mane and Patten lifted the reins. "Shall I return to pick her up?"

"No," she said, steadying her voice. "Tell Queenie we'll bring her home in time for supper."

With no further words, he turned and guided the mare around the ancient oak that divided the road. Like the brothers who had divided her heart.

Jincy called from the front yard where everyone gathered. "Hurry, Miss O'Quinn."

She smiled at all of those she'd come to love. John Henry, grinning, holding up the rusty cow bells. Nellie and Jincy waving their cake and pie tins, and dear old Alex flipping open her uncle's pocket watch, her recent gift to him.

"Nineteen minutes to go, Miss Aletha. Then it gonna be our eleventh hour over here."

Yes, she thought, the guns of war were silenced. And everyone would celebrate the end of the Great War with relief and happiness. But it would be with a heavy heart for the millions of young men who had perished. Nearly a whole generation lost forever to the slaughter of war.

THAT EVENING, she lingered over Frank's heavily censored letter, savoring the small rounded script with its occasional curlicues, his scrolled g's and the way he looped his l's. The handwriting not at all like his daredevil larger-than-life self. She still didn't know where he was in France. Any information that revealed location or tactics that could fall into enemy hands had been deleted. But she felt sure he'd been part of the Meuse-Argonne offensive that began on September 26. Four of the nine American divisions took part in the assault and the newspapers said that the Germans put up such a desperate resistance in Argonne Forest that the Americans had to fight for the forest one tree at a time. She turned up the kerosene lamp to read it again.

Somewhere in France
October 9, 1918

Dear Sis,

It's true that you never hear the one that wings you. We'd barely installed the radio antenna when the shelling began. I was trying to signal the position of the Germans and advise our artillery of the effect of their shells when something slammed into my shoulder. It felt like a hot branding iron and then my left arm went numb. Although my arm is still useless, the doctor says once the shoulder wound heals, the nerve damage might improve. They call it going West if you don't make it and I'm just grateful I made it.

The heavy rains and mud are relentless. We are being moved to [censored] for convalescence. We hear the influenza is rampant there too. Just as many men are being taken off the field with fever here as with mortar and shells. But the tide of war has finally turned. You and the family stay well and I hope to see you all by spring.

Your loving brother,
Frank

A GRAY FOG wrapped the morning in mist after the previous night's storm, and the shock of cold air surprised her when she stepped out to sweep the front porch. She shivered, remembering the chilly chamber pot in the middle of the night, and realized that soon she'd need a fire in the bedroom for heat.

Since the Armistice a week earlier, life was returning to normal. There had been no new influenza cases in Ray's Mill for over three weeks, and for the first time since it began, Alex and Nellie had hitched Sulky to the wagon and gone into town to collect laundry.

Goosebumps pricked her skin and she tucked her hands beneath her arms, surveying the storm's remnants. Water still dripped from the eaves and the air smelled of wet pine. Sweet gum balls littered the porch and a blanket of pine needles carpeted the front yard. Only the morning glory vine on the porch railing, its vivid blue blossoms beaded with rain droplets, remained unscathed. Until first frost, she thought. Then overnight, the vine would wither to a desiccated eyesore that she and Nellie would have to yank down. But they would save the seeds for replanting in the spring. If only she could be here.

She sighed and picked up the broom. Even the steady drumming of rain on the window panes had done little to soothe her and allow her to sleep. She reproached herself for so many things. Couldn't she have shown more interest in the neighbors and been more discreet with some of her convictions? She had gone against the social order and made herself an outcast. What a fool she'd been to think she wouldn't be ostracized.

The worn oak broom handle felt smooth in her hand and she stabbed at the cobwebs in the corners thinking of Elmore Jenkins. She didn't regret defending Willa Mae, nor did she regret walking out of New Ramah. And she was proud of protecting John Henry. Like her uncle, she believed with moral certainty that racial hatred and injustice were wrong. But her intent to deed the land had been a mistake. Neville was right. Courage was doing what needed to be done, but wisdom was knowing what to defend.

A dead cicada lay among the prickly balls and she stooped to pick up the colorful insect, marveling at its intricately patterned green body and gossamer wings. She would miss its sounds of summer. Placing it as a keepsake on the windowsill, she began sweeping the sweet gum balls and debris into small piles and swishing them from the porch into the camellia bushes.

Geese honked in the distance, and she cocked her head to listen. They were flying low, probably on their way to the millpond, but the fog was too dense to see them.

No Name nibbled the resurrection fern at the base of the oak tree. He followed her everywhere now, bleating and sometimes making a sneezing sound of alarm if she was out of sight. Soon, when he reached puberty, he'd be smelly, but she didn't mind.

The noise grew louder over her sweeping and she paused. It wasn't geese. She put down the broom and walked toward the lane. No Name followed her, but she didn't have the heart to turn him away.

The loud chatter continued until like a pied piper walking out of the mist, William, the oldest Sirmans boy, led a small group of children down the lane. Timothy, the youngest, busied himself demonstrating how far he could spit through his missing front tooth. Puckering his mouth and swishing his spit, he aimed a large glob into the mud puddle in front of him. The middle brother copied him. Her heart ached at the sight of the motherless boys.

Behind them, Cora Lee's girls walked arm in arm, the older with hair the color of Cora's, gently nudging her younger sibling forward. William, with deep-set brown eyes like his father, stopped before her. "Papa says if you're willing to teach us, others will follow."

Jincy brought up the rear, grinning with her well-kept secret. "Uncle Neville says you'll probably have to teach us in the parlor for now."

Timothy tugged on her apron. "Teacher, do you believe in switching?"

She smiled, tousling his hair. "Not well behaved little boys like you."

No Name approached her side, butting his head against her hand.

"What's your goat's name?" asked Timothy. "Can I pet him?"

"Yes, you may. He doesn't have a name yet, but he needs one."

No Name's little white tail wagged as Timothy stroked his long floppy ears. Cora's youngest approached, cautious but curious, rubbing his long nose as the other children took turns petting him.

"You can play with him at recess, but he doesn't like loud noises and you mustn't move too quickly toward him. Just remember that he likes to eat paper and will snatch penmanship papers out of your pockets if you aren't careful."

Pleased with his newfound playmates, No Name turned toward home.

Jincy fell into step beside her, and Anne Aletha gave her shoulder a quick squeeze. The fog that obscured the road earlier lifted and the first shafts of sunlight glinted in the rain puddles and on Anne Aletha's lashes. "Tell your uncle the parlor will do just fine," said Anne Aletha, as the children and No Name cavorted down the lane.

END

Reader's Guide for *Anne Aletha*

Discussion Questions

1. Anne Aletha stands up for her convictions. She stomps out of church when the Klan marches down the aisle of church, demands Elmore Jenkin's arrest after he assaults Willa Mae, and defends John Henry with a shotgun when a posse threatens to take him for questioning. What did you think of her actions?

2. Anne Aletha is outraged over the horrific lynchings, especially the young woman, Mary Turner. Neville Clements warns her against confronting the Klan. He tells her that this new Klan is presenting themselves as decent Christian men and duping an amazing number of people into thinking they are protecting the home front while America's young soldiers are fighting overseas. Do you think the townspeople did not speak out against the Klan because they condoned the Klan, feared its reprisal, or had family members in the Klan? Did the racial injustice and violence in the novel shock you?

3. The twin brothers divide Anne Aletha's heart. Patten stirs her passion and Neville her intellect. Anne Aletha is physically attracted to Patten, but Neville shares her interests and makes her feel special. What did you think of her choices regarding the brothers?

4. In 1918 we first meet Anne Aletha on the train wearing a yellow rose (yellow for suffrage, red if opposed). She supports the federal amendment that demands suffrage for all women, including African American women. At the time, women had very little power and could not even vote. Were you surprised that the amendment did not have widespread support even among women in 1918?

5. John Henry is the brightest pupil, white or black, that Anne Aletha has ever taught, and she hopes he will someday go to a black college in Atlanta. Ralph Attaway is the town gossip, and though Anne Aletha takes an immediate dislike to him, she later softens toward him. What roles did these two characters play in the novel?

6. As soon as Anne Aletha settles in Ray's Mill she is ostracized by many of the townspeople. What could she have done differently to gain acceptance?

7. Against Neville's advice, Anne Aletha decides to deed Alex and Nellie their tenant cottage with a little land, even after he reminds her that in Plato's *Republic* justice requires courage but also moderation and wisdom. Do you think this was the cause of the Klan's final retribution of torching the schoolhouse?

8. During the deadly Spanish Influenza, Anne Aletha fights against her own cowardice when she is asked to nurse the Sirmans boys. She feels she can't refuse, and remembers her Uncle Carter saying that courage is sometimes having no choice. Do you think her act of selflessness is what caused the town's final acceptance?

9. Frank's letters from France are based on real events and stories of the Great War. He writes Anne Aletha of the mud, stench, death, and fear. What insights did his letters give you about World War I?

10. The reader is introduced to a small Southern town in the early 1900s. We see all facets of the town: the beauty of the millpond, the ruined earth of the lumber mill, and the ugliness of racism. Though *Anne Aletha* is a work of fiction, the setting and historical events are real. Did the sense of place enrich the story for you?

About the Author

BORN AND RAISED IN THE SOUTH, *Camille N. Wright has deep roots in Georgia's red clay. Although a lifelong bookworm, she did not begin writing until middle age. Her story idea was conceived when as a small antiques dealer she acquired a trunk of Victorian love letters. Writing in the tradition of Ferrol Sams, Olive Ann Burns, Sue Monk Kidd, Robert Morgan, and other Southern authors, Wright draws on family history, diaries, and letters to create her own fictional world.*

Visit Anne Aletha online at:

www.annealetha.com.

CPSIA information can be obtained
at www.ICGtesting.com
Printed in the USA
LVHW082330250420
654463LV00014B/424/J